A ROGUE COWBOY'S SECOND CHANCE

The Hart Ranch Billionaires

STEPHANIE ROWE

COPYRIGHT

A Rogue Cowboy's Second Chance. Copyright © 2021 by Stephanie Rowe

Print ISBN: 9798540292085

Publisher: Authenticity Playground, LLC

Cover design © 2021 by Kelli Ann Morgan, Inspire Creative Services.

All rights reserved. No part of this publication may be reproduced, disseminated, or transmitted in any form or by any means or for any use, including recording or any information storage and retrieval system, without the prior written consent of the author and/or the artist. The only exception is short excerpts or the cover image in reviews. **Please be a leading force in respecting the right of authors and artists to protect their work.** This is a work of fiction. All the names, characters, organizations, places and events portrayed in this novel or on the cover are either products of the author's or artist's imagination or are used fictitiously. Any similarity to real persons, living or dead, is purely coincidental and not intended by the author or the artist. There are excerpts from other books by the author in the back of the book.

CHAPTER ONE

Tatum Crosby held up her arms and bowed again, grinning as the crowd cheered. This was why she hadn't walked away from her life. Her soul needed this to thrive, and whenever she thought of what she would lose without it, she couldn't even breathe.

She waved again, inhaling the energy of the stadium, of all the people pouring love into her. "Thank you again," she shouted. "I love you guys." She blew a few kisses, then jogged down off the stage into the tunnel lined with her people, high-fiving them as she ran.

It had been one of the best shows she'd had in months, maybe all year. She'd felt free and energized. Happy almost. She—

"Tatum."

She stopped, tension gripping her as a man stepped out of the shadows in front of her. "Donny."

She hadn't seen her manager, and ex-husband, Donny Evans, in almost a month. The moment she saw him, she realized that was why she'd had a good show tonight. Because he hadn't been around. "You're back."

He looked bigger than the last time she'd seen him. He'd bulked up, his muscles coiled beneath his black tee shirt. His ice blue eyes were such a contrast to his dark hair. Those blue eyes had wooed her when she was seventeen. Now she knew they were the windows to hell.

"I heard you contacted a lawyer again," he said.

She bit her lip. How had he found out? She'd sworn everyone to secrecy. "Look, Donny, it's not a big deal. I just wanted to know what my options were—"

"You know your options. Your only job is to sing. I take care of everything else." His icy blue eyes flashed. "Don't make this difficult, Tatum. We're good together. Let's fix it. Be a team in the bedroom as well as out of it. I know you miss me."

She took a step back as he reached for her. "Don't touch me."

His jaw tightened. "It was a one-time mistake. She didn't mean anything to me. You'd been on tour for months, and I missed you."

"I know." She'd heard it too many times before. She also knew that his infidelity didn't even scratch the surface on why she didn't want him near her. "I'm exhausted." She started inching past him, trying to keep as much distance between them as possible. "The doctor told me I need to rest my vocal cords as much as possible. Are you staying around for long this time?"

"I'll be joining you for the rest of the tour."

"No." Her stomach dropped, and she clenched her fists. "Don't stay."

"I'm staying. I'm concerned about your stalker." He fell in beside her, keeping pace as she walked. "I miss you, Tatum. We'll work this out."

She didn't look at him. "You're not my husband anymore. And I don't want you as my manager. Let me go."

"It doesn't work like that, sweetheart."

The way he said "sweetheart" made chills clamp down on her spine. "Don't call me that—"

"Tatum!" Her tour manager, Nora Smith, hurried up. "Do you have a moment to go over some details about tomorrow's concert? We need to switch a few things up due to venue restrictions. Can you come with me?"

"Yeah, of course." Tatum nodded at Donny as Nora took her arm. "Gotta go." She didn't look back as Nora hurried her down the hall. The moment they put distance between her and Donny, she felt relief rush through her. "Thanks," she whispered.

"No problem." Nora flashed her a worried look. "The stalker got in your dressing room again," she said. "While you were on stage."

Fear congealed in Tatum's belly. "How? How is he getting in? Someone must be letting him in." Her first thought was Donny. Was he trying to terrorize her into taking him back?

"I don't know, but we're going to change things up for the show tomorrow to give you better security." Nora raised her brows. "Unless you want to cancel?"

"You know I can't. Donny won't let me."

"You need to fire him."

"You know I can't do that either." She'd tried, but the contracts she'd signed when she was eighteen had trapped her far beyond what she'd understood was even possible at the time.

Nora sighed as they reached the end of the hallway, where her security team was waiting to get her out of the stadium. "You've got to do something, Tatum. You're breaking. I can see it."

She thought she'd been hiding it. But maybe she hadn't. Maybe she was so close to the edge that there was no way to keep up the façade she'd practiced for so long. "I know. I'll figure something out. Where are we tomorrow?"

"Portland, Oregon."

Tatum stopped and stared at Nora. "Oregon?"

"Yes, why?"

Tatum let out her breath, and then made an instant decision. "Can you get a VIP ticket and backstage pass for tomorrow's concert to someone? It needs to arrive by seven tomorrow morning." Would that even be enough lead time for him? She knew how full his life probably was.

Nora raised her brows. "In less than eight hours?"

"Yeah. Can you do that?"

"I'm magical. Of course I can." Nora pulled out her phone. "Who?"

Tatum hesitated for a split second, then blurted out the name before she could change her mind. "Brody Hart. He has a ranch in eastern Oregon. I don't know the address."

Nora stared at her. "Brody Hart? *The* Brody Hart? The reclusive tech genius who was part of a band of homeless kids, then made billions and now lives on some horse ranch in the middle of nowhere?"

"Yeah." She'd been part of that group of homeless kids a very, very long time ago. She'd known Brody before he'd become rich, and he'd known her before she'd become famous. And then everything between them had broken. "Can you find him and get him the ticket?"

"Honey, that man gets invites to everything, and he never goes."

Tatum grimaced. "I know. But can you find him and get him the ticket by morning? It's important."

Nora sighed. "Yes, but don't get your hopes up that he'll come."

"Too late. They're already up."

CHAPTER TWO

Brody Hart ran his hand over the gleaming chestnut hair on Stormy's neck. "Looking good, kid."

Stormy snorted and swished her tail, impatient to get released from the crossties.

"I know. I'm almost done." Whenever Brody was in town, he did the shoeing for the horses who needed extra care. He'd made a study of methods and honed his skills to best help the animals they rescued and brought onto the Hart Ranch.

He trusted no one with Stormy's feet, and his care had made a difference. She'd barely been able to walk when she arrived, afraid to put weight on her broken hooves.

Now she galloped through their extensive pastures, tail held high, the purest freedom of spirit. She was why he had this ranch. She and all the others like her. Broken horses with no real home, just like he and his family had been so long ago.

He ran his hand down her back leg and leaned his shoulder into her hip, shifting her weight off her hoof so he could lift it and work on it. He was humming quietly to himself when he heard footsteps behind him.

He didn't have to look up to know who it was. He recognized the gait of all eight of his brothers and sisters. He'd trained himself to do that back when they were homeless kids, hiding under the bridge in the dark. It had been imperative that he knew who was coming, so that he would know how to keep those under his care safe.

The habit remained today, even though they were all adults and no one was after them, trying to drag them back into foster homes, or worse. "Hey, Keegan."

His brother spoke without preamble. "Did you sleep last night? At all? Your light was on all night."

"You stalking me?" Brody set the lightweight, high-tech shoe on Stormy's foot to test the shape. Most horseshoes were steel. A few racehorses used aluminum. He'd experimented on a lightweight, durable plastic compound. It was too expensive to ever become popular, but he didn't care about money.

He cared about his horses. And his innovations had saved Stormy's feet.

"No." Keegan leaned against the wall, his booted feet in Brody's line of vision. "Just keeping an eye on my bro." He let out his breath. "Did you find anything?"

"Nothing new." Brody lined up a high-tech nail and tapped it through the shoe and the outer rim of Stormy's hoof. "It was a false trail." Although only nine of the under-the-bridge kids had stuck together, taking the last name of Hart and claiming legal status as a family, a number of others had gone through their pack during the five years Brody had held them together.

After one of the women had been murdered a few years ago, Brody had made it a point to track down everyone he could find and make sure they were all doing okay. He'd located most of them, touched base, and helped out where he could. But there were a few he couldn't find, and he wasn't planning on resting until he found them all. He thought he'd found one of the girls, but he'd run into a dead end last night.

Keegan sighed. "We're all adults now, Brody. It's not your job to continue to hold us all together."

Brody shrugged. "It's not a job. It's what I do."

"I know. But you don't need to be the guardian of everyone anymore."

Brody finished securing Stormy's shoe and set her hoof down. He stretched his back as he turned to face his brother. Keegan was wearing a dusty cowboy hat, faded jeans, and a loose flannel shirt. His short blond hair was neat, and his blue eyes blazed with the warmth that was a hallmark of every Hart.

Keegan looked like a working cowboy, not one of the Hart billionaires who had gotten lucky with security software when they were teenagers. The world saw his family as billionaire celebrity recluses. Brody saw his family as the only people who mattered to him, real people who were all still fighting to escape the childhood that had sent them running for their lives to hide out under a bridge as kids.

The shadows still ran deep for all of them. But the family they had formed had given all of them the safe space they needed, no matter what demons crawled out of their pasts after them. The Harts had a rule, one Brody had made when they were all under the bridge: no one could hold out. Emotions had to be shared. Secrets had to be revealed. No one carried their burdens alone.

It was why they'd survived, and why the Harts were thriving now.

Which was why he answered Keegan's question. "Every night I go to bed, I see Katie Crowley's face. I wonder what I could have done to save her. If I hadn't let her go to Boston—"

"Stop." Keegan held up his hand. "You have to stop that

shit. You're not a god, Brody. You never had the right to tell any of us what to do or how to live. Those who stayed chose to stay. Those who chose to leave were following their paths. However it turns out isn't your fault."

"But she's dead—"

"Yeah, it was shitty. You don't need to tell me that. I think about her, too. But she died years after leaving us. I hate to tell you this, bro, but you aren't responsible for the entire lives of every person you've ever met."

Brody scowled at him. "She's *dead*."

"And the rest of us are alive." Keegan put his hand on Brody's shoulder. "We're all here, Brody. Eight of us, plus you. Several hundred if you include the Stocktons, now that Hannah married into their family. Katie was Hannah's sister, but Hannah fought to find a life again, happiness, and a family. Learn from her. Let yourself be happy, Brody. That's what you're always telling us."

"I know." Brody shoved his cowboy hat back from his head and wiped his wrist over the perspiration beading on his brow. "It's different for me. It's my job to hold everything together."

"Yeah, well, not if it wrecks you." Keegan lightly punched Brody in the shoulder. "Family meeting tonight, bro. You're the topic. I just thought I'd warn you."

Brody frowned. "Why me?"

"Because we all think you're turning into an old shit, and you need to get a life." Keegan grinned and ducked when Brody tossed a rag at him. "Seriously. You better come in your party pants or you're going to get your ass kicked. We're tired of your crap, old man."

Brody laughed, his spirit already lighter. "Who's house?"

"Bella's hosting tonight."

Bella was the older of the two Hart sisters. She was the

chef at the guest portion of their ranch that was for high-end guests seeking a dude ranch vacation. "Is she cooking?"

"She is."

"Well, damn. I wouldn't miss it if she's cooking."

"You wouldn't miss it anyway." Keegan tossed an envelope at him. "By the way, this arrived this morning by personal courier. Looks important so I opened it."

Brody took the envelope, which was, indeed, torn open. He didn't care. He had no secrets from his family. "What is it?" As he asked, he noticed the grin on Keegan's face. He stopped. "What?"

"Open it."

Brody shot Keegan a suspicious look, then slid his fingers into the envelope and pulled out a small white envelope with his name on it. That envelope was also open. He lifted the flap and saw it was a concert ticket.

Covering the name of the performer was a yellow sticky note. Someone had jotted in purple pen, "Personal invite from Tatum. She hopes you'll come."

He froze. "Tatum?"

"Tatum," Keegan confirmed.

Brody ripped the sticky note away and saw Tatum Crosby listed as the headliner for the concert. His seat was row one. Behind the ticket was a backstage pass. "The concert's tonight in Portland," he said, scanning the details.

"I saw that. You can't go, obviously. Family meeting and all."

Brody couldn't take his gaze off the ticket. Tatum Crosby. She'd swept through his little group when she was seventeen, a brilliant flash of fire, passion, and energy. She'd stayed for a summer.

A summer he'd never forgotten.

And then he fucked up, she'd left, and she'd never spoken to him again. He'd kept track of her, though. Watching her ascent to the realization of her dreams. "This can't be from her. She'd never invite me."

"Is it her writing?"

"No." She'd left Brody a note when she'd taken off. A note he'd kept for a long time as a reminder of how badly he could fuck up if he wasn't careful. A reminder that had helped keep him focused on being the protector that all those in his care had needed.

He shoved the ticket back into the envelope and held it out to Keegan. "Toss it. I'll be at the family meeting tonight."

Keegan didn't take it. "I can't. I texted the Hart chat. We think you should go to the concert. See her. Family consensus."

"No." Brody tossed the envelope into a nearby trash can. "It's not from her."

"What if it is?"

He paused and looked at his brother. "She's married."

"Divorced. You know that."

Brody let out his breath. "Our fling was a long time ago."

"It wasn't a fling, and it might have been a long time ago, but she still haunts you. She's the reason why you've never met anyone else. We all know it." Keegan plucked the envelope out of the trash. "You're always telling us we deserve love. You're the one trying to marry all of us off because we all deserve the family we didn't have. But you're the one who won't even try. Because of her."

Brody walked to the end of the aisle and stared across their expansive ranch at the sun quickly rising in the sky. Tatum Crosby. Keegan was right. She had become his world fifteen years ago, and that hadn't ended when she'd left.

"You have to go, Brody. You always say that the universe hands you what you need, not necessarily what you want. Well, guess what?" He shoved the ticket back into Brody's hand. "You got handed a ticket, so you gotta go."

Brody scowled at his brother. "Why do you remember the things I tell you only when it's convenient?"

"Because I'm smart. I booked the penthouse at the Ritz in Portland for you already. They're *so* delighted that Brody Hart will be gracing them with his presence this evening." He grinned. "We're still going to eat Bella's dinner, but we're doing it without you, so you better have a good time, or you'll miss her dinner for nothing."

Brody grabbed a brush and began brushing Stormy's neck. "I'm not going. It's not from Tatum."

Keegan laughed. "Of course you're going. There's no way in hell that you could possibly walk away from this invite without knowing that for sure."

Brody ground his jaw. "I fucked up. She was right to leave."

"Yeah, an eighteen-year-old, homeless, runaway trying to keep a bunch of kids alive and together made a mistake. He definitely deserves to pay for that for the rest of his life, right?"

Brody looked over at his brother. And said nothing.

"How many of her songs do you know every word to?" Keegan asked.

Brody replied without hesitation. "All of them."

"Then you need to go see her, or you'll never be free."

CHAPTER THREE

Brody was late.

And he still wasn't sure if he was staying.

He kept his head down, his shoulders hunched, and his cowboy hat tilted as he strode through the quiet tunnels leading into the stadium.

There were a few people in line for beer or pretzels, but it was mostly empty.

Everyone was in their seats, screaming for Tatum, who had been on stage for a half hour already.

Brody knew, because he'd sat in his truck and watched the social media feeds. He wasn't about to go in before she was on stage. But once she came on...he'd just sat there in his truck, watching as fans posted grainy clips of her performance.

Then, thirty minutes in, someone had posted a clip from up close, close enough for Brody to see her face. She'd looked up, as if she were looking right at him, telling him to come in.

So he'd shoved his phone in his pocket and gotten out of his truck.

And now, he could hear the thud of the music as he neared the doorway that led to Floor Section 4, Rows 1-10.

He paused to show his ticket to the usher, and then was waved inside.

He shoved his hands in his front pockets and stepped inside the stadium. The music hit him like a wave of raw power. The lights flashed. Smoke rose from the stage. An assault on his senses that he ignored, his gaze going right to the stage to find her.

His breath seemed to catch in his chest when he saw her in person, for the first time in fifteen years. She was at the far end of the stage, one arm over her head, her stance wide and strong in red, sparkling heels. Her halter top matched the shoes, showing off her muscled torso, while her black leather pants showed off every curve. She radiated a passion and gloriousness that the photographs never did justice to.

She was moving to the fierce beat, working the fans up into a frenzy.

Her voice was glorious, radiating through the stadium like heaven itself had unleashed its greatest glory through her. It wasn't country. It wasn't soul. It wasn't pop. It was all of those together, mixed with a magic that no one else had ever been able to mimic.

Tatum Crosby was legend, and she was right there, fifty feet from him.

The front row was less than five feet from the stage. She would see him. And the moment she did, he would be close enough to read her expression and know if she'd sent the ticket and backstage pass. He would know whether to stay.

But still he didn't move.

He stood there, silently, watching. Breathing in the woman who had been a part of his soul for fifteen years. With the lights from the stage, he knew she wouldn't be able to see him from where he was standing.

He could watch her entire concert, and then slide away into the night.

She would never know.

But then, neither would he.

Keegan was right. He had to know. This was his chance to begin to live again.

He waited until she was at the far end of the stage again, singing to the crowd on that side of the stadium. The moment she turned her back on him, he pulled his hat down to hide his face, and then he went on the move.

Brody wasn't coming.

The realization wound tight around Tatum's chest, making it difficult to get enough air to sing.

She fought for the energy her fans deserved. She shouted her love for them. She poured all she had into her music. But she couldn't keep looking at the empty seat in the front row.

She'd known it was a long shot he would come. It had been so long since she'd seen him. Since everything had fallen apart. Since she'd run.

Movement in the wings caught her eye, and she saw Donny shouting at her, gesturing with his palms up for her to step up the energy. He would be angry at her performance.

Her chest tightened even more, dreading the after-show recap with him.

Beside him stood Nora, her clipboard clutched to her chest. She shrugged at Tatum, indicating that she, too, had noticed the empty seat in the front row.

He wasn't coming.

She had to get over it. She'd come this far on her own. She didn't need him. Wasn't that the point she'd been trying to prove her whole life? That she didn't need anyone?

Her mom had quit on her, choosing drugs over her own daughter. Her dad? She didn't even know who he was. Foster care? All hell, except for a gray-haired old man named Roger who had given her his old guitar and changed her life.

No. The guitar hadn't changed her life. *She'd* changed her life, and she didn't need anyone.

It was fine if Brody didn't show. Absolutely fine.

She could do this. She'd been on her own since she was ten, tossed between foster homes when her mom was in jail for drugs, sitting in their crappy apartment, watching her mom's chest to see if she was still breathing, or if she'd finally died of a life not worth living.

Her mom had finally died. And on that rainy day in June so long ago, Tatum had decided she was going to become the star she'd always dreamed of, the celebrity who was so incredible that everyone would love her. That everyone would see how special she was.

And she'd done it.

She had money. She had success. She was a star. She didn't need anyone or anything, especially not Brody. But even as Tatum told herself that, she stumbled, panic starting to close in around her.

Emotion caught in her throat, filling her eyes with the tears she worked so hard to keep at bay every moment of every day. The loneliness, the fear, the isolation—they were all lies and illusions. She *had* what she needed. She was *enough*, all on her own.

She spun away from the wings, away from Donny and Nora. She focused on her fans, on the people who filled her soul and kept her going.

Still singing, she moved to the edge of the stage and bent down, holding out her hand for a high-five. A woman in her forties with red hair screamed and high-fived her, making

Tatum smile. She moved along, holding out her hand to her fans.

Two adorable young men, early twenties, stopped holding hands long enough to high-five her. "We love you, Tatum!" One of them yelled.

"I love you, too!" she shouted back.

The next in line were three girls that looked like they were in college, screaming and shouting and jumping up and down, filming her as she high-fived them.

Next up, a man in a cowboy hat with his head down.

In Brody's seat.

At that moment, he raised his head and met her gaze, dark brown eyes that she'd never forget.

Brody.

Tatum was so shocked she forgot the words for a second, the music thundering on without her. She caught up almost immediately, and she knew that no one except Donny would notice, but she couldn't take her gaze off Brody.

He looked the same. And different. A beard. Muscles. Heavier. Fancier.

Still singing, she held out her hand to him for a high-five, her heart pounding.

He reached up and caught her hand. It was a split second of skin brushing over skin, but it was the touch of a man she'd never forgotten. Her entire body seemed to come alive at his touch, and suddenly, her spirit was back.

She leapt back to her feet and took off across the stage, her voice richer and stronger than it had been in years. The music became a part of her, filling every cell of her body with its magic.

For the rest of the concert, she sang to the crowd, but she was *singing* to him.

Tatum was aware of Brody every second, his face always in her peripheral vision, afraid that if she took her gaze off him, he'd disappear into the night and be gone again, for another fifteen years.

She finished her set, the concert, but she didn't leave the stage. She turned to her band. "One more. Do you guys know *Under the Bridge?*" It was an earlier song. One that had never been released as a single. One that no one cared about. Only her die-hard fans knew it. Her label hadn't let her perform it on tour, because no one cared.

But Brody would know what it was about.

Her band nodded. Her drummer, Victoria Rose, tossed her black hair and started the beat. Her bass player, Ace, joined in. And then the others started in.

She grinned. Of course they knew it. Victoria and Ace would know it because they'd been with her from the start. The rest of the band was paid well enough to make sure they knew every single one of her songs.

Tatum spun around and raised her hands over her head, trying to galvanize the crowd for the song. A few of her superfans started screaming. They knew they were about to get a treat that no one had ever had.

Others were cheering just on principle.

But there were a few boos, too. People annoyed that she wasn't finishing with their favorite song.

Well, too bad. Because it was her favorite song.

She walked over and held out her hand to Brody. His brows shot up, and a slow smile curved the edge of his mouth. He shook his head. He was as famous as she was, but he stayed off the radar. No way would he want to be on stage in front of everyone.

The music played on, and she started to sing the first verse.

The day my life began.

Was the day I found the bridge.
The laughter. The joy.
The freedom beneath that bridge.

Brody's face became shuttered, but she held out her hand. "Brody Hart's in the audience," she shouted to the crowd. "Let's give him a little encouragement. Come on up, Brody. Sing with me."

They'd sung the song together so many times. Written it together. Laughed over its silliness together. Cried over its power together.

The crowd began to chant Brody's name, and she could hear the women screaming for the legendary bachelor that no woman had ever been able to snag.

Tatum went down on one knee and held out her hand. "Sing with me, Brody." The music raged forward, not waiting for either one of them.

He met her gaze, searching her face. Suddenly, he stood up, braced his hands on the stage, and vaulted up beside her.

The crowd went wild, screaming for both of them. The lights blazed down on him, lighting up the handsome face that she'd followed in the papers for so long. One of the techs ran on stage and handed her a microphone.

She grabbed it and held it toward Brody.

Instead of taking it from her, Brody wrapped his hand around hers and leaned in, his beautiful voice joining her in the words they'd created together. As they had so long ago, their voices blended perfectly, entwined like invisible lovers.

The music surged through the stadium, growing in power as they sang together. She couldn't take her gaze off his, lost in the tumultuous brown eyes that had kept her company in her dreams for so many years.

They got to the silly part, the part that had sent them

into hysterics as teenagers. She stalked away from him, acting it out as they once had, turning playful curses into music filled with heart.

He followed her, grabbed her wrist, and yanked her against his body, teasing her with the lyrics that started making her laugh again. The crowd roared with laughter, cheers, and whistles, and she knew her fans were, for the first time ever, experiencing the song the way it was meant to be sung.

She knew now why no one had ever liked it.

Because without Brody, it wasn't complete.

He twirled her around and dipped her, pretending to nuzzle her throat, and the crowd screamed again as she laughed.

He tossed her back to her feet, and they leaned in toward each other, their voices reaching up to the crazy heights of wild, teenage freedom as they carried the final notes of the song together until they faded into the night.

When the song ended, the place went wild.

Tatum raised Brody's hand in victory. "Let's hear it for Brody Hart! Who says tech geeks can't sing, right?"

He tipped his hat to the crowd, then leaned in. "I'll see you backstage later," he said, his lips brushing against her ear as he shouted to be heard over the screaming.

He was coming backstage. She nodded, her heart leaping as he waved to the crowd one more time, then hopped off the stage back into the crowd. People surged around him, and she quickly lost sight of him in the light and the crowd.

Joy leaping in her heart, she raised her arms to the crowd. "One more. You guys want one more?"

The place went nuts, and her heart soared as she sang the song they'd come there to hear.

But she couldn't stop grinning.

Brody was back.

CHAPTER FOUR

An hour later, Tatum was still giddy with excitement as she arrived backstage for the meet and greet that Donny and Nora always made the band do after every concert. She was usually the last one there, but tonight, she was first of her band to arrive.

One look told her that Brody wasn't there yet. In fact, no one was there other than staff, preparing to let people in.

Victoria was the first one of the band to arrive. "What the hell, girl! Since when do you know Brody Hart?'

Tatum grinned. "I met him when we were teenagers. I haven't seen him in fifteen years."

"Fifteen years? No way, girl." Her bass player, Ace Stevens, strode in with his husband, Jackson O'Hare. Ace was still wearing his black leather pants and matching vest, but his husband was wearing a dress shirt, pressed jeans, and polished loafers, as always. "There was so much heat between the two of you that you practically set the stadium on fire."

"Amen to that," Jackson said. "I couldn't decide whether to get a fire extinguisher or a mattress."

Heat blazed in Tatum's cheeks. "Shut up. It's not like that. I literally haven't seen him since I was seventeen."

"It was definitely like that," Ace said. "Donny's going to be furious. He won't like any man looking at you like Brody Hart just did."

Sudden tension chased away Tatum's jubilation. "He's not my husband anymore."

Ace put his arm around her shoulders. "Oh, shit, girl. I didn't mean to pop your bubble. You looked so happy out there." He grabbed her chin and wiggled. "Where's my Tatum smile? I want it back."

Ace and Victoria had been with Tatum since the beginning. The rest of the band had been shuttled through by Donny to try to up her sales. Only Ace and Victoria had survived, and now Tatum had made it clear that without them, she wouldn't perform.

So far, Donny hadn't called her on it to see if she would really give up singing to keep them. Mostly because Ace and Victoria were amazing, and they had their own fan bases as well. They helped sales, and as long as they helped with the profit margin, Donny left them alone.

Tatum managed a smile for Ace, trying to put Donny out of her mind.

Nora walked in then, and headed straight for Tatum. "You know him," she said, a hint of accusation in her voice. "You already knew Brody Hart when you asked me to send him the ticket."

"I hadn't seen him in years. I didn't know if he'd come."

Nora looked annoyed. "I need to know these things. We could have leveraged this so much better. Former boyfriend? Reunite on stage? This is big stuff. It could really help boost the sales for this tour. Is he coming backstage? I need to talk to him."

Suddenly, Tatum wasn't so sure having Brody backstage

had been the right idea. Donny would be there momentarily. If everyone else thought she and Brody had a past, Donny would, too.

And he could make things really ugly in a hurry.

She cleared her throat. "I don't know if he's coming backstage. And he's not an old boyfriend. We were friends as kids. That's it. Just friends." Until they'd slept together, declared their love for each other, and sworn eternity, of course. Except for that, just friends.

The rest of the band ambled in. Hired musicians that had already been swapped out twice during this tour. They kept to themselves and hadn't been interested in getting to know Tatum.

She didn't like that.

She liked to have a team around her. Music worked better that way.

"Hang on." Jackson, Ace's husband and the one with business sense, held up his hand. "Ticket sales aren't going well?"

"No." Nora eyed Tatum. "We all know Tatum's been off, and the word gets ahead. Ticket sales have been going down all tour. Tonight with Brody was big. You got the crowd going again. Maybe he can join us for that song for the rest of the tour? Do a joint promo?"

Crap. Brody wouldn't like that. He was intensely private, and very sensitive about people who wanted something from him because of his money. That was one reason she'd never contacted him. She didn't want to be one of those people who swarmed him now that he was someone. "Don't ask him. Tonight was just a gift for an old friend."

"Oh, I'll ask him. You need it." Nora looked at her watch. "I'll go see if he's in line out there. I'll escort him back."

"No!" Tatum leapt ahead of Nora. "I'll go check."

"You need to be here. You're the star people have paid to see." Nora held up her hand.

"But—"

"Your contract requires you to meet and greet. I will go." Nora turned to leave, but Victoria intercepted.

"Hey, Nora. I've got a little situation with my drums."

"You do?" Nora swore and turned to Victoria. "What's going on?"

Victoria winked at Tatum before drawing Nora away. Ace and Jackson waved her off as they too headed after Nora.

Tatum blew them all a kiss and sprinted for the door. She paused by one of the security guards. "Which way to the VIP entrance?"

He pointed to the left, and she took off at a run. The hall was empty, which she loved. She was never alone anymore. Never got her own space. This emptiness of the hallway felt like a breath of fresh air, and she grinned as she ran.

She'd arrange to meet Brody later. Just them. Just...why? What would she say to him?

She slowed down to a walk. Why *did* she invite him? Wasn't it because she *did* want something from him? For him to use his clout and somehow free her from the contract she'd signed, from the manager who wouldn't leave her alone?

Tatum stopped, alone in the empty hall.

How could she ask Brody to solve the problems she'd created for herself? A man she hadn't seen in fifteen years? It wasn't his job to save her. How pathetic did that make her, to run to him for help?

She laced her fingers together and rested them on the top of her head, sudden guilt pressing down upon her.

"Tatum."

She tensed as Donny walked around the corner, coming from the direction of the VIP entrance. "What?"

"What the fuck was that with Brody Hart and that song? Neither of those were pre-approved."

Tatum pulled her shoulders back and put her hands on

her hips. "It's called art. The best art isn't always scripted. Everyone loved it."

"It doesn't matter. That was a bullshit move. What if it had backfired? What if he sues us? We didn't get a release to film him or use his voice for profit."

"He won't sue me. He chose to get on the stage—"

"Why'd he do that?" Donny reached her, glaring down at her. "You guys had that little dance perfectly choreographed. You know him? You've been sleeping with him? Is that why you filed for divorce? Because you've been sleeping around with him? Are there others?"

There was an edge to his voice that made Tatum freeze.

He'd hit her only once. And then she'd walked out of his office and straight into the lawyer's office.

But he scared her ever since. It felt like the anger was mounting inside him, and at some point, he was going to snap.

Like right now. Right now, there was an edge to Donny's voice that made all the hair on her arms stand up. They were alone in the tunnel. No one was around. Just them.

So, instead of shouting at him that he had no right to accuse her, she took a moment to gather herself. "Unlike you," she said evenly. "I never had an affair outside our marriage. What I do now is none of your business. If it is too difficult for you to handle, I would love to buy you out of the contract."

He stared at her, her words hanging between them. "I'm not going anywhere."

She pressed her lips together to keep from screaming in frustration. "I'm going to go meet Brody. Nora invited him backstage—"

"He's not coming. I told him to leave."

Anger shot through Tatum. "What?"

"I told him that you felt that he pushed the boundaries

during that song, and you didn't want to see him. He didn't argue. Didn't fight to see you. So whatever dreams you have of snagging that rich bastard, give 'em up, Tatum. He's not interested."

She could barely keep from shouting at him. Instead, she silently turned away and walked down the hall toward the VIP entrance.

Donny followed her, still talking, but she ignored him.

When she rounded the corner, the fans all started shouting for her.

She ignored them, searching the crowd for Brody. There weren't that many people in line, and it took only moments for her to see that he wasn't there. She hurried over to the security guard. "Do you know who Brody Hart is? Was he here?"

The guard nodded at Donny. "Mr. Evans asked him to leave."

Of course he had. "How long ago?"

"Maybe fifteen minutes."

Fifteen minutes. Maybe she could still catch him. "Which way did he go?"

The security guard pointed. She didn't hesitate. She ducked under the rope into the middle of the fans. "I'll be right back," she shouted. "Go backstage. I'll be right there."

Then she took off running down the hall. She could hear Donny shouting at her to come back, and a few fans started running after her, but she didn't slow down.

She sprinted around a corner, then threw her shoulder into the stairwell door. Brody would have parked in the VIP parking. She ran down the stairs and raced out into another tunnel.

This one was full of fans, and she was spotted immediately.

People converged around her, shouting and waving pens.

She could smell alcohol on their breath. Intoxicated superfans closed in around her.

She suddenly couldn't move. Couldn't breathe. People were touching her. A hand actually went in her mouth.

Shit. She batted it away as another hand landed on her breast. "Get back, please. Get back!" She waved her hands to try to get them back, but they crushed in even more. Panic surged in around her, and she ducked her head, trying to shove her way through them, but there was no way through it.

Dear God. What had she been thinking? Donny always told her she wasn't normal, that she couldn't lead a normal life. She hated him for trying to trap her, but now, she could see what he meant.

Tatum tried to see over the crowd to find help, but she was much too short. All she could see were the bodies closest to her. She didn't even know which way was the doorway she'd come out of.

A hand grabbed her ass, and pens were shoved in her face. People were screaming questions at her. One guy ripped off his shirt and tried to shove a marker in her hand to sign his chest. She wanted to go down on her knees and curl into a ball to protect herself, but she knew she couldn't.

She had to get out. Which way was out?

"Hey! Get the hell back!" A man in a blue security guard uniform suddenly shoved his way in beside her. He was tall and heavy, and he used bulk to create a blockade for her. "Let's go, Tatum." He put his arm over her shoulders and crushed her against him, driving a wedge through the crowd as he plowed forward.

She ducked her head against him, keeping her head down as he propelled them through the crowd. She could feel people pushing against them, but he was so big that it didn't seem to affect him.

It took only a moment, then he shoved them through a door and slammed it behind them, cutting off the crowd. The silence was breathtaking, and Tatum sucked in a breath. "Thank you—"

Her savior suddenly flung her aside. She crashed into a counter, sending pots crashing to the ground. Pain shot through her left wrist, and tears sprung to her eyes as she spun around, holding her arm to her chest. They were in what looked like a kitchen, but they were the only ones in it. One of the restaurants that had closed once the concert had started. "We need to call security—"

"No, we don't." His voice was thick with disdain and hate, and she spun around in alarm to look at him.

He was standing a few feet from her, his hands by his sides, his weight balanced between his feet, as if he were ready to launch himself at her. Aggressive. Not protective.

Alarm shot through her. "We need to go upstairs," she said, trying to ignore the throbbing pain in her wrist "It's time to go."

"Tatum Crosby." He said her name like it was a curse word.

Her heart started hammering. "What do you want?" She frantically took stock of her surroundings, trying to find something to protect herself with. Her hand was numb, and she couldn't move her fingers.

"You don't know? Of course you know. It's our game. We've been playing it. I leave you messages. You pretend not to see them."

Her stalker? Was this her stalker? She'd been so sure it was Donny messing with her. Maybe it was still Donny. Maybe he'd hired this guy. Or maybe this guy was crazy on his own. "You're the one who broke into my dressing room?"

"You forgot to leave it unlocked. That was the deal."

It wasn't the deal. Who had told him it would be unlocked?

"I had to break in." He moved in closer. "And now we finally get to play together."

Oh, shit. Shit. Shit. She reached behind her with her good arm. Her fingers closed around the handle of a pot that she hadn't knocked off. "I need to go upstairs," she said, trying to keep her voice calm. "I have to go greet my fans. Let's meet later in my dressing room. I'll leave the door unlocked this time."

"Later works. And so does now." He made a sudden move for her, and she swung the pot, slamming him in the side of the head.

He stumbled and crashed into the pot counter.

She threw the pot at him and ran for the door.

CHAPTER FIVE

ONE-HANDED, Tatum fumbled for the lock and then flung the door open. Much of the crowd had already been cleared, and the security team had arrived, dispersing the crowds.

One of the security guards saw her, but she didn't go to him for help. He was wearing the same uniform as the man she'd left in the kitchen.

She grabbed a hat off a souvenir stand and yanked it over her head as she ran down the hall, keeping her head down. Tears blurred her vision, as she cradled her arm to her chest. She was sure it was broken.

She didn't know where to go. Who to trust. She couldn't go back upstairs. What if Donny had set it up? What if other security guards were working with him?

She saw a black sweatshirt on the ground, covered in footprints. She snatched it up and yanked it over her head. It smelled like body odor and beer, but she didn't care. She got her right arm through the sleeve, but didn't even try the left. She got the hat back on her head, yanked the hood up, and then ducked her head.

She couldn't fight the tears, so she didn't try. She just ran for the exit and hurried outside.

Rideshare cars were lined up outside, and she ran to the front of the line, where security guards were trying to make for an orderly dismissal. She pulled her hood down and ripped off the hat. His eyes widened when he recognized her. "Ms. Crosby."

"It's an emergency. I need to get out of here. Right now."

"In here." He yanked open the door of the first car, waving off a couple who were about to get in. "Get in."

She dove into the SUV and hunkered down in the backseat as the security guard closed the door. The driver, a guy in his early twenties with a ball cap from one of her tours, started protesting, and the people started yelling that it was their car.

Tatum leaned over the console and grabbed the driver's arm. "Hey."

He looked down at her, then his eyes widened. "No shit."

"Please. Help me. I need to get out of here."

"Fuck yeah." He punched a button on his phone to decline the ride, then he hit the gas and peeled out.

Tatum rolled onto her back on the seat, holding her arm to her chest as she tried to breathe against the pain.

"Where do you need to go?"

She closed her eyes. What she needed was to go to the hospital, but she didn't dare, because she didn't know who she needed to hide from. Was it Donny who had sent that guy after her?

"Tatum? Fuck. I can't believe Tatum Crosby is in my car."

"I'll give you as many VIP tickets as you want for life if you don't tell anyone I'm with you."

"Shit, yeah. You bet." The car rolled to a stop. "I'm at the edge of the parking lot. Where are we going?"

Where to go? She had no money. She hadn't managed

her own life in years. She had no friends outside the little circle that Donny had kept her inside for so long. The crowd had just shown her she couldn't run around the city by herself.

"Tatum?"

She was in trouble. Desperate. No money. No one to trust. Where had she gone fifteen years ago when she was in that situation?

To a guy who lived under a bridge and took care of people.

Brody. She needed Brody. She had no idea how to find him.

But she'd followed him in the paper for years. If he wasn't planning to drive back to the ranch tonight, there was one place he'd be. "Take me to the Ritz," she said.

"You bet."

The car began to move again, and Tatum continued to lie on her back on the seat. She closed her eyes, trying not to gasp every time the car hit a bump. "How far is the Ritz?"

"About twenty minutes normally, but there's a lot of concert traffic."

Twenty minutes. She had to hang on for twenty minutes.

She tried to breathe through the pain.

Twenty minutes. If he was even there when she arrived.

Please let him be there.

Brody swung his truck into the drop-off circle at the Ritz, swearing when his tires screeched.

Shit. He needed to calm down.

He pulled up in front of the other cars and parked. He swore and leaned back in the seat. What the fuck had happened at the stadium? Being on stage with Tatum had been electrifying. The energy rushing between them had been off the charts, as if it had been amassing for the last fifteen years.

He'd thought the connection between them was long gone.

Wrong didn't even begin to describe how off base he'd been with that one.

He'd been so jacked up to go backstage and talk to her. To connect.

And then... His fists bunched as he recalled Tatum's manager intercepting him.

He'd come on too strong? He'd crossed lines? What the fuck did that even mean? He was sure the connection with Tatum had been mutual. He would have argued with the guy, but there were fans all around. People taking pictures of him.

No way was he going to make a scene. Not in public. And not in a venue that could adversely impact Tatum.

But what the fuck? Brody hit his hand on the steering wheel, frustrated that he'd left without hearing it from her.

The man was her manager, but he was also her ex-husband. Brody should have insisted on hearing it from Tatum...but for what purpose? To make her suffer? If she didn't want to see him, he'd be a dick to make her see him anyway.

He wasn't a dick.

But he also didn't understand how it was possible that she could have changed tides so fast. He might have known her for only a summer, but he knew her. He knew her vibe. He *knew* they'd been on the same page.

He slammed his fist on the steering wheel again, then shoved the door open. No way was he staying in town tonight. He was getting his shit from the room and then leaving. He was too fired up to sleep, and he'd rather crash in his own bed at four in the morning than a hotel at midnight.

A valet hurried up. "Mr. Hart. Shall I park your car, sir?"

"No. I'll be back down in a couple minutes. Leave it here." He handed the woman a hundred. "Keep an eye on it."

"Yes, sir." She tucked the money in her pocket and took up residency next to his truck.

A hundred bucks got a lot of respect.

Brody pulled his hat over his head and strode into the lobby, keeping his head down so no one dared approach him. Usually, he tried to be cool with people who wanted a moment of his time, but he wasn't in the mood right now.

His cowboy boots thudded as he strode across the polished marble floor toward the penthouse elevators. He punched the button and shoved his hands in his pockets as he waited, watching the floors click by on the lighted display above the doors.

The elevator was down to the third floor when Brody heard Tatum's voice.

He tensed and spun around, searching the lobby, but he didn't see her.

He waited for a moment, but he didn't hear her voice again.

Shit. He was now hallucinating her.

The elevator doors opened, and he strode inside.

He was out of there.

∼

It was all Tatum could do to keep from bursting into tears. Her arm hurt so much she could barely think, she smelled like beer and someone else's body odor, and she was scared. "Please," she said again. "At least call Brody's room. He'll tell you that it's okay."

The hotel manager's face was tight. "I've told you already. We protect the security of our guests at all costs. I'm going to have to insist you leave." He nodded at two security guards.

"I'm going to have my team escort you outside. Please don't make a scene and force us to call the police."

"No. Please. I'm Tatum Crosby. Surely you recognize me."

His gaze swept over her outfit. "Do you have identification?"

"No, I left without my wallet."

"How unfortunate." He nodded at two burly men. "It's time to leave."

And go where? She had no money. No phone. Nothing. "I can't leave. Please, call Brody. He'll be so furious with you if you don't call. He'll want to know."

"I'll take that chance." The manager nodded at his team. "Take her now."

The security guard took her arm, and she gasped as pain shot through it. "Don't!" she snapped, unable to keep the tears back. "Don't touch me! I'll go." She lifted her chin, ignoring the tears streaking her face. "Fine. I'll go."

∽

The doors were just sliding shut when Brody thought he heard Tatum's voice again.

This time, he didn't hesitate. He jumped out of the elevator as the doors were closing and paused, listening, but he didn't hear her voice again.

Brody wasn't crazy. He didn't believe he'd imagined it. Adrenaline rushing through him, he walked out of the elevator hall and back toward the main lobby. He stood at the edge, scanning the room.

There weren't many people there. A middle-aged couple walking through in black tie clothes. A family with a couple of snoozing toddlers and weary-looking parents. A businessman who looked like he'd found a new friend for the night.

No Tatum.

Scowling, Brody walked over to the reception desk. "Excuse me."

A clean-cut guy about his age looked up from the computer. When he saw Brody, he straightened up. "Mr. Hart. I'm sorry about the disturbance. I assure you, we safeguard your privacy."

He frowned. "What disturbance?"

"The woman—"

Tension shot through Brody. "What woman?"

The front desk attendant glanced toward his left. "She said you knew her, but we are escorting her out—"

"Shit." Brody sprinted around the corner and almost ran straight into the hotel manager and two men flanking a tiny figure in a hooded black sweatshirt.

"Tatum!"

She looked up, and Brody's gut went cold when he saw the tears streaking her cheeks. Her eyes were wide, and there was fear and pain etched all over her face. "Brody?" she whispered his name in almost disbelief.

He sprinted over to her. "I'm here, Tatum. I've got you. You're all right, now." He went to gather her in his arms, but she yelped and jerked back.

"My arm," she whispered, holding it to her chest. "I think my wrist is broken."

Fuck. Anger tore through him, a raw, visceral fury. What the fuck had happened to her? He put his arm around her shoulders, tucking her against him carefully, so as not to bump her arm. When he felt her body trembling against his, something inside him snapped.

He levered a hard gaze on the manager. "You were going to kick her out?"

The hotel manager looked horrified. "I'm sorry, sir. I didn't know you knew her—"

"A woman is in your hotel, desperate, terrified, and crying, with a broken arm, and you're going to throw her out in the fucking street?" He couldn't keep the disgust out of his voice. "It doesn't matter if I knew her or not. Your responsibility as a human being is to take care of people who need help. No matter what. Even if it gets dirt in your fucking hallway."

Tatum put her hand on his chest. "Brody," she whispered. "Get me out of here."

It was the tiniest plea, the faintest whisper, and it got his full attention instantly. All his anger at the manager vanished, and Tatum became his entire world. He yanked his coat off and wrapped it gently around her shoulders. "Let's go."

He kept her shielded against his body as he helped her through the lobby. "I'll drive you to the hospital—"

"No!" She jerked and pulled back. "We need to get out of town. I can't go to the hospital."

He ground his jaw. "You said your arm is broken—"

"He'll find me at the hospital. We need to leave town. Now. Is your truck here?"

He swore. "He, who?" It was all Brody could do to keep his voice calm. "The man who broke your arm?" Simply saying the words made Brody want to hunt him down right then.

"I don't know. Please. I just need to get out of here. It won't take long. People are already taking pictures."

He glanced over his shoulder and saw that the mom of the little family was holding up her phone, as were a couple others. "Shit. Let's go up to my room. I need to grab my stuff."

"How long will it take?"

"Five minutes. Tops." He guided her toward the elevators.

"Okay, but no longer."

"It won't be longer." He punched the elevator button, and

it opened immediately, still on the ground floor from when he'd called it before.

He guided her inside, swiped his keycard for the penthouse, and then pulled the woman he'd missed for fifteen years into his arms.

CHAPTER SIX

Tatum didn't push him away.

She said nothing, but she pressed her face into his chest, her breath heaving as she tried to control her sobs.

Brody had a thousand questions, and emotions roiled through him, but he shoved them all aside and focused on the woman in his arms.

He kissed the top of her head and gently stroked her hair, even while he kept his other arm tight around her waist. "It's all right, Tatum," he whispered. "Breathe, baby, breathe. I'm here now."

She still didn't say anything, and she was trembling.

Anger built inside Brody again, a need to go after whoever had scared her and hurt her, but again, he forced it aside, knowing that his first job, his only job right now, was to help Tatum.

The elevator door slid open, and he used his keycard to open the penthouse. "This is my room. Let's go."

She nodded and ducked past him. Her shoulders were hunched, and it was clear from the way she was holding her arm that it was painful. "You want to sit while I pack?"

"No. I'm too antsy to sit. Do you have ibuprofen? Water?"

He nodded and grabbed a bottle of water from the fridge. "The ibuprofen is in the bedroom." There was a time where he would have given his soul to have Tatum in his bedroom, but right now, that was so far off the table.

He put his hand on her back and guided her into his bedroom. She stood awkwardly in the middle of the room, clutching the water bottle, while he grabbed the medicine. "How many?"

"The whole bottle, please."

He laughed softly and shook out three for her. "Where did you get the sweatshirt?"

"I found it on the floor of the stadium. I was trying to disguise myself."

"Want something that smells better?"

She managed a laugh. "Yeah, actually, that would be great." She looked up at him, her big brown eyes wide with pain. "I need help to get this off, I think."

"Sure." He helped her get her right arm out of the sleeve, and then gently tugged the dirty garment over her head. She was still wearing her tight, sparkly outfit from the concert. "You look fantastic, but how about some sweats? I have some with drawstrings we should be able to tighten enough that they stay up."

She looked down at her pants. "There's no way I can get these off with one hand."

Brody tried for a neutral tone. "I've seen you naked before. I'm fine with it if you are."

Her cheeks turned pink, but she shrugged. "Emergency situations call for emergency actions. Disrobe me, my minion."

He laughed and walked behind her to unzip the top. It fell away, revealing her bare back, the hourglass curve of her waist and hips. He sucked in his breath as he carefully slid the strap over her right arm.

Tatum met his gaze as she let him grasp her left upper arm and lift it enough to carefully lift the strap over her wrist. He somehow managed to keep his gaze on her wrist, and not her breasts. "It's swelling."

"And purple. You know I like pretty colors."

He smiled. "I do remember that, but we need to get you to the hospital." He grabbed a soft, flannel shirt and carefully slid her broken wrist through the sleeve, but even being his most careful, she still flinched and fresh tears filled her eyes. "Shit, Tatum. Sorry."

"No, it's perfect." She got her right arm through the sleeve, and then stood patiently while he quickly buttoned it up. The back of his hand brushed over her breast, and they met gazes for a moment.

God, he'd missed her. It was like no time had passed. She'd never left her place deep inside his soul, the place he'd kept open for her.

And now, she was back. And she needed him.

This time, he wasn't going to let her down.

He crouched down in front of her and undid the straps on her sandals. Her toes were painted a hot pink, and he smiled. "I remember when you stole that bottle of nail polish so you could have pink toes," he said.

"It wasn't pink. It was salmon. And you made me take it back," she said. "You said that just because we were homeless didn't mean we were criminals."

"Yeah, well, sorry about that."

She braced her hand on his shoulder as she lifted her foot for him to take off the shoes. "Why?"

"Because the nail polish gave you joy. I understand a lot more about how important the little moments of joy are. Without them—" He cut himself off.

"Without them, what?"

"The past can overwhelm you," he said succinctly as he set the shoes aside. "Pants." His voice was rougher than he intended as he unzipped her pants and pulled them down. Her underwear was a tiny scrap, and he left it in place.

Tatum rested her right hand on his shoulder as she pulled her feet out of the tight pants. Her legs were long and toned, not the scrawny teenager he'd known before. She had the body of a woman now, with curves and...bruises.

He brushed his thumb over a purple mark on her thigh. "What's this from?"

She looked down. "I don't know. It's just a bruise." There was a hint of laughter in her voice. "You're still the same, aren't you? The protector."

"I am." He grabbed his running pants. They were the smallest thing he had with him, but they were still huge on her. He laughed as he tied the bow. "They might literally be twice as big as you are."

"They're perfect." She suddenly sat down heavily on the bed, as if she were too tired to stand. "These smell so much better."

"They do." He tossed the old sweatshirt in the trash, then folded up her clothes and put them in his travel bag. It took him only a few minutes to pack, but by the time he was ready, she'd already curled up on her side into a tiny ball, hugging her broken wrist to her chest. "Tatum?"

She didn't open her eyes, and her breathing was heavy.

God, she looked exhausted. Brody wanted to let her sleep. He wanted to pull the covers over her, then climb in with her and pull her into his arms. Make her feel safe.

But there were a thousand reasons why he couldn't do that, the most important one being that she appeared to be on the run. So, he sat down next to her on the bed, and touched her shoulder. "Tatum, baby. It's time to go."

Her eyes opened and for a second, she looked confused. Then she saw him, and recognition flooded her face. "Right. Okay. Great." She sat up too quickly, and gasped in pain.

Brody swore as he helped her off the bed. "You need to get that looked at."

"Not in town. We need to get out of the area." She sighed as he strapped her sandals back on her feet.

He grabbed his bag, tossed some cash on the bed for housekeeping, and then tucked his hand around Tatum's elbow to support her. "Where are we going?" he asked as they stepped into the elevator.

She bit her lip and said nothing.

"Tatum?"

She finally looked up at him as the elevator hit the first floor. "I don't have a place to go. I left my wallet and my phone and everything behind. I don't have anything with me."

Brody had to remind himself to stay calm. What the fuck had happened tonight to make her bolt without even her phone or wallet? "And you don't want to go back and get it?" He was impressed he'd managed to keep his voice even.

She shook her head.

"Even if I go with you?"

She shook her head again.

What the fuck? She knew what he was capable of, that he could keep her safe. And yet it wasn't enough? He wanted to ask more, but the elevator doors started to slide open. He put his cowboy hat on her head and pulled it low so it would hide her face. She turned into him, tucking her face against his chest, hiding it from anyone who might recognize her.

He put his arm around her and guided her across the lobby. He knew she couldn't even see where they were going with her head down like that. She had to depend on him.

This was her life. Not just tonight, but all the time.

Always hiding. Never able to live, except when she was on that stage.

He reached his truck and gave the valet another tip. He helped Tatum into the passenger side, tossed his bag in the back seat, then jogged around to the driver's side.

Tatum had slunk low in the seat, the hat pulled down, completely covering her face.

Swearing under his breath, Brody started his truck and pulled out.

"Where are we going?" she asked. "I know you have a plan. You always do."

That used to piss her off. Right now, she sounded grateful for it. He wasn't sure he liked seeing her depend on him. It was the role he'd always wanted in her life, but it wasn't taking a whole lot for him to realize that a shrinking Tatum wasn't right.

She needed to find her way back to herself.

"Home. My home. The ranch," he answered. And stopping at the regional hospital near his house. That wasn't optional. "Is that cool?"

She pulled the hat off and looked at him. "Really? I can stay with you? It won't be for long—"

He wanted to tell her that she could stay with him forever. He wanted to say a lot of things that he hadn't said before. But she'd left him once, and for good reason. He didn't have the right to say a lot of things right now. So, instead, he simply nodded. "You can stay as long as you need to. You know that."

She bit her lip. "I wasn't sure. It's been so long since...you know."

He looked over at her as he paused at a stop light.

The light from the streetlights was illuminating her face, casting shadows across her cheeks. She looked exhausted and in pain. And beautiful. God, she was beautiful. And she was here. With him. Trusting him again, even if it was only to keep her physically safe. He wanted to apologize, to explain, but the past didn't belong with them right here. Not right now. "You can always reach out to me, Tatum. *Always*."

She nodded, a half-smile at the corner of her mouth. "Still the same Brody," she said as she closed her eyes and leaned her head back. "Is it okay if I sleep?"

"You bet." He reached over into the back and grabbed a blanket. "Here." He helped arrange it around her, and then she closed her eyes and leaned her head back, still holding her arm to her chest.

The light changed to green, but it took Brody a moment to pry his gaze off the woman resting beside him. She's been in his dreams for fifteen years. A figment of his imagination. An elusive memory of a time when life had tried to hand him something beautiful. A wisp that slipped out of his fingers.

Tatum was back. In trouble. But back.

He had a second chance. And he was going to give it everything he had.

CHAPTER SEVEN

By the time Brody drove under the sign for Hart Ranch hours later, Tatum was beyond exhausted. The sun had risen while they were in the local hospital, and even Brody's charm hadn't sped up the wait time.

Three and a half hours of driving.

Four hours at the hospital.

But now she had a cast, painkillers, and a place to sleep without worrying that anyone was going to come after her. Keeping anonymity for both of them, Brody had checked her in at the hospital as his wife, Josie McMillan, and paid cash, so there was no record that they'd been there.

He hadn't asked any questions.

He'd just taken care of everything for her.

She knew the questions were coming, but for now, he was giving her space. She sighed and rested her head on the seat as they drove down a dirt road. "Is all this yours?"

"Yep, we've got a bunch of land. We keep buying up adjacent lots when they become available. We all have houses on it, but we're spread out."

There were grassy pastures stretching on both sides of the

road. Horses were grazing in the morning sunlight, and wooden post-and-rail fences kept them in. Beyond them rose pine trees, lush and green. "It's beautiful."

"Thanks. We've done a lot with it." Pride was evident in his voice, making her smile.

Brody was a homemaker. He'd created a home under the bridge when they'd had nothing, and now, he'd created a masterpiece.

To the left, she could see barns rising high and a couple huge, beautiful houses. But Brody turned right at a fork. In front of them there was only one house, which looked like a big log cabin. A huge deck wrapped around the entire home, and big picture windows looked out on the expansive grounds. It was too big to be called charming, but that's what it felt like. It was so homey. "Is that yours?"

"Yep." He pulled around back and hit a button beside the dome light. There were five rustic garage doors, but only the one further to the left opened. He pulled right into a gleaming garage and punched the button to close it as soon as he parked.

Yep. He said it so casually, as if he hadn't created the most beautiful home she'd ever seen. She had no doubt that he'd had it designed and built to his exact specifications. He was brilliant. A visionary. She'd forgotten just how much.

Brody hopped out of the truck and walked around to open her door. He offered his hand to help her down, and she took it.

The minute his fingers closed over hers, her stomach jumped. She met his gaze and saw the heat in his eyes. It was still there. The magic between them. The magic that had blinded her before.

The magic that was already trying to pull her right into his spell, into his arms, into his kisses.

She couldn't go there. Not again. Not right now.

As soon as Tatum's feet hit the ground, she pulled her hand free. Needing her space from him.

Brody escorted her to the steps that led into the house. "I need to know how you want to handle this." His face was serious, his brown eyes so dark.

God, she remembered how he used to look at her like that. So serious. Like he was carrying the weight of the entire world on his shoulders. "What do you mean?"

He took his gaze off her to punch in an alarm code. "Can I let my family know that you're here?"

She bit her lip as he opened the door. "I don't know if my life is in danger. I'm not sure what's going on, exactly." She wasn't up to facing the rest of the Harts. Leaving them had been...not her best moment. "I guess maybe give us a day to figure it out."

He nodded. "I'll see if I can keep you off the radar for that long."

She knew what that meant. If one of them asked, he'd tell the truth. But if no one asked, if no one showed up, he wasn't going to send out the alert. It was big that he'd even offered that much, because she knew how much he believed in open communication with his family.

He gestured for her to enter. "After you."

She stepped over the threshold, sucking in her breath at her first glimpse of the interior of his home. It was as cozy and welcoming as it had looked from the outside. Exposed wood beams. A cathedral ceiling. Huge windows on all sides of the open-plan first floor. Expansive couches that looked like she could get lost in them. An enormous stone fireplace that looked so inviting for cozying up in front of all winter long.

She could totally imagine the Harts gathering here, lighting up the place with their laughter and warmth. The house had clearly been built for entertaining a lot of people on the first floor, but it didn't feel huge or too much for just the two of them either.

It was perfect. "It's so amazing to see you living in such a beautiful home," she said. "The last time I saw you guys, you were all living under a bridge, and now...this. It's fantastic."

Brody smiled as he headed toward the kitchen. "A lot can happen in fifteen years."

Her smile faded. "Fifteen years. I can't believe it's been that long since we saw each other. It feels like forever, and at the same time, it feels like yesterday."

He slanted her a look she couldn't decipher. "That it does." He pulled out a pitcher and poured some water into two glasses. "You hungry?"

"No, the food we got at the hospital filled me up." She yawned as she took the glass from him. "Just tired. It's been a long time since I pulled an all-nighter."

"I'll show you to the guest room." He led the way to a gorgeous staircase that curved up to a second floor. "The biggest guest bedroom is on the opposite end of the house from my room, but I'd rather put you next to my room, so I can hear you if you need anything. Is that all right with you?"

He was so formal. Keeping a distance between them. The connection on the stage was gone. The intensity between them when he'd first found her in the hotel had faded. Now that the music was over and the danger not so imminent, he was pulling back faster than she could even track. It was probably for the best, but having him so close and yet so unreachable actually made her heart hurt. "It's fine to put me next to you."

"All right." He turned right at the top of the stairs and led the way down a hallway until he got to a door on the right. "This has its own bathroom, so you have privacy." He led the way inside, and she followed him in.

The room was small, as he'd said, but it was perfect. A big

picture window opened to the fields, and she could see horses grazing in a nearby pasture. The bedframe was made of old logs, and a thick carpet filled the center of the room, protecting the most beautiful wood floor she'd ever seen. The boards were wide and thick, as if they had once been part of a barn. "It's gorgeous."

"Thanks. I'm proud of that bed. It's my favorite of all the ones I've made."

She looked at the bed more closely. "You built that?"

"Yep." He set the glass of water on the nightstand. "I don't cut the trees. I just go out in the woods and collect wood that has already fallen."

Of course he wouldn't take down a tree. Brody was a giver of life, not a taker. She cocked her head. "A billionaire who makes his own beds out of logs."

"A kid who was once homeless who now has the time to make art whenever he feels like it," Brody corrected. "The money means nothing. You know that."

She sighed. "I do." She knew so much about money now, so many things she wished she didn't have to know. "But at the same time, it means everything. It means security."

"Does it?" He looked pointedly at her arm.

She bit her lip. "Maybe not all the time."

Brody walked over to her and slid two fingers under her chin. Her heart started to pound as he looked down at her, so close she could see the golden flecks in his dark eyes. "A girl who was once homeless who now brightens the world with her music," he said quietly.

She swallowed. The feel of his fingers against her skin was almost too much. *I missed you*. The words whispered through her mind, but she kept them to herself. She had to.

"Two artists who once knew each other," he said. "And now...here we are."

"Yeah." She met his gaze, and silence fell between them. So much to say. But where to even start? Or finish. "Brody—"

He cleared his throat, as if her voice had broken the spell. "Later. We'll talk later. You're about to pass out on your feet."

As if on cue, she yawned again, and they both laughed, breaking the tension between them.

"My point proven." Brody nodded at the bathroom. "I keep a new toothbrush and toothpaste in every bathroom, in case anyone needs to crash here. Sometimes Bella and Meg leave stuff around. I'll see what I can scrounge up for you to wear."

Bella and Meg were the two Hart sisters. Tatum had known both of them when she'd been with Brody. Bella... they'd been best friends that summer. The kind of best friend she'd never found again. And Meg...sweet Meg. A few years younger, she'd been like the little sister Tatum had never had.

Brody paused and then handed her his phone. "If you need to call anyone, use this. The number is blocked. No one can track you. The passcode is the address under the bridge. Do you remember that?"

She nodded. "I do." The Hart kids had made up an address for their hideaway to put on school paperwork and other places that needed proof that they had a home. She clutched his phone in her hand. "Thanks."

"No problem." He headed toward the door, then turned to face her. "I'd like to tell them you're here. They know I went to see you. I know they're wondering what happened."

She knew he was talking about his family.

She bit her lip. She knew how important honesty was to him. He'd fought hard to open the lines of communication between everyone, believing that working together was their only chance of survival back then. She'd fallen under that spell, and it had burned her.

She didn't believe in sharing all her secrets anymore. He'd taught her that. "Can we wait?"

"There's power in numbers," he said.

She raised her chin. "There's also power in intimacy, Brody. Two people who have their own secrets, their own whispers. There's power in that, too."

"If they ask me, I can't lie to them," he said again. "And they're going to ask."

She sighed. "I know. I know." He was right. "That's fine. Just...can you give me time before I have to talk to them?"

Understanding softened his face. "Of course. That, I can do."

Relief rushed through her. "All right, then."

"Good?"

"Yeah."

"I'll grab a plastic bag and some tape for your cast so you can shower. I'll be back in a few minutes." He reached for the door, then paused again. "Tatum?"

Her heart started to race at the look on his face. "What?" Fifteen years. *Fifteen years.*

"I'm glad you came to me for help. Whatever's going on, we'll fix it."

She sighed. "Thanks."

He nodded and shut the door behind him.

Instead of heading for the bathroom to get the grime off, Tatum simply sank down onto the bed and curled up on her side, staring at the door that had just shut behind Brody.

She'd never thought she'd see him in person again.

She'd never thought she'd speak to him again.

And yet, here she was. In his house.

She'd thought he was going to say that he was glad she was there. Or it was good to see her. Or that the song had been magical.

But he hadn't. He'd said he was glad she'd called him for help.

Because that was what Brody was. The man who helped everyone. A trait that made him a hero.

But it was that trait that had broken her heart and made her leave him behind forever.

Until now.

She was back. With a heart that maybe hadn't recovered from the past nearly as much as she'd thought. And a man who was still the guy who'd broken it in the first place.

CHAPTER EIGHT

Brody was back at Tatum's door in less than five minutes. He'd found one of Bella's sweatshirts hanging in the entry, so he'd grabbed that, then jogged back up the stairs.

Tatum was in his house.

She was back.

Here.

With him.

The thought was staggering.

"Tatum?" He knocked lightly at her door and then opened it.

She was asleep on the bed, curled up in a ball, her hands tucked under her chin.

She looked tiny and vulnerable. His gaze settled on the cast, and he swore under his breath. He had to stay focused. Her being in his house wasn't about rekindling a romance that he'd screwed up.

It was about finding out what the hell was going on and making sure she was safe.

He set the plastic bag and tape on the bathroom counter, then grabbed a heavy blanket from the closet. He set it over

53

her, but as he was tucking it around her, her eyes flickered open.

His heart seemed to stutter when those sleepy brown eyes settled on him. "Stay with me," she whispered.

He let out his breath. "Tatum—"

"Hold me, Brody." She closed her eyes again. "Like before. Like none of this ever happened."

For a long moment, he didn't move. He just stood there, staring down at her. Lie down with her? In bed?

She opened her eyes again. "Never mind. Forget it. It's fine." She rolled away from him, turning her back on him, just like she'd done fifteen years ago, when he'd refused to be there for her.

Fuck that. If she needed him, he was going to be there for her. Whatever it was.

He kicked off his boots, then slid onto the bed, tucking himself up behind her as he wrapped his arm around her waist. She immediately scooted backward, pressing her back against his chest.

Brody draped his leg over her hips and pulled her tighter against him, being careful not to bump her arm. Tatum wrapped her fingers around his wrist and tugged his hand against her chest, pulling his arm even tighter around her.

He let out his breath, relaxing into the warmth of her body. Listening to the sound of her breathing. Feeling the rise and fall of her ribs under his arm. Her hair tickled his face. He pressed a kiss into her hair, then buried his face against the back of her head.

Like he used to do.

Only back then, he hadn't slowed down to appreciate the moment. To realize she could be gone in a moment, and what that would do to him if it happened.

But now he knew.

So this time, he let down all his shields, and he breathed

her in. He concentrated on everywhere their bodies touched. On the scent of her shampoo. On the feel of her breast against his forearm. On the curve of her hip beneath his thigh. On the way her foot wrapped around his other calf. On the feel of her fingers wrapped so tightly around his wrist, holding onto him as if she'd never let him go.

He breathed in every sensation. Every single detail he could.

Because this time, he knew he might never hold her like this again.

That this might be his last time. Forever.

∽

Tatum was running, running, running, terrified. Someone was hunting her. She could hear his footsteps behind her, echoing in the empty stadium tunnel. His breath was loud. Close. Getting closer. She screamed for help, but no sound would come. Just silence. He was going to get her. He wanted to hurt her. She could feel his intent pressing down on her. He had a knife. She couldn't see it, but she knew he did.

"Tatum. Baby. Wake up." Brody's voice drifted faintly, but she couldn't see him.

She spun around, frantically searching for him. She tried to scream Brody's name, but again, her voice had no sound. Just helpless, wordless silence. Footsteps were getting closer. Heavy boots. Running her down. He was coming for her.

"Tatum. Come on. Wake up." Brody's voice was louder now.

Brody! Help! She screamed silently as a hand came down on her shoulder. She screamed and spun around, but it was too late. She couldn't see his face as he grabbed her and threw her into a wall—

"Tatum!" Brody's voice broke through, jerking her out of

the darkness. Her eyes snapped open, and she saw Brody leaning over her, his brow furrowed.

She stared at him, her breath heaving in her chest. Tears were running down her face, and she could feel sweat dripping down her temples.

"It was a dream." He brushed her hair back from her face. "You're okay. You're in my house. You're safe. Do you hear me?"

She nodded, and rolled onto her side, pressing her face into his chest, breathing him in. "I can still hear him. Running after me. He was going to kill me. I know it."

He kept stroking her hair, but she felt his body tense. "Who was chasing you?"

"I don't know. I couldn't see his face. But in my dream, I knew who it was." She closed her eyes. Her heart was still pounding. "It was just a dream," she said out loud. "Not real."

"Just a dream," Brody agreed, his voice deceptively mild. "How did you break your arm, Tatum?"

She needed to talk about it. She needed to tell him. But she didn't want to give it space in her mind. Or her heart. "I wish it would just go away," she whispered. "All of it. Can I live in your barn with the horses?"

He laughed softly, his fingers still drifting through her hair. "It's a great barn, but I'm not sure that's quite up to your standards."

"My standards are pretty simple right now." She pulled back. He was stretched out on his side, facing her, his head on the same pillow as hers. So close. Close enough to touch.

So, she did.

She reached out and pressed her hand to his chest. "It's been a long time since I've woken up and felt safe like this."

Something flickered in his eyes, and he put his hand over hers, holding it to him. "I need to know what's going on, Tatum. It's not just last night, is it?"

She bit her lip and shook her head. "I try not to think about it. To give him power by thinking about him."

"Him? Who?"

She met his gaze. His dark eyes were fixed on her face, wholly focused on her. There was nothing else on his mind. No one else he was worried about helping. Right now, it was just her. "I'm not sure what's going on. Not exactly. Just...I'm not sure I'm safe. I'm...trapped."

He smiled. "Baby, you need to stop dancing around the topic and just blurt it out. I can't help if I don't know. You're safe right now. Completely safe." He pressed a kiss to her fingertips that were poking out of the end of the cast. "Start with last night. What happened to your wrist?"

Tatum drummed her fingers on his chest. Brody recognized the action. It was what she used to do when she was thinking hard on something important to her. Like, when she was working on a new song. Or trying to figure out how to tell him that she loved him—

Shit. He didn't need to think of that right now. Of that night.

"Tatum, tell me about your injury."

She finally met his gaze. "I was waiting for you backstage."

Something stilled inside him. "Your manager said you didn't want to see me."

She raised her brows. "Really, Brody? After that song, you thought I didn't want to see you?"

He ground his jaw, knowing damn well that he hadn't fully bought it. He'd used it as an excuse to bail. "It was a mistake to leave," he said.

She searched his gaze, her fingers still drumming on his chest. He loved the feel of her fingers tapping against him. "I heard he told you to leave, so I went to find you."

Brody let out his breath. She'd come after him *before* she'd gotten hurt. Before she'd needed his help. Why had she come after him? Why had she sent the tickets? He had a thousand questions, but he knew not to push her. She held things close and would retreat if pushed.

So, he forced himself to be patient. "And then what?"

"I ran into a stairwell. When I came out in the exit tunnel, I was swarmed by fans. A security guard was there, and he got me into one of the kitchens in the stadium." She shrugged. "And then he got aggressive. He threw me against a table, and that's when my wrist broke."

Brody had to focus on staying calm. "How did you get away?"

She grinned. "I hit him in the head with a pot. Knocked him right out."

He smiled. "Nice."

She stopped drumming her fingers, and he knew she was starting to relax into the story. "I stole someone's Uber ride and had him bring me to the Ritz. I owe the driver a lifetime of front row tickets."

"That seems fair." He studied her face. The short story wasn't complete. He could tell. "What else?"

She rolled onto her back and stared at the ceiling. "I'm probably imagining things."

"Probably not." He propped himself up on his elbow so he could see her face. "What's up?"

She bit her lip and glanced at him. "My ex-husband, Donny, is also my manager. I signed a contract with him when I was eighteen, and it pretty much trapped me for life. I can't get out of it. I've been trying and it's...pissing him off."

The bastard who had told Brody to leave. Shit. He should have had better instincts. He usually did. But Tatum was hell on his equilibrium. "Has he threatened you?"

She shrugged. "Not exactly, but he's getting increasingly aggressive. I don't feel comfortable around him." She glanced at Brody again. "I also have a stalker. He's been getting in my dressing room at concerts. He got into my tour bus. And the security guard who attacked me made a comment that made me think that he was my stalker. I think—" She stopped. "What do you think?"

He knew what she'd been about to say. "You think Donny is behind the stalker? Trying to coerce you into going back to him for help?"

She nodded and rolled back to face him. "I've been thinking that someone has to be helping the stalker. How else is he able to get into my dressing room and bus? And get a security guard uniform at the stadium? It's probably Donny, but if not, then it has to be someone else, and I don't know who." She held up her casted arm. "Or how far they'll take it."

Brody wrapped his hand around the cast and lowered her arm. "Have you contacted the police?"

"Yes, but we move from state to state, so they can't really help. We're gone before they can find anything."

"How long has this been going on?"

"The stalker surfaced a year ago, but he's been getting bolder and bolder. Reaching closer and closer to me. More and more aggressive." She chewed her lower lip. "Between him and Donny, I'm on edge all the time. I can't sleep. I have nightmares. The only time I feel alive is when I'm on stage, but even that...when I look over and see Donny standing there...I just want to walk away."

"From him?"

"From singing. From touring. From that whole life." She laughed softly. "I meant it about living in your barn, Brody. That sounds like such a gift to me now." She paused. "Sleeping today with you was the first time I felt safe in a very long time."

And yet she'd still had a nightmare. He pressed a kiss to her cast. "Is that why you sent the ticket?"

She nodded. "It was a spontaneous idea. Nora, my tour manager, told me our next stop was Portland, and I thought of you, and I asked her to send you the ticket. I didn't know if you'd come or how you could help me..." She shrugged. "But as it turned out, I'm very glad that I asked her to send the ticket."

"Me, too." He rubbed her knuckles over his jaw, thinking.

She smiled. "You still do that?"

"Do what?"

"Rub my knuckles over your whiskers when you're thinking."

He stopped. "Sorry."

"No, it's okay. Keep doing it. It makes me feel like I've come home."

Brody met her gaze, losing himself in her familiar brown eyes. "I missed you, Tatum. Every fucking day."

Her eyes darkened. "I missed you, too, Brody. You were my world once."

He wanted to kiss her. He wanted to kiss her so fucking badly.

Tatum's gaze flicked to his lips, and then back to his face.

Silence stretched between them, long, taut silence filled with longing, need, and fifteen years of wanting.

Brody knew he should get out of the bed. Right now. She'd come to him for help. She was scared. On edge. Vulnerable. He needed to be the hero she needed and take himself out of the equation.

But he couldn't. There was literally no way he could make himself walk away from her.

Tatum searched his face. "How can I need you to kiss me so badly, when I haven't seen you for fifteen years? We knew each other as kids, Brody. *Kids*. We're strangers now, but—"

"Not strangers. Never strangers. Not us." He brought her hand to his lips and kissed each knuckle. "I feel the same way,

Tatum." His voice was rougher than he meant, raw with need he could barely even grasp. "I should get up."

"No!" She gripped his shirt with her right hand. "Stay." Without any more words, she pulled him toward her, drawing his face down to hers.

He went willingly, meeting her halfway.

The minute his lips touched hers, his world exploded.

CHAPTER NINE

Brody's kiss seemed to reach inside Tatum's heart the minute his lips touched hers. It was everything she'd dreamed of for so long, and so much more.

She wrapped her good arm around his neck, holding him close as she kissed him back. She felt starved for him, for his kiss, for his touch, for the feeling of safety she felt in his arms.

Brody draped his leg over her hips and drew her against him as they kissed. The feel of his body against hers was incredible. It had been so long since she'd been held, since she'd wanted to be held.

She was afraid to break the kiss, afraid that if she gave him a chance to think about what he was doing, that he'd stop. He was always the good guy, the responsible one, the one who did what was right, and she knew that this wasn't right.

She was a mess.

He was in protector mode.

Their parting fifteen years ago had been a hell from which her heart had never healed.

There was no way that making love with him right now was a smart thing to do.

But now, in his arms, kissing him, none of that mattered. All she knew was that she needed to lose herself in him, one more time, one more glorious time.

She slid her hand under his shirt and spread her palm over his chest. She felt his muscles tense, and excitement soared through her at his response. He might have tossed her aside fifteen years ago, but the connection was still there. Their bond might be threadbare and neglected, but it was still there, holding onto the faintest bit of light.

"Take it off," she whispered into the kiss, tugging at his shirt. "Please, take it off."

His eyes were dark as he ripped it over his head. Before she could worry that he'd realize they shouldn't do this, he was back kissing her, his fingers unfastening the top button on the flannel shirt he'd given her.

Her heart began to race. His knuckles brushed over the swell of her breast as he worked his way down the buttons. He kissed her collarbone, then traced kisses down her sternum, between her breasts, following the path of his hand as he unfastened each button.

He reached the bottom, and the shirt fell open. Brody pulled back to look at her. She watched his face, suddenly nervous. The last time she'd been with him, she'd had a seventeen-year-old body. Fifteen years had changed her body, given her curves, scars, and softness that she hadn't once had.

But then he smiled, a reverent smile that made her relax. "Beauty that still takes my breath away," he whispered, as he bent down and kissed her breast.

Tatum ran her fingers through his soft hair, closing her eyes as he evoked sensations in her that she'd forgotten even existed. She was so lost in his touch that she barely even noticed when he untied the drawstring of her sweatpants and tugged them over her hips. His moves were pure seduction now, slower, savoring, relishing as he explored her body, taking his time, until she couldn't hold back, moving under him. "Make love to me, Brody."

"Tatum." Her name was a rough growl on his lips as he rolled off her and ditched the rest of his clothes.

When he came back, it was skin against skin everywhere. She ran her foot over his muscled calf as he moved over her, her hands roaming across his chest, biceps, and shoulders, unable to get enough of him.

He kissed her again. Long. Deep. Tender.

Then he slid inside her. They both sucked in their breath, and her eyes snapped open. The expression on his face was raw and vulnerable, matching the painful crack in her soul. She pulled him down to her, showering him with kisses as he began to move inside her, kissing him until she couldn't. Until all she could do was hang onto him, completely consumed by the sensations whirling through her, more and more and more until—

The orgasm tore through her, and she bit her lip to keep from screaming. But when Brody whispered her name as the orgasm took him, she felt her heart tumble again, right into his hands, into his everything, stripping her of the shields she'd spent fifteen years building.

As Brody collapsed beside her and pulled her into his arms, she realized she'd made a terrible mistake.

One time wouldn't be enough with him. She wanted more. She wanted forever.

But she had to remember this was Brody, the man who could never give her what she needed from him.

He was the one man she couldn't afford to love.

But she also couldn't leave him either. Not now. Not until she was safe.

Last time, after she'd fallen for him, she'd left.

But this time, she couldn't run.

This time, she had to stay.

∼

Brody felt Tatum tense immediately, and he swore silently as fear ripped through him. She wanted to leave again. He could feel it in the tension in her body, in the way she held her breath, in the way she kept her gaze focused on the ceiling instead of him.

He couldn't screw this up again. He had to keep her steady until he could find a way to untangle the past that had tripped them up so badly.

He wanted to tell her how much he'd missed her. How she still shook his world. And a thousand other things.

But he didn't.

He knew he had to play it cool. Distract her. "Did you call anyone to let them know you haven't been kidnapped?"

She shook her head, still tense. "No. I don't know anyone's number. They're all in my phone. Listen, Brody—"

"Isn't there anyone that will alert the police that you're missing? The police will find you if they want."

For a moment, she didn't respond, then he saw her forehead furrow in thought. "Victoria and Ace will worry. But I don't have their numbers. They're in my phone."

"Social media?"

She looked over at him. "I don't have my login info. I literally have nothing with me." She frowned. "That's so weird to be completely cut off from my life." She paused. "It actually feels kind of good. I've been accountable to others every second of my life since I was eighteen."

He grinned. "I hate accountability. I get that. So, let's call someone so the police don't hunt you down."

She bit her lip, then brightened. "My bass player's husband has an advertising agency. I can look that up."

"Great." He unlocked his phone and handed it to her.

Her fingers brushed against his, and she shot a look at him as she took the phone. She pulled the covers over her chest and turned away as she looked up the company online.

Brody took the opportunity to grab his pants. It went against every part of him to pretend they hadn't just made love, but he could tell how tense she was, and he knew he had to back off. There would be a right time, but it wasn't now.

She glanced over at him as he got dressed. "Hi, Jackson O'Hare please. This is Tatum Crosby. I know he's out of town. Please connect me. Thanks." She put the phone on speaker and set it on the bed as she grabbed his shirt.

Brody handed her Bella's sweatshirt. "This might fit you better. It's all I could find. We'll get you clothes today."

"This is fine." She continued to button his shirt, not noticing his relief that she'd chosen his shirt instead of Bella's. She was halfway through the buttons when a man's voice came on the phone.

"Tatum! Where the hell are you? We're so worried! What happened?"

Brody could hear the panic in the man's voice, and it made him smile. As scared and solo as Tatum was, she had at least one person who legitimately cared about her.

Tatum finished buttoning the bottom button. "I'm fine. I'm with a friend."

"What friend? How do you know it's a friend? We're your friends!"

"I know you are." Tatum glanced at Brody. "But I don't want anyone to know where I am."

"Fine, we won't tell. Where are you?"

"Jackson," she said as she looked around the bed. "I think

my stalker has been hired, or at least given help, by someone inside our team. He almost got me after the show."

There was silence for a moment. "Holy shit, Tatum. You're serious? You think it's Donny?"

"I don't know. But I'm not coming back until I figure it out." She paused. "It was close, Jackson. He broke my arm when I was fighting him." Her voice became tense again, and she hugged her cast to her chest.

Brody ground his jaw as he found the sweatpants she'd been wearing and handed them to her. He didn't like her scared. He didn't like her in danger.

"Holy shit, Tatum," Jackson said. "You need to call the police."

"I will." She rolled out of bed, and the shirt slid up just enough to reveal a long expanse of thigh that made Brody suck in his breath. "Tell people I'm fine, but that I'm taking a break. Tell them not to look for me. Don't tell them why."

"Where are you staying? I need to know how to reach you."

She looked at Brody and raised her brows.

Brody found her underwear and handed it to her, grinning when her cheeks turned pink. "I'm Tatum's friend she's staying with," he said, leaning over the phone.

There was a pause. "A man? You're with a *man*? What male friend do you have? Are you safe? Who are you? Tatum, give me the secret code to tell me you're safe."

"We don't have a secret code," she said as she slid her foot through the scrap of silk. "Relax. It's fine. I've known him for almost fifteen years."

"Fifteen years? Who have you known for fifteen years?"

"Jackson, you're a good friend to Tatum," Brody interrupted. "I appreciate that you're looking out for her, but I promise I'll keep her safe. I'll give you a phone number. Call it, leave a message for Tatum, and she'll get it. Got a pen?"

"Oh, holy shit, Tatum! You said last night at the show that you hadn't seen Brody Hart for fifteen years. Are you with him?"

Tatum's eyes widened as she finished pulling her underwear on, and she looked at Brody.

He swore under his breath. They'd screwed up.

Tatum bit her lip. "Jackson. Listen to me. I don't know how much danger I'm in, or who on my team is responsible for it. You can't tell anyone. You can't trust anyone." She sat back on the bed and hugged her knees to her chest. "Not even Ace."

There was silence. "He's my husband, Tatum."

"I know, but he works with them. If he sees Victoria freaking out, he'll want to reassure her. And if he tells her, then she might tell someone, and—"

"No. You knew when you called me that I would tell Ace anything you said. You know he's not the one responsible. If you think someone on the team is responsible, then we can keep an eye out. Help. He won't tell Victoria if you don't want him to." He paused. "I'm going to call him and tell him the minute we get off the phone, so you can either be on board or not."

Tatum looked up at Brody, questions on her face.

He hit mute on the phone. "Do you trust him and Ace?"

She nodded. "I do, but what if I'm wrong?"

"Then we'll know it's them. We'll put out a trail of breadcrumbs and see who follows." Brody unmuted the phone. "Jackson?"

"Yeah."

"This is Brody Hart."

He swore. "I knew it. I fucking knew it. You and Tatum set the stadium on fire when you guys sang together. Where are you guys?"

Brody paused for a moment to consider strategy, then

answered. "We're at my ranch in eastern Oregon." Tatum's face paled, and Brody put his hand on her knee to reassure her. "I took her to the hospital out here last night to get her wrist casted. She's all right. She's safe for the moment."

Jackson paused. "Some guy really broke her arm?"

"Yeah." Brody rubbed Tatum's leg. "If he's willing to break her arm, he's probably willing to hurt you and Ace, too, so don't go around asking questions. You don't know what you'll stir up."

"I don't want you to get hurt," Tatum added.

"I was in the Marines for five years," Jackson said. "I can handle myself. What can we do?"

"Listen," Brody said. "Someone knows something, and you may overhear something. People on her side will want to find her to make sure she's safe. Whoever is stalking her will want to find her so they can get to her. There will be a difference in how they talk about her, even if it's simply the emotions underlying their words. Listen."

"I can do that. What else?"

"That's it for now. Once we get some leads, we'll have you leak her location to whoever we suspect. We'll see what they do. But not yet. We need to get prepared."

"Got it. Where can I reach you?"

Brody rattled off his phone number. "That's my phone number. Text me your number so I have it."

"Right on. Got it."

Tatum leaned forward. "Can you grab my phone and all my stuff? I left it at the stadium."

"You bet. Nora probably grabbed it, but I'll find it and send it to you. What's the address?"

Brody gave it to him.

"Got it." He paused. "Tatum, be careful."

She looked at Brody. "I am."

"She's not alone," Brody said. "She's safe here."

"For now, but you both are celebrities. Someone had to have seen the two of you together. Someone's going to spill, and people are going to find you. I'm guessing you maybe have twenty-four hours before people know the two of you are together."

Brody swore under his breath, but he knew that Jackson was right. "Keep us posted as people figure stuff out. We'll be ready."

She took a breath and nodded. "Yeah, we will."

"All right," Jackson said. "I'm going to call Ace now, and then head over to find your stuff. We'll see what we can find out."

"Be careful," Tatum said. "I love you guys. I want you safe."

"We love you, too, baby. Don't worry about us. No one's going to mess with me or Ace. Call or text if you need anything. We'll be in touch." He disconnected.

Brody picked up his phone and shoved it in his back pocket, watching Tatum. Her face was tense. "How are you doing?"

She let out her breath. "I'm a little freaked out that the ball is already rolling, honestly. It makes me nervous that someone on my team knows that I'm here. You even gave him the address."

He frowned. "You don't trust Jackson?"

"It's not that. I absolutely believe he's not my stalker, but I don't want him to get hurt. He's always very protective of Ace, and I'm worried he's going to go into protector mode for me as well, and get in trouble."

"If he's been in the Marines, he's not helpless, but yeah. We need to find out more, fast. He's right. It won't take long for people to track you here."

"And then someone will come for me." She searched his gaze. "Someone from my team. It's so weird not to know who

I can trust. I mean, I'm guessing it's Donny, but I don't know for sure."

He wanted her to be right about trusting Jackson, but life had taught him that it was easy to get fooled if your heart was involved. "We'll find out soon enough."

She bit her lip. "So, what do we do?"

"We'll bring in the rest of my family. Alert people and—" He stopped when she grimaced. "What?"

She paused. "If you don't mind, I'd rather not bring your family into this. Can I just lay low at your house?"

He frowned. "Why?"

Her gaze flicked to him. "I didn't leave under the best of circumstances."

There it was. The past. Finally laid out between them. Tension flooded him. He wasn't ready to rock their fragile reconciliation by going back into the ugly past. "You're part of us, Tatum. You always will be. They know that. Especially Bella. You guys were so close."

She shook her head empathically. "No, I don't think—"

There were sudden footsteps in the hallway, but before either of them could move, his sister Bella appeared in the doorway. She was wearing jeans, cowboy boots, and a Bella's Café tee shirt. "Brody, I heard you up here. Do you have—" She stopped and stared at them.

Brody realized the covers were still tossed, he was barefoot and shirtless, and Tatum was wearing his shirt and no pants. It didn't take a genius to realize what they'd been doing, and he knew Bella wasn't going to pretend she hadn't figured it out. "Hey, sis—"

"Holy shit. You guys are back together."

Tatum scrambled to her feet, near panic on her face. "No, we're not," she said quickly. "I just—"

"What were you thinking?" Bella spun to Brody, her hands on her hips. "You were supposed to go to Portland to finally get her out of your system, not bring her back here!" She glared at Tatum. "Keep away from my brother. You've done enough damage already."

Then she spun around, stalked out, and slammed the door behind her.

CHAPTER TEN

Tatum felt like running for Brody's truck. Embarrassment flooded her cheeks, and she fumbled for Brody's sweats, tears blurring her eyes. "I shouldn't have come. It was stupid. I'll call an Uber or something—"

"Tatum." Brody's hands closed over hers, holding her still. "No."

"No, it's fine. I know that your family is your priority. I don't expect anything different." Of course she knew that. She'd been stupid to think that she had a chance putting herself back in his life again. "Go talk to her. She's upset."

"This isn't about her. It's about us."

Tatum tried to get her foot into the sweatpants, but they kept swaying out of the way. "There is no us, Brody. There can't be an us—" She tried to grab the waistband with her broken arm, and pain shot through her. She gasped and went down to her knees, holding her arm to her chest. "God, that hurt."

"Let me help."

"No!" She staggered to her feet, still clutching her arm to

her chest to protect it. "It's fine. I don't need anything. Jackson will take care of me—"

"Tatum." He caught her good elbow, his fingers closing gently around it. "It's okay."

"It's not! Not at all. I thought it was. I pretended it was, but it's not. I can't—"

"Let me help you get the pants on." He picked up the sweats, opened the waistband for her and crouched in front of her. "Come on."

"I can't do this with you." Her hand shaking with emotion, she set it on Brody's shoulder while she put her foot into the pants.

"Yes, you can." Brody pulled the leg of the pants over her foot, then she set her foot down.

He was still the same. Refusing to talk about her emotions. Refusing to validate them. "Always the peacemaker, aren't you Brody?"

He glanced up at her as he guided her other foot into the pants. "Is that bad?"

"Yes! I mean, no, I know it's what you had to do to survive, to pull people together, so it's fine." She helped him pull her sweats up and then stood there like some helpless fool while he tied the drawstring.

"Clearly, it's not fine," he said evenly. "What's the problem?"

"You." She put her hand on her hip as he rose to his feet. "Your only goal, ever, is to protect your family, to make sure everyone is good and happy. You want everything to work perfectly. There's no room for anything else."

He ground his jaw. "You're in that circle, too, Tatum—"

"No, I'm not. I'll always be on the outside of it. There's no room for anyone inside that circle."

He frowned. "There is, actually. There always has been. I welcomed everyone who came to us. I still do."

He didn't get it. Tatum stared into his beautiful face, the one she had dreamed of for so long, and she knew she'd been right to leave him, no matter how badly it had broken her heart. His protector nature was part of what she'd fallen in love with, and it was the part of his character that made it impossible for them to ever be together. "I know you think that," she said softly.

His brow knitted. "I don't understand."

"I know." She took a breath. "Look, it's fine. I don't want to upset Bella. I'll call Jackson back and we'll figure out something." She held out her hand for his phone.

He didn't hand it to her, and she could see the indecision on his face. If he didn't give her his phone, he'd be trapping her, and taking away her choices. If he did give her the phone, she would leave. He wouldn't want either of those. But those were his choices. "Brody. The phone."

"I'm sorry," he said instead.

Oh, no. She wasn't going back to that place. "Just give me the phone."

"I'm sorry that I put her before you fifteen years ago. I've regretted it every moment of the last fifteen years what I did that night."

Her chest tightened. She didn't want to relive that night. "The phone, please."

"I was wrong," he said, his voice rough. "I thought I had time with you. I thought that you would wait for me while I helped the others."

Her gaze snapped to his face. "That's why you're sorry? Because I *left* and didn't wait around for you to finally treat me like I mattered? You're sorry that your choice made me leave, and *not* about what you did?" She stalked over to him, anger suddenly pouring through her. "I *loved* you, Brody. I was seventeen, and so head over heels for you that all I wanted was to be with you for the rest of my life."

He grimaced. "I know—"

"Do you? Do you know?" She hit his chest with her good hand. "We made love that night. We told each other we loved each other. You promised me forever. And then, what did you do? You offered to marry someone else two days later. What the hell, Brody? *What the hell?*"

"I'm deeply sorry for that, and I regret it. It was wrong to do that without preparing you—"

"Without *preparing* me? Are you kidding?" This was the apology she'd dreamed of for so long? *This?* "Brody, you don't do that. There are certain things you don't do, and one of them is offering to marry someone other than the woman you just announced you'll love forever."

His jaw flexed. "Her father was coming after her. I was giving her the safety of a husband so he couldn't get her. I couldn't let her go back—"

"I know." She held up her hands to silence him. "I've heard it all before, Brody. I get it. You're a guardian of others. You protect everyone. You'll sacrifice yourself completely to save others. You're a hero. Whoever is in the most danger gets your attention. Like today. You let Bella run away in tears because someone might kill me. I win right now. Yay for me. Are you going to offer to marry me next, not because you love me, but to keep me safe?"

Brody scowled. "I wouldn't make that choice now. If I offer to marry you, it's because I love you—"

"Here's the thing, Brody. I don't want to spend the rest of my life in such dire straits that I come first. I want to be happy, stable, and good. But if I am, then I know that I will never come first for you. Whoever is in the most trouble comes first."

"I'm not going to walk away from someone in danger—"

"No. I know."

"Then what do you want?"

A ROGUE COWBOY'S SECOND CHANCE

She met his gaze. "I just wanted to be your special person, Brody. It's all anyone wants. To be that special someone to the person they love. But there won't ever be space for that person in your life. Family is family. I get that. But at the end of the day, there's a special bond with that person you love. Like Jackson. He loves me. But he wasn't going to lie to his husband. Because Ace comes first for him. Period. I want that, and that's not who you are. It's not who you will ever be."

Brody's jaw flexed as he stared at her. "There's room for both in my life, Tatum. I let Bella leave not because you are in danger, but because there is no other you. There never has been. I fucked up when I was eighteen. Would I do it again? Probably. I didn't know what else to do back then. Would I do it now? No. Now, I'll stand here in this room with you for as long as it takes to get another chance with you."

It was her turn to stare at him. "Another chance? You want...another chance?"

He nodded and walked over to her. "When Bella said she wanted me to go to Portland to get you out of my system, she was referring to the fact that I've never gotten over you. You're still the woman I let get away, the woman I never stopped loving."

She swallowed. "We were kids, Brody. Kids in a desperate situation. You have no idea who I am now."

"Then show me. Let me see. Let's try this again."

God, she wanted to. She wanted to so badly. Brody was her safe haven, her first love. Maybe her only love. But she knew what drove him. "You want me right now because I'm in danger again," she said, her voice breaking. "It's not about me. And maybe I want you right now because I'm scared."

He slid his hand into her hair. "And maybe we are drawn together because our souls have always been connected, and we're right for each other."

Tatum wrapped her hand around his wrist. "I can't do this, Brody. I can't do this with you right now. I have an ex-husband who is giving me actual nightmares, and maybe trying to get me killed. There's no way I can do this with you. I just can't."

He said nothing, but his dark brown eyes searched her face. She felt like he was trying to see inside her soul, and she instinctively put up her shields. She didn't let anyone get that close to her anymore. Brody had once, and he was the only one, and that had ripped her heart open. No more. Never again.

"All right," he said finally.

"All right?" She was startled by the wave of crushing disappointment that swept through her. He hadn't fought for her before. He'd let her go. And now, with one speech, he wasn't fighting for her again? She took a breath. "Great."

"But I would like you to stay so I can protect you." Irony flashed across his face. "It's what I do best, right?"

Tatum bit her lip. She was so off kilter right now that she wanted to run, but the truth was, she didn't know where to go. She didn't know who she could count on for help. She might not be able to trust Brody with her heart, but her life? As he said, it was what he was good at. Maybe, when all this was over, she could get her life back, the way she wanted it, not the way it had been for the last five years. "I'll stay...if you'll help me with something else, too."

A grin crooked the corner of his mouth. "You're bribing me to let me keep you safe?"

"Yep. I know you live to protect, so you'll do whatever it takes to get the chance. Is it a deal?"

He cocked an eyebrow at her. "What do I need to do to earn the chance to protect you?"

"Help me find a way to get out of my contract with Donny as my manager. I've had lawyers go over the language, and there's no out that anyone can find. But if I can't get away from him..." She paused, her throat tightening as she spoke the words that had been weighing on her with increasing pressure lately. "If I can't, I'm going to have to stop singing. I have to get away from him, Brody, and that's the only path I see."

His jaw flexed. "Singing is what keeps your soul alive."

"I know." She couldn't hold back the sudden tears. "He's killing me, Brody. I can't do it anymore."

He swore under his breath, but nodded. "Of course I'll help."

She nodded, feeling stupid with her tears. "Thanks. It's just that—"

"I know, baby." He reached out and pulled her into his arms. "I know."

Tatum let herself surrender to Brody's hug. She needed him as a friend, as a support system, as the only one she'd ever trusted with her true self. With Brody, she didn't have to pretend. "I missed you," she whispered.

"I missed you, too, Tatum." He kissed the top of her head, a kiss that was about support and friendship, not seduction. "I'm glad you're here. We'll get this straightened out, and then you can go back to what you love."

"Thanks." She nodded, breathing in the warmth of his body. Go back to what she loved? It was singing...but it was also the man holding her. *Just friends*. How could she keep herself from being near him and falling for him again when he was doing his protector thing with her?

She loved his protector side, even if it was what had broken her heart.

One summer. That was all they'd had together. One summer when she was seventeen.

How could one summer fifteen years ago have such power over her? Over him?

And how could they finally get past it?

Maybe it was finally time for both of them to be free and move on.

Maybe that was why she'd come back. Not to love him. Not to rekindle the romance they'd once had.

But to finally be able to leave him. Physically and emotionally.

Maybe this was supposed to be their final farewell.

CHAPTER ELEVEN

He was going to keep Tatum this time.

Or at least try like hell.

For years, Brody had wondered if he'd imagined their connection. If he'd turned her into a goddess that didn't really exist. If their summer romance really had been nothing more than a teenage fling between two desperate, hopeless kids that had clung to the breath of hope they'd given each other.

But as he leaned back in his deck chair, listening to Tatum talk as she finished up the chicken he'd grilled for their late afternoon dinner, he knew the answer.

They weren't kids anymore. They were adults with lives, success, and stability. They weren't desperate anymore. And yet, their connection was still there, deeper than it had been. He didn't know how it had become deeper when they'd been apart, but it had.

He'd backed off to give Tatum the space she needed, but he knew that she was feeling the same things he was. Was it enough? He'd heard what she said about him being a protector, never putting her first, and the truth was, he didn't know if she was correct in her evaluation of him. Was it impossible for him to put a woman first? For him to treasure her above all else. And to make sure she knew it?

He thought he could. And he was committed to finding out, to taking this as far as it could go. To taking this second chance with her and giving it everything he had.

The afternoon sun was illuminating golden highlights in her dark brown hair, streaks he remembered from that summer so long ago. Her face wasn't as lean as it had once been. She had curves now where she had been sinewy before. He loved her body now. He loved the changes in her. He wanted to tell her how beautiful she was, but he didn't dare.

He knew she would bolt at the first excuse, and he wasn't going to give her one.

She'd kept the conversation neutral, asking questions about the ranch and horses. Not about him, his life, or his family. But she'd been willing to answer questions about her music, about her tours, about her life.

Her passion for her music was as strong as it had been when she was a teenager. He loved watching the way she lit up when she talked about it. But his gut clamped down in anger whenever her stories got too close to Donny, and she retreated emotionally.

Donny was under her skin. He could feel it. The man may not have hit her, but he controlled her, and had abused her emotionally. And that shit was going to end now.

Every time Tatum moved her left hand and winced in pain, anger pulsed through Brody. Someone had broken her arm. Donny? Someone else? He was going to find out. Make sure she was safe. Help her get her life back...even if it meant she left him when she was free again.

He didn't want her to stay because she had to.

He wanted her to stay with him because she wanted to.

Tatum finished her meal and leaned back. "That was fantastic. I didn't know you could cook."

He smiled. "One of my many skills acquired later in life. How are you doing? All right?"

She shrugged. "Sleeping half the day and the food perked me up. I'm good." She raised her brows. "So, what next? About this." She held up her arm, as if to make sure she wasn't trying to open the door to their relationship.

He knew, but regret still pulsed through him anyway. He had to work through not only their own past, but the fifteen years under Donny's thumb. Trust him? Trust men? Trust relationships?

He doubted there was any willingness to trust left in her, but he was going to find it anyway.

So, he gave her a neutral smile that gave her the space she needed. He had his computer out and ready, the cursor blinking at him. He'd already taken notes while he'd been cooking. "First, I need you to send me the contract. I know a specialist who will look at it for you. Good?"

She nodded. "I've had a couple top attorneys look at it already."

"Well, we'll see. I have some incredibly brilliant minds at my disposal." He handed her his phone, and she called her attorney, and then they called his.

He called her cell phone directly, and she answered immediately, as always. "Brody," she said. "How can I help you today?"

"Eliana, I'm here with Tatum Crosby. Tatum, this is Eliana Tiernan."

There was a pause. "The singer?" Eliana said.

"Yes. She's got a situation she needs help with. Tatum?"

Tatum leaned forward. "Hi, Ms. Tiernan—"

"Call me Eliana. I'm on your side, Tatum. What's up?" Eliana was one of the most brilliant people Brody knew, highly respected, and an absolute badass, but she was also one of the most down to earth people he'd ever met. Other attorneys showed up to meetings in suits. Eliana wore jeans, sneakers, and tank tops, and then blew them all away.

Tatum bit her lip. "I'd like to get out of the management contract that I signed when I was eighteen. I've had a bunch of attorneys look at it, and no one can find a way for me to get out of it."

He could hear Eliana's fingers typing. "Hang on. I'm Googling you right now. Your ex-husband is your manager?"

Tatum glanced at Brody, a sheepish expression on her face, as if she were embarrassed she'd gotten herself stuck with him. "Yeah."

"What's he like?"

Tatum frowned, but Brody nodded at her to continue. Eliana was special. That was part of the reason he'd put Tatum on the call with her. He had a feeling Tatum needed a little bit of Eliana in her life.

"He's a controlling bastard who might be arranging for a stalker to terrorize me so I take him back," Tatum blurted out, then her cheeks turned red. "I mean, I don't know that. I just—"

"Oh, Tatum." Eliana sighed. "I had a husband like that. You gotta get away from him or he's going to suck the life out of your soul."

Tears suddenly filled Tatum's eyes. "You had one?"

"Honey, lots of women have one of those." She paused. "Brody didn't tell you one of my specialties, did he?"

Tatum glanced at Brody. "No."

"I'm the best in the country at untangling egregious contracts between married couples that screw over the wife. It's my favorite thing I do. There's nothing like setting a woman free. You're not alone, honey. Not by a long shot."

Brody smiled as Tatum's shoulders seemed to sag as she let go of the tension she'd been holding. "It's not your fault you signed that contract, Tatum," he said gently. "He had all the power. You were a starry-eyed teenager who wanted the world. Don't blame yourself."

She looked at him, tears still brimming in her eyes, and then back at the phone sitting on the table between them. "You think...you think you can do something?"

"I never make promises," Eliana said, "but I pretty much always find a way to make it better. I'm very good at what I do. It matters to me."

Tatum bit her lip. "Thank you."

"You got it, honey. Now, send me that contract and I'll get on it. What's the timing?"

Tatum picked up the phone, making Brody grin. It was a small act, but it was a powerful one. A taking control for herself. "Right now, I'm sitting on Brody's back deck with a cast on my arm, hiding out until we figure out if Donny sent the stalker after me who broke my arm last night."

There was a pause for a moment. "All right then, to the top of the pile your case goes. Do you have an email address? I'll send you a contract for my services. I'm extremely expensive. Can you pay? If you can't, I will, of course, do it for free, but—"

"I can pay," Tatum interrupted. "I'll pay double to make up for the women who can't pay you."

Brody could almost see the smile that came over Eliana's face. "Women like you are the reason that I can help others for free. Double my fee it is. Thank you for that."

"Any time," Tatum said, her smile widening.

Brody knew where that smile was coming from. It was that feeling that came from helping others. Best damned feeling in the world. If Tatum's situation could help others, that would help take the sting out of it, and she needed some serious balm right now.

"Tatum doesn't have access to any of her accounts right

now," he told Eliana. "She took off without any of her stuff," Brody said. "Email the contract to me."

"Got it." Eliana paused. "Tatum?"

"Yes?"

"I'm taking off my lawyer hat right now. This isn't legal advice. It's a tip, woman to woman."

A small smile played at Tatum's lips. "All right."

"Brody's one of the good guys out there. I've taken down a lot of assholes, and I can see 'em from a hundred miles away. Brody's one you can trust."

Tatum's cheeks turned pink. "I'm not dating him—"

"I know you had a thing with him. I would have made a move on him long ago if he weren't so hung up on you. I have no idea if you feel the way about him as he feels about you, and I know that you probably aren't interested in ever giving a guy a chance again. But if you're tempted by him, I just want to tell you that he won't hold you back the way most men do."

Brody laughed and leaned in toward the phone. "You never would have made a move on me, Eliana," he said, trying to distract Tatum from the advice she'd just been given, advice he would have paid Eliana a shit ton of money to give, if he'd known it was an option. "You won't touch a relationship with a ten-foot-pole."

Eliana chuckled. "This is true, but it's easier to blame you for it than my own emotional baggage. Tatum, you still there?"

"I am."

"Go find that bastard who broke your arm. I'll take care of your ex. We'll hit 'em from both sides and you'll be walking free before you know it. Got it?"

Tatum smiled. "Got it. And, Eliana? Woman to woman?"

"What's up?"

"Thanks."

Eliana laughed. "You got it, girl. Life is good when you have a badass woman at your back. Never forget it."

"I won't. Front row tickets to any of my shows for life."

"That's fantastic," Eliana said cheerfully. "I'll be there, for sure. Can't wait to meet you. You're as cool as Brody claimed you were."

Tatum raised her brows at Brody. "I'm definitely cooler than Brody said I was."

"Of course you are. Men have no idea how fantastic women are. I'll be in touch. Give Brody a kiss for me, since Lord knows I'll never kiss the man, but he's about as kissable as they get." She disconnected.

Tatum was grinning as she handed the phone back to Brody. "I think I might want to marry Eliana."

Brody smiled. "I thought you'd like her. She's tough as hell and has one of the biggest hearts I know."

Tatum gave him a speculative look. "She seems to adore you, as well."

"I'm pretty adorable," he agreed.

"You guys never dated?" Her question was casual, but with just enough of an edge to make Brody have to stifle a grin.

Tatum was a little jealous about the possibility of him dating Eliana. He liked that. He liked that *a lot*. Tatum might put on an aloof front, but she still cared. That meant there was hope. "We never dated," he confirmed.

"Why not?"

He shrugged. "Because she's not you."

CHAPTER TWELVE

TATUM'S CHEEKS turned pink at Brody's declaration, but she didn't turn away. She studied him. "What does that mean?"

He leaned back in his chair and stretched his arm out on the back of the adjacent chair, intentionally keeping his stance and tone casual. "You set the gold standard for me, Tatum. It's the way it is."

"It's been fifteen years, Brody. We knew each other for a summer." But she was searching his face, as if she wanted to know. Not recoiling from his feelings. Not right now.

So, he met her gaze. "Tatum, I've spent my life taking care of others. You know that, right?"

She nodded. "It's who you are."

"I feel like I walk around with my arms out, ready to catch anyone who starts to fall. That's my job. That's what I'm here to do. I love it. It gives my life meaning."

She pressed her lips together. "I know it does—"

"But who catches me?"

She frowned. "What?"

"You, Tatum. You're the one who held her arms out for

me. You're the one who makes me whole, who holds me up, the one I need to keep me together."

Her face softened. "You don't need anyone to hold you up, Brody."

"Not true." He swore under his breath and leaned forward. "I hold up the world, and you hold me up. No one else. Just you. It will always be you, no matter what happens between us. You're the light that keeps my soul whole."

She stared at him. "I don't do anything for you. I haven't seen you in fifteen years. And that summer...that summer you were the one who took care of me. It wasn't equal. I didn't give you anything—"

"You're wrong." He took her hand, the one without the cast, pressing it between his palms. "I was a homeless kid fighting to stay alive and free. I had a bunch of kids counting on me, and I was a kid myself, running away from an abusive stepfather after my mom died. I had no money, no family, nowhere to go. I was scared all the time. Scared I would fail and someone would pay for my mistake. I didn't ask to become a hero, but I was suddenly in that role, and I was absolutely fucking terrified I would fail."

Tatum's face softened. "Oh, Brody—"

"The reason I had to make everyone else safe, was because I needed to protect them from going through what I went through. It was as if by keeping them safe, I could somehow protect the little boy that I'd once been. It was this desperate compulsion. Still is, in a way. Like I need to overcompensate and be that protector I never had when I was little, when I needed it."

Tears filled her eyes. "Brody—"

He played with her fingers. "Here's the thing, Tatum. It didn't work, though. I tried to make others safe, but *I* never felt safe. I never let down my guard. Ever. The harder I worked to protect them, the less safe I felt, because I was so fucking scared I'd fuck it up." He met her gaze. "Except when I was with you. That was what you gave me, Tatum. You gave my heart a place where it could breathe again, recover, and find its strength to go on. You made me feel safe. And you still do."

She searched his face. "I...I had no idea. You never told me that."

He laughed softly. "Of course not. I was eighteen. I had to be tough."

She smiled. "And now?"

"I'm a total softie who cries at the drop of the hat."

She burst out laughing. "You're such a liar." She sat back. "Anyone could have done that for you, Brody. It wasn't me. It was just that I was there at that time."

"I'll never know, because you were the one who did it." He paused, unsure whether to continue, to say the rest. Would it push her away? It might. It might be too soon. He forced himself to pull back, to not go where he wanted to go. "You're my star, Tatum. You were then, and you still are," he said, trying to keep his tone light so he didn't scare her. "Which means, even though Eliana is fantastic, she's got no chance with me, and she knows it." He tapped Tatum's nose. "You are singlehandedly responsible for the fact that Eliana will never land the man she has pined for her entire adult life."

Tatum laughed again, a beautiful sound that made him smile. "I don't think Eliana would pine for anyone. She's not the pining type."

"I'm sure she pines for me."

"I'm pretty sure she doesn't—"

"Eliana?" The deck slider opened. "You were talking to Eliana? Did she ask for my number yet?"

Tatum's smile vanished as her gaze shot to the man walking onto the deck.

"She never asks for your number. You're going to have to go after her yourself." Brody had heard the truck pull up in front of his house, and he knew whose footsteps were coming through the house. He stood up as the kitchen slider opened and one of his brothers walked out. "Dylan. You remember Tatum Crosby. Tatum, this is Dylan."

Tatum bit her lip, wariness etched on her features, no doubt expecting another welcome like she'd received from Bella. "Hi," she said hesitantly.

Dylan was wearing a black tee shirt, jeans, and hiking books. His cowboy hat was pulled low over his brow, but not low enough to hide the row of stud earrings in his left ear, the tattoo on the side of his neck, or the way his dark hair curled a little long and ragged. He carried himself like he had a chip on his shoulder, and most strangers believed it and kept their distance. "Tatum."

He strode over to the table, set his backpack and a duffel bag on a chair, and held out his arms. "It's been too fucking long."

Relief rushed through Brody at the warmth in Dylan's voice, and he could see Tatum visibly relax. "Dylan," she whispered, barely getting his name out before he swept her up in a fierce hug.

She hugged him back, closing her eyes. "I missed you," she whispered.

A hint of jealousy shot through Brody at how tightly they were hugging, which made him scowl. What the hell? Since when was he jealous of his brothers? But he was. He could definitely feel his tension mounting the longer they hugged. He cleared his throat. "All right, let's move on with this. We have a lot to do."

"Fuck, Tatum." Dylan finally let her go, pausing with his hands on her upper arms as he inspected her, totally ignoring Brody. "You look like hell. Who told you that plaster casts are fashionable? It's going to kill your brand."

She laughed and patted his cheeks. "Did you know there are professionals that will actually cut your hair? You don't need to use kitchen scissors."

"I like my hair the way it is. It scares all the nice girls away." He pulled a black marker out of his back pocket and held up her arm. "No one else has signed it. I'll be your first."

Her first? Dylan wasn't going to be Tatum's first at anything. "Give it a rest, Dylan," Brody said.

Still ignoring Brody, Dylan scrawled *Never forget you're a star!* in big, bold letters, and then signed his name with a flourish. He tossed the marker at Brody as he sat down. "Always coming in second with Tatum, Brody. Always second."

Brody caught the marker and glared at his brother. "Shut up." He said it with a smile, but he couldn't quite keep the irritation out of his voice, which made Dylan grin.

"He's still not over you," Dylan said cheerfully. "Never has been. That's that Tatum magic for you. Hangs around forever even after she's long gone. Did you know that brother of mine put an emotional wall up the day you left, and he's never taken it down?"

Tatum's smile faded, and she glanced at Brody.

Shit. He didn't want to put the pressure on her. "Dylan—"

"Just kidding." Dylan picked up his backpack. "All right. Let's talk, kiddos."

Tatum frowned. "About what?"

"I asked Dylan to stop by," Brody said, almost wishing he hadn't. He'd forgotten how close she and Dylan had once been. There had never been anything romantic about their relationship, but they'd shared many private jokes and had always had a bond he'd been a little jealous of. "He's a private investigator."

Tatum raised her brows as Dylan opened his backpack and pulled out his computer. "Really? You're a PI? That's kind of funny after all the times you wound up in jail."

Dylan grinned. "Irony at its finest. I love to be unpredictable." He booted up the computer. "I've taken the liberty of getting started. You don't mind, do you?"

Tatum glanced at Brody. "Getting started with what?"

"Your case," Dylan said. "I've managed to obtain copies of the security footage from the stadium, and I've isolated the footage of the attack. If the two of you could adjust your chairs to see the screen, I'll show you what I've found."

Tatum's eyes widened, and she sat back, holding her casted arm to her chest. "I don't want to watch that."

"I get that." Dylan's voice was gentle, but firm. "It would be helpful if you did. You might notice something we won't."

She shook her head, and Brody could see her practically shrinking into her chair. *Shit.* She was retreating into the fear of the night before, when she'd been so panicked. "Tatum?" he said gently.

She looked at him and silently shook her head, a tiny little head shake that spoke volumes.

Brody swore and pulled his chair up between her and Dylan, and took her hand. Her fingers were cold, and she wrapped her hand tightly around his as he leaned in toward her. "Baby, it's time for this to be over. You deserve better than to live in fear. Right?"

Tatum stared at her hand, wrapped up in Brody's, then looked up at him. "Yes," she whispered. Then she cleared her throat and said it again, louder this time. "Yes."

He smiled. God, he loved her courage. Still the same

Tatum. Vulnerable, but brave. Gentle but strong. Sassy but sweet. "If there's any chance you can see something that could help us figure out who is behind it, we need you to watch. Not to relive it. But to help catch that fucker and shut him down."

The corner of her mouth twisted. "Such profanity, Mr. Hart. What kind of a role model are you?"

"Profanity is a sign of genius. I read that on a meme, so it must be true."

She laughed softly. "Everything on the internet is true. Always."

"Of course it is. According to the internet, I've had at least ten girlfriends who I've never actually met. And several kids as well."

She grinned. "I dated all three Hemsworth brothers, and I never even knew it. That was such a bummer I missed out on that once-in-a-lifetime experience, right?"

"Absolutely. Even I would date a Hemsworth brother if I had a chance," Dylan said.

Brody could see Tatum relaxing, and he knew they almost had her. "If Dylan and I both promise to watch the video with our guns ready to shoot the fucker through the screen, you think you can watch it?"

"You're not shooting my computer," Dylan said.

"Not even for Tatum's well-being?"

"That's what yoga is for."

Tatum laughed aloud at Dylan's joke, which poked at Brody ever so slightly. Dammit. He wanted to be in a good place with her, not getting some macho jealous streak tainting their interaction. He forced himself to chuckle at Dylan's joke.

"All right," she said. "I'll watch it, but if I freak out and run to the corner of the patio and start throwing up from PTSD, consider turning it off. Cool?"

"Deal." Brody kept Tatum's hand in his, noting that she didn't try to pull it away. "Give it a go, Dylan."

"You got it." He pulled up a grainy video on the screen and hit play.

CHAPTER THIRTEEN

Tatum gripped Brody's hand as the video began to play.

They were on the camera in the hallway where the crowd had attacked her. She searched the crowd for the security guard who had grabbed her. There were so many people. No security guards. "That's weird," she said. "There isn't any security. Usually we have them all over."

But that made sense why she hadn't been able to find one when she'd needed it.

She leaned forward. "Which door do I come out of?"

Dylan pointed at the center of the screen. "That one."

Tatum scanned the crowd at the edge of the camera, and then she saw him. Chills shot down her spine, and fear gripped her belly. "That one. There he is." She watched as he shoved his way through people, moving fast, clearly focused and on a mission— "He knows I'm going to come out of there," she said suddenly. "Look at the way he's moving. He's trying to get there before me."

Dylan nodded. "That's what I thought as well."

She watched as she flung the door open and burst out into the hall. The crowd surged around her immediately, and that sense of claustrophobia closed in on her. She disappeared from view, swallowed up by the aggressive crowd.

"That's your life?" Brody said quietly.

She nodded. "Not always that bad, but yeah."

The security guard shoved his way through the crowd. He even punched one guy to get him out of the way. "He's so much taller than the others."

"He's a big man." Brody's hand tightened around hers. "He looks like hired muscle. Look at his shoulders and the way he's handling the crowd." He swore. "That's no ordinary stalker, Tatum. I'd wager your gut was right. He was hired."

As they watched, the security guard emerged from the crowd with Tatum tucked against his torso. "He shielded me like a bodyguard," she said. "He knew what to do." She'd been wondering if she should have realized there was something wrong before going in the kitchen with him, but watching the video, she knew she would have done the same thing again.

The crowd had been fierce, and the guy knew how to protect.

"It's going to make me hesitant to trust security again," she said.

Brody tightened his arm around her. "We can set up a better process for you to know who's been hired."

She bit her lip and nodded, but she wasn't sure if that would work. Her ability to do her career depended on her ability to trust her security guards. If she couldn't...then she couldn't be who she was.

She watched as the security guard took her to a closed door, pulled it open, and then yanked it shut behind them, shoving a few arms out of the way. A few fans tried to open the door behind him, but it was locked.

She let out her breath. "What about the video in the kitchen?"

"There's no footage," Dylan said. "The camera was off. Never recorded."

She looked over at Dylan. "Really?"

"Yeah. He could have done anything to you in there."

Chills ran down her spine and she shivered. Brody put his arm around her, and she instinctively slid onto his lap and tucked herself against his chest. He immediately enfolded her in his strong arms, and she leaned into him, grounding herself in his strength. Not that she was weak. She wasn't. But she was scared again, scared about what could have happened last night. And scared about what could happen in the future. And Brody made her feel safe.

She laughed to herself. Maybe it wasn't so bad that he liked to be a protector, right?

Silently, they watched as time ticked by. She knew what was happening behind that door, how she was fighting for her life, but the hallway was normal life. The crowd dispersed. Other security appeared and began moving the crowd along.

So many people so close. And no one had any idea what was happening only a few feet away. "It's chilling," she said. "No one knew I was there. No one knew I needed help."

Brody's arms tightened around her, and he pressed a kiss to her shoulder. "We'll figure out what's going on, I promise."

At that moment, she burst out of the door. Her eyes were wide with panic, and she was cradling her arm. Instinctively, Tatum hugged her cast to her chest as she watched. She could see the terror and desperation in her face, and the same feeling rushed over her as she watched herself plunge into the crowd and disappear out of sight.

Brody brushed his thumb over her cheek, wiping away tears she hadn't even noticed. "You're strong as hell," he said. "That guy was trained, at least on some level, and you got away."

She nodded. "Because I had a pot. I don't usually travel

around with pots."

"I have a lot. I'm happy to lend you some."

She managed a smile. "I could start a line of kitchen cookware, a combination of dinner prep and self-defense. We can call it the Tatum Attack."

Brody chuckled as he brushed his thumb over her other cheek. "I like it. I'll be your first investor."

She raised her brows. "I've learned not to mix business with pleasure."

His smile faded. "Then let's not do business together. Ever."

For a moment, they stared at each other, their laughter fading into the weight of his words, then Dylan interrupted.

"Watch this." Dylan nodded at the screen. "Watch when he comes out."

Tatum dragged her gaze off Brody's face and looked at the computer. It took a few more seconds, but the door finally opened. He staggered out, holding his head. Blood was trickling down his temple.

She grinned. "I hope he suffered a lot."

"Nice work," Brody said.

Dylan grinned. "It made my day when I saw that."

As they watched, he looked both ways, clearly searching for her. When he didn't see her, he pulled out his phone and called someone. He spoke for a minute, then hung up.

Then he pulled off his security guard hat and jacket and tossed them in a nearby trash can. He then blended into the crowd in a plain black tee shirt, looking like any other concert goer.

The transformation was shocking. "He looks like any other guy now." Again, the realization was chilling. "He could have been right next to me in any crowd, and I never would have noticed him. No alarm would have sounded that he was there to cause me harm."

Brody's arms were still tight around her. "He's good," he agreed as he rested his chin on her shoulder. "My guess is that he's not cheap. He knows what he's doing. He was definitely working for someone. He got instructions there to abort."

"That's what I think as well," Dylan said. "I was able to get enough footage to see that he left the building and went into the parking lot. I didn't see where he went from there, and I wasn't able to get an ID on him. I have some folks running his face through their databases to see if they can find a match, but nothing so far."

"What about Donny?" Tatum asked. "Is he on camera anywhere when the security guard made that call?"

Dylan grinned. "Not bad thinking for an artsy-fartsy girl."

She managed a small laugh. "An artsy-fartsy girl who has made over a hundred million dollars being artsy," she retorted.

"Money doesn't impress us around here." Dylan pounded his fist over his heart. "It's all about what's in here, and you've got the goods, even if you are one of those crazy artist types."

She smiled, starting to relax again. Sitting here, on Brody's deck, with two of the Hart brothers, she was safe. Unless a sniper was after her, no one could get to her. She sat up. "What if he's a sniper?"

Brody didn't laugh at her. "Our property is too big, and we have cameras set up everywhere. He'd never get close enough to shoot without us seeing him. You're fine."

"But you don't have a gate or fences."

He shrugged. "We don't believe in locking people out. If anyone needs us, ever, they are welcome to come."

She smiled. "You haven't changed."

"Nope." He cocked his head. "But that's why we have all the cameras. Anyone can come on the property, but we'll know they're there."

She took a breath. "You're sure we're safe?"

"Positive." He smiled. "We're not without our own issues, Tatum. We live with precautions, and you're inside them now. All right?"

She nodded. "We spent our childhoods hiding from truant officers and social workers, and we're still hiding. We just have nicer prisons."

"Nope," Brody said. "Not hiding. Choosing what we let into it. There's a difference. We're free now."

She looked around the beautiful ranch, with its seemingly endless pastures. The ranch felt like freedom, and she never felt like that. "Not for me," she said slowly, understanding of her life beginning to dawn. "It's still the same for me."

Brody frowned. "Well, maybe it's time to change that."

"I can't. It's the way it is." She turned away from the beautiful fields. "So, Dylan," she said briskly. "I assume you checked videos or whatever to see if Donny was on the phone when that guy called."

He glanced at Brody, and something passed between the two men before he focused on Tatum and answered her question. "I checked your whole team. Everyone associated with you. Four people were on the phone during the time that security guard was making that call."

"Four?" Tatum's heart started to pound. "Who?"

He hit a button, and the screen shifted to a four-way screen split. Four people talking on the phone, with the same time stamp.

She pointed at the top left. "Donny. My ex. My manager." Then her gaze slid to the right. The woman on the phone had her hand over her mouth, covering it so Tatum couldn't see what she was saying.

"That's your drummer? Victoria Rose?" Dylan said.

Tatum frowned. "I've known her since I was eighteen. She was the first drummer they gave me. She would never hurt me."

Neither Hart brother agreed with her, which sent chills down her spine. "She's my friend," she said stubbornly.

"Friends can make the worst enemies," Dylan said. "What about her?" He pointed to the image below Victoria.

"Nora Smith. My tour manager." She frowned. "She's been with us for five years. I like her. She takes care of everything. She helps keep Donny away from me." But she couldn't take her gaze off the still grainy image. "She has access to everything on the tour," she said slowly. "It would be easy for her to arrange everything that has happened."

"And what about him?" Dylan pointed to the image on the bottom right.

Her stomach dropped. "It's Jackson. My bass player's husband."

"The one we called earlier?" Brody asked.

She nodded, then suddenly got up and walked away from the table, hugging herself. "These people are my friends. I trust them. With the exception of Donny, I love them. There's no way it's them." She put her hands on her hips. "It has to be Donny. There's no point in looking at any of them." She couldn't keep the tension out of her voice. "Those people are my *friends*."

The brothers exchanged glances, but it was Brody who spoke. "We'll focus on Donny. He's the most likely candidate."

"But you're going to look at the others, aren't you? My friends." At their silent nods, she laced her fingers on top of her head. "You guys don't understand. I don't have a lot of friends. Donny kept me isolated, and I can't exactly run around meeting people in cafés. My circle is so small. I don't have enough friends for one of them to be trying to get me killed!"

Brody's face softened. "I understand—"

"No, you don't. You have this huge family and this huge

life. You probably have a massive circle of people you can count on. I don't." She held up her hands. "No, I don't want to hear it. It's not them. It's Donny." But even saying that it was Donny who was after her hurt.

She'd given her heart to him once. She'd turned her dreams over to him. He'd already broken enough. She wasn't sure she could take more.

Dylan shut his computer and shoved it in the backpack. "I'm going to get started on this." He slung his backpack over his shoulder and walked over to her. "Tatum."

She looked up at him, trying to pull herself together. "I appreciate your help—"

"I know," he interrupted. "We'll figure out what's going on, and then you can go forward with whatever we find. And you're not alone. You have all of us."

Her throat tightened. "No, I don't. Bella hates me—"

"She doesn't hate you. She's hurt."

Tatum frowned. "Hurt about what?"

"You were her best friend, and you left her when you left Brody." He glanced at Brody. "Yeah, Brody was an ass to you, but the rest of us weren't. You left all of us."

She stared at him, her heart sinking. "I didn't leave you—"

"You did. You took off. No one had any idea how to find you. And no one ever heard from you again. Not even once. You could have found us easily, but you didn't."

Her mouth fell open. "I thought you all hated me for leaving. None of you reached out to me, either."

Guilt flickered over his face. "You're right. It was a two-way street." He pulled out his phone. "What's your phone number?"

"I don't have my phone—"

"You'll have it back eventually. What is it?"

She rattled it off, watching as he typed it into his phone.

He shoved his phone in his pocket and looked over at Brody. "You got that marker?"

Brody flipped it to him, and then Dylan gently took her arm, and wrote his phone number in permanent marker on her cast. "Don't let anyone see that. It's unlisted." He tossed the marker on the table, his dark eyes penetrating. "You have enemies, Tatum. It's impossible not to have some when you are as successful as you are. But you also have friends. Remember that." He paused. "I'm sorry."

Tears filled her eyes. "I'm sorry, too."

He reached for her, and he pulled her into a hug. His arms were strong and warm, holding her tightly as she clung to him. "What about the others? Bella?"

Dylan pulled back. "Bella was crushed. You're going to have to work it out with her." He touched her face. "Welcome back, Tatum."

"I'm not back. I'm leaving."

"Not the way you did before. Never again." He bumped his fist on his chest, over his heart. "I'll be in touch." He indicated the duffel bag still on the chair. "I brought some clothes from Meg. I think they'll fit all right." He nodded at Brody, then headed back into the house, pulling the slider shut behind him.

Tatum stared after him, her mind whirling as Brody came up behind her and slid his arm around her waist. She spun out of his reach. "Is that why someone on my team is after me? Am I that bad of a friend? Of a person? Do I hurt people, but not realize it? I was embarrassed by how I left. I thought they would be mad. But I never thought...I never thought they'd be hurt." She lifted her hand to brush her hair back and was startled to find her fingers were trembling. "Brody? Be honest with me."

He walked over to her and took her hands. His touch felt so warm against hers, and she realized her hands were freezing, even though it was warm out. "Tatum." His voice was gentle. "You have one of the biggest, kindest hearts I've ever met. That's why I fell in love with you, and that's why I still love you. You're a survivor, and sometimes you need to do brave things to survive."

She searched his face. "So, I've done things to hurt people. I just had a good reason for it? That doesn't help."

He laughed and kissed her lightly. "Come on. Let's go for a ride."

"A ride? What? Where?"

"One of our cameras along the southeast pasture is offline this morning. I want to check it out." He released her hand and began to gather their dishes.

"A camera is *offline*?" A cold chill gripped her. "How do you know it wasn't tampered with?"

"That's why I want to check it out." He headed inside with the dishes.

She hurried after him. "What if someone is waiting out there for us? What if it's a trap?"

"That's what I'm hoping." He set the dishes in the sink.

"Hoping? You're *hoping* that there's a stalker waiting for us?" Panic started to close in around her. "How can you say that?"

Brody walked over to her and grasped her shoulder. "I'm not just a software geek who struck it rich. I also have skills. I made it a point to acquire them, so I could protect my family. If someone is waiting for us..." He smiled, a focused, amused smile that sent chills down her spine. "He's the one who will be in trouble. I sincerely hope he, or she, is there."

Tatum searched his face, and saw only absolute confidence in his gaze. Some of her fear dissipated. "You've changed," she said.

He shrugged. "I think I've simply become more of who I

always was." He slanted a glance at her. "A protector," he said quietly. "Always the hero, right?"

Her words hung in the air between them, that he was a protector first, and she would always come second. The very thing that she was using to justify leaving him was the same thing she was taking advantage of.

He'd said he still loved her. His family made it clear he'd never gotten over her. And yet, she was standing here, allowing him to help her, and still planning to leave him again.

The thought struck her hard, leaving her reeling. Maybe she was a bad person. Maybe she was selfish. Maybe...

"Come on." Brody picked up the duffel bag. "Let's get you into something ranch-friendly and go find a couple horses." Before she could protest, he kissed her lightly and took her hand.

"I think you need to get out of here."

She did.

But riding out into the fields toward a camera that might be a trap wasn't what she wanted to do. Spending more time with Brody felt horribly selfish, and she didn't want to be that person anymore. "I don't think that's a good idea—"

"We have to go." He squeezed her hand. "It's time to take your freedom back, Tatum. No more running. No more hiding."

She bit her lip. "I'm so tired of living in fear."

"Then let's do this." He put his hand on her lower back to guide her to the stairs. "It's time to fight back, Tatum. It's *your* time."

She didn't want to fight.

She didn't want to face down her stalker.

She didn't want to have to deal with the truth that someone she trusted was terrorizing her.

Which meant Brody was right.

She had to do it. And that time was now.

CHAPTER FOURTEEN

Brody was quiet as he rode beside Tatum along the south trail of the ranch.

He had his Glock at his hip, and a rifle across his thighs, which was both reassuring and alarming. Her Brody could be dangerous. He had evolved from the protector he'd once been to a complete badass.

And a part of her really liked it.

The man was already pure heat. He rode his horse like he was part of it. His muscular legs relaxed in the saddle, his body moving easily with the lope of his mount's gait. His cowboy hat was ridiculously sexy, and his biceps were the stuff of a woman's dreams.

He looked over at her, then grinned and raised his brows. "Thank you."

"For what?"

"For looking at me like that."

"I'm not looking at you at all," she retorted, immediately forcing her gaze off him. "I was admiring your ranch."

Which was also true. His lands were gorgeous. Acres and acres of beautiful horse pastures stretched as far as Tatum could see, with big mountains in the distance. The evening sky was radiant, and the air smelled clean and light.

It was pure heaven. Freedom. Beauty. The luxury of peace and time, with no one wanting anything from her.

But she couldn't quite relax.

Not surprising, given that they were traipsing across the gorgeous landscape in hopes of surprising her stalker. Which sounded like fun. And she was doing it with the man that she desperately wanted to let herself fall for again.

Brody looked like a man ready for battle. He was constantly scanning their surroundings, with a focused vigilance that was far from casual.

"You think someone's here," she said. Her horse, a dark bay named Cecil, was loping easily along. His stride was comfortable, making it easy for her to settle in despite her minimal horse skills.

Brody glanced at her before scanning the woods to their right again. "Our cameras never go out like that." His horse was a majestic black horse with a beautiful white blaze across his face. The two of them moved with stunning grace, perfection at its finest. Brody, a former street kid, had evolved into a true cowboy.

He looked dangerous, rugged, and devastatingly hot.

He flashed her a grin. "I love it when you look at me like that."

Heat flooded her cheeks. "Like what?"

"Like you're thinking thoughts that I'd like."

She pulled her gaze off him and watched the trees they were passing. "I don't know what you're talking about."

He laughed softly. "Liar." He suddenly reined his horse to a halt and signaled her to do the same.

She reined Cecil to a halt as Brody swung to the ground and knelt on the dusty trail, inspected it closely. He looked up. "Boot prints."

Oh, man. "Not yours?"

"No. No one in my family, either. Too big." He mounted again, pulled out his phone, and hit send. "How fast can you get down to Camera 26?" He paused, listening. "Bring anyone you can find. Stealth mode. We might have a visitor."

Tatum's heart started to pound. "Shouldn't we call the police?"

He shook his head. "The police will scare him off. We want to catch him." He lowered his voice. "If he's here, he's watching us." He leaned in. "Kiss me like you don't know he's watching."

Tatum stared at Brody. "Seriously?"

"He'll get careless if he thinks we're not paying attention. Criminals love easy targets." He let his rifle drop down by his hip. "Look easy."

"I'm not easy." But she leaned in toward him, patting Cecil's neck when her horse shifted.

Brody laughed softly. "No, not easy. But worth it." He slid his hand behind her neck and kissed her.

His kiss was slow, hot, and pure temptation. It might be a kiss for show, but it lit her up like wildfire. She put her hand on his shoulder, feeling his muscles flex under her hand as she kissed him back.

Her memories of his kisses had made them seem incredible. Her memories had made every kiss since feel inadequate. She'd thought she was making it up.

She hadn't been.

Kissing Brody was incredible. It was...perfect. It was pure inferno and passion, but also a feeling of rightness, of safety, of being where she was meant to be.

Brody pulled back a tiny bit, enough so he could whisper against her lips. "This stalker situation is personal," he whispered. "That means he's not going to shoot us from a distance. It's going to be up close and personal."

She swallowed. "That sounds fun."

He kissed her again, speaking between kisses. "Stay close to me. And don't get off your horse, no matter what. Keep Cecil moving. No man is as fast as a horse."

Her heart started to hammer. "What about you?"

"I'll be here, but if something happens, I want you to know what to do." He cupped her cheek and kissed her again, tender little kisses that didn't feel so safe anymore. "Keegan will be here shortly, but right now, it's us, and I want him to make a move. Got it?"

Oh, *God*. They were literally using themselves as bait. "What if you're wrong? What if he shoots us? He might shoot you."

"He won't. That's not how stalkers work."

"But if he's paid by someone else—"

"Then he's being paid to terrorize you, not kill you."

"What about killing you?"

"Cold-blooded murder is different than stalking. Usually not the same criminal."

"Usually?" Because that wasn't nearly as reassuring as she would have liked.

"Yeah." He kissed her again, a longer, hotter kiss that made desire mix with the tension gripping her. He leaned in, brushing his lips over her ear. "There's a bunch of trees up ahead. It's a good place to hide. You stay on the other side of me. Laugh. Sound happy. It'll piss him off."

Her mouth was dry, but she nodded. "All right." She managed a laugh and hit him in the chest with her cast, which sent pain shooting through her arm. *Shit*. That had been stupid. "Brody," she said loudly. "You're so dirty." Dirty? Really? She'd called him *dirty*.

He smiled devilishly, flashing her a grin so devastating that her heart felt like it skipped a beat. "I want you naked again," he announced. "Right now."

She laughed, even as heat pooled in her belly. "I'm not getting naked outside. There are bugs."

"Bugs? There are no bugs. This is Oregon. We don't have bugs." He moved his horse closer, wrapped his arm around her, and grabbed her ass. "Ride double with me, Tatum."

Oh, God. That actually sounded really fun. "Really?" Wait, no. She needed Brody to have his arms free to save her life. He'd told her to stay on her horse, no matter what. "No. Never. I need my space, cowboy."

She pulled away and urged Cecil into an easy lope. The gelding moved easily beneath her, his muscles flexing as he moved.

Brody's deep laugh echoed, and he urged his horse after her. "As soon as we get this camera fixed, I'm getting you naked. Off screen, of course."

"You have to catch me first." They were riding past the cluster of trees now, the ones that Brody had said would make a great hiding place. She tried not to look over at them, but she couldn't keep from glancing sideways at them.

"Stop." Brody's command was quick.

She immediately reined in Cecil. "What?"

"This." He rode up, leaned in, and kissed her. Hard, deep, tantalizing.

His chest was muscled and hard, his thigh corded where she put her hand on it for balance. She thought he'd stop, but he didn't. He kept kissing her, stripping away at her defenses, until she was leaning into him, hanging on for dear life. He broke the kiss and nibbled the side of her neck. "I'm going to dismount," he whispered. "No matter what I say, don't get off. Got it?"

She swallowed. "Got it."

"Good." He went back to her mouth, kissing her again, turning the horses while he did it, so that his horse was between her and the woods. He finally broke the kiss. "Fuck the camera," he said. "Let's take a break." He swung his leg off his horse and dropped to the ground, his back to the woods. "Let's get sweaty, sweetheart."

Making love to Brody outdoors? The thought was incredible. "You want to have sex outside? There's way too much dirt."

He grinned and unstrapped a rolled-up blanket from the back of his saddle. "I came prepared. The blanket's soft." He draped it over his shoulder and extended his hand toward her. "Come on. It's been too long, Tatum. I need to be with you."

There was an edge of honesty to his voice that seemed to reach inside her. "I need you, too, Brody."

Something flickered in his eyes. "Then come on down. No one's around."

God, she wanted to. "Not outdoors," she retorted. "I'm not an outdoorsy kind of girl."

Brody set his rifle across his saddle and then held up both hands to her. "Come on."

Oh, God. He'd put his rifle down. She assumed it was to tempt her stalker into taking action, but come on! It wasn't like Brody was a trained professional. "Brody—"

"Let me make love to you, Tatum." He walked over to her, set his hand on her thigh. "Lean down and kiss me."

Her heart was pounding, and she tightened the grip on the reins. She quickly scanned behind Brody, but she didn't see anyone. Did Brody sense anyone? Were they being watched? It was so freaking creepy not to know. "I'm not getting down."

"One kiss, then." He squeezed her thigh. "One kiss, and then decide."

Her throat felt like she couldn't swallow, but she nodded. "One kiss." Her heart thundering, she leaned down.

Brody slid his hand behind her neck and kissed her, drawing her in. His kiss was measured and precise, and she could feel he wasn't paying any attention to it. His focus was elsewhere. She slitted her eyes open and saw that his right hand was on his hip, on the butt of his gun, even though his left hand was still in her hair.

"Kiss me like you mean it," he whispered. "Like you're not aware of anything else in this entire world."

She was so tense she wasn't sure she could even stay on her horse, but she gripped the collar of his jacket and kissed him deeper. His hand slid up her thigh to her waist, then slipped along her ribs, then to her breast. Heat pooled immediately at his touch, even as fear wrapped around her. He kneaded her breast, his knuckles evoking a need that had no place in that moment—

Brody suddenly jerked away from her and spun around with a grunt as her attacker from the stadium swung a thick metal bar right at Brody's head.

She yelped as Cecil spooked to the side, jumping away from the men.

Brody turned swiftly, and the metal bar slammed into the side of his upper arm with a crack that made her gasp. Cecil danced away, and she fumbled for her reins, gasping as pain shot through her wrist.

Brody was several inches shorter than her assailant, and probably thirty pounds lighter, but he was quick and agile as he danced out of reach, holding his upper arm. Oh, God. Was he hurt?

Her assailant came hard and fast at Brody, and Brody ducked around his horse to the other side. Her stalker followed fast, striking hard, but then Brody suddenly switched to the offensive. He moved quickly, striking hard and fast, backing him off. The stalker stumbled, and by the time he was back on his feet, Brody had his Glock out, aimed right at his chest.

"Don't move." Brody's voice was low and hard. "Or I will

make you pay for breaking Tatum's arm." His anger was tightly coiled, but seething.

The stalker stared at him, then silently clasped his hands behind his head and dropped to his knees.

Tatum's heart was pounding as she watched.

Brody didn't lower the gun. "Face down on the ground. Now."

But he didn't move. Instead, he looked up at Tatum, and smiled. "This is just the start. You don't know what's coming for you."

"No one's coming for her," Brody said. "You're done."

His gaze went back to Brody. "It's not me you need to worry about. It's never been me." He smiled at Tatum, a creepy, terrifying smile. "The nightmare is just beginning."

CHAPTER FIFTEEN

"Well, that was a pretty asshole thing to say," Keegan said as he rode up behind Brody.

Brody grinned as his brother reined in beside him. "I agree." He raised his voice, unwilling to take his gaze off the man on the ground. "Tatum? You all right?"

"Yes." Her voice was tight.

Brody swore under his breath, wanting to go to her and check on her. Or at least turn to her, but he didn't dare take his gaze off his prisoner. "Did you bring a gun, Keegan?"

"I always bring a gun with me." Keegan dismounted, landed easily beside Brody. "Want me to shoot him?"

"Not yet. Just hold him there."

"You're never any fun." Keegan helped himself to his own Glock and aimed it. "Now there's two of us, and only one of you. Don't you think you should go face down on the ground like my brother asked? I'm not as understanding of theatrical displays meant to terrify women."

The man glared at Keegan, then finally dropped to the ground, face down, hands by his head.

"Got him?" Brody asked.

"I do. I sincerely hope he goes for the pipe again, though, so I can shoot him."

"Call 911 instead. Better the police shoot him. Less paperwork."

"We pay people to do our paperwork," Keegan said. "But fine." He pulled out his phone and dialed as Brody lowered his gun.

Tatum was still sitting on Cecil, and she was frowning at the man on the ground. When he saw the frown, he relaxed slightly. She wasn't terrified. She was mad.

He walked over to her and touched her thigh, bringing her gaze back to him. "Tatum? You okay?"

She looked down at him, pain in her eyes. "It's Jackson, isn't it? It had to be Jackson who sent him. No one else knew I was here."

"It would be close. It's barely been four hours since we called Jackson. Barely enough time for him to call this guy and get him over here."

"But it could have happened." She looked crushed. "I thought it had to be Donny—"

"It might be." He squeezed her knee. "For this guy to be here this fast, it's more likely that someone saw us leave the hotel together and whoever sent this guy knew you were with me long before we called Jackson."

"Or not." She glanced over at the guy again. "Can I go talk to him?"

Brody let out his breath. "Yeah, but don't get too close."

"All right." She dismounted, then lifted her chin and pulled her shoulders back. "Come on." She walked toward the man on the ground, and Brody stayed right next to her, his gun ready. He raised his brows at Keegan, who moved slightly so that he still had a clear shot at the trespasser.

Tatum got within a couple yards of the man, and Brody caught her arm to stop her. "That's close enough."

She crouched in the dirt, her shoulder by Brody's calf. He went down on one knee beside her, keeping his body slightly in front of hers. The man on the ground looked over at her, his eyes dark with threat. On his right temple was a row of neat stitches, and Brody couldn't help but grin.

Tatum smiled. "I sent you to the hospital, huh?"

He said nothing.

She raised her arm. "You sent me, too. That's assault."

There was no reaction from the man on the ground, but Brody was impressed with Tatum staring him down. He could see her hands shaking, so he put his hand on her lower back.

She leaned into his touch, making him realize that her courage in dealing with this guy was because he and Keegan were there to protect her. He was giving her the space to find her strength.

He liked that. He liked that a lot.

She rested her broken arm on Brody's thigh. "Did you ransack my dressing room those three times?"

The man on the ground raised his head and looked at her. "You don't get it, do you?"

"Tell me, and then I will."

Brody's phone rang suddenly, and he pulled it out. "It's Dylan." He answered it, and Tatum leaned closer to him so she could listen. "What's up?"

Dylan's voice was brisk. "Got an ID on the guy who broke Tatum's arm. His name is Hank Davoe. Prison name is Street. Ex-con, but been out for a year. Was in jail for assaulting his ex-girlfriend and putting her into a coma. Three of his ex-girlfriends have restraining orders against him."

Tatum stiffened, and Brody took her arm and drew her to her feet, pulling her backward. "Who does he work for?"

"He freelances. Nothing I can pin down."

Tension gripped Brody. "Is he paid, or a stalker?"

"I don't know yet. Still working on it. Cops are looking for him."

"We have him."

Dylan paused. "Where?"

"Camera 26. Keegan already called the police."

"Shit. I'll be right over." Dylan disconnected, and Brody shoved his phone back in his pocket.

Brody looked at the man with new disgust. "You hurt women." Of course he did. No man would break Tatum's arm unless he was all right with doing that, which meant he'd done it before.

Hank said nothing.

Brody gestured for Tatum to stay back, then he walked over and crouched next to the guy. "Who paid you to hurt her?" He let his anger infiltrate his voice. He allowed the threat to hang in his words.

Hank didn't answer.

Brody leaned in, his fingers relaxed on his gun...and ready. "I'll ask you again," he said. "Who paid you to hurt her?"

"Was it Jackson?" Tatum asked. "Did Jackson pay you?"

Hank looked up at her. "You don't get to walk away. That's not how this works." He smiled, the same creepy smile he'd given her before. "Don't go to sleep. Don't ever go to sleep."

"All right." Brody stood up. "That's it." He walked back over to Tatum, who had wrapped her arms around her torso. "Tatum, why don't you head back to the house? We'll deal with this here."

"Alone? No." She walked over to a nearby rock and sat down. "I'm not going anywhere alone." Instinctively, she cradled her cast to her chest. "I'll wait."

Brody hated to see her scared. As much as he loved that she trusted him to keep her safe, to have her sitting near him, never at the cost of her freedom.

She wasn't free right now. She had all the money and success in the world, but she wasn't free.

And he hated that for her.

He realized that his job wasn't to be her protector. His job was to set her free.

He'd spent his life holding those he loved close to him. Building a wall for them to hide behind.

And with Tatum, he was going to have to do the opposite...which meant setting her loose to fly.

He let out his breath. He'd just found her again, but he wasn't going to be able to keep her.

Unless he could find another way.

CHAPTER SIXTEEN

Tatum pulled her knees up to her chest and rested her chin on them as she watched Brody and Keegan deal with Hank.

She refused to watch Hank.

Instead, she kept her gaze focused on Brody. He was moving a little stiffly, and she had a feeling that his arm was pretty bruised from the pipe. But he was using his arm, so it was clearly not broken. He'd made himself vulnerable to tempt Hank into attacking.

He'd literally put his body between her and her stalker, without hesitation. Without agenda.

Because that was who he was. After not seeing her for fifteen years, he hadn't hesitated for even a moment to take care of her. She sighed. She was such a liar that she didn't want him to be her protector, wasn't she? Wasn't that why she'd asked Nora to track him down?

He grounded her. He made her feel safe. With Hank lying on the ground over there, she still felt safe, which was crazy.

It had been a very long time since she'd felt safe.

The low voices of Keegan and Brody settling her, she looked around at the beautiful ranch. The beautiful white plank fences surrounded acres and acres of lush green grass. In the distance were snow-capped mountains, even though it was early summer. Above her head...she looked up and smiled at the two horses who were leaning over the fence, watching the action.

Cecil was ground-tied, napping in the shade beside Brody's and Keegan's horses.

No one was bothering her.

No one was trying to get her autograph.

No one was waving a clipboard at her, announcing her agenda for the day.

No emails or texts.

Just...breathing.

It had been a long time since she'd simply sat.

Without guilt. Without stress. Without purpose.

Just sat.

Her gaze fell on Keegan. He hadn't said anything to her when he'd arrived on the scene. She knew he'd been focused on dealing with Hank. Would he welcome her or hate her?

She heard the sound of hoofbeats, and she looked over as Dylan rode up. He flashed a grin at her as he dismounted. "Tatum. You all right?"

"I'm great. Brody might be hurt though."

Dylan frowned. "Hey, Brody. You okay?" He walked over to Brody, and Tatum could see the flash of a gun at his hip.

Were they all armed? Why? What kind of life did they live?

She heard an engine approaching, and this time, she saw a pink camo four-wheeler coming down the trail. On it was a woman. Not Bella.

Meg.

She scrambled to her feet as she watched Meg drive up. Her brown skin was gorgeous, her thick hair bouncing around her shoulders. Meg was a few years younger than Tatum, and she'd followed Tatum around during that summer, like the little sister Tatum had never had. Bella had been the only other girl in the group at the time, and the three of them had been tight.

Tatum had taught Meg how to French braid her curls to keep them from tangling.

She'd given Meg her own diary because she hadn't had one.

And then she'd left her, too. Dylan's words had made her aware that the pain of rejection might not have been only on her side.

Meg pulled up, stopping the four-wheeler with an awkward jerk, almost running over Tatum. She whipped off her helmet and stared at Tatum, her dark brown eyes wide. God, she looked the same...and older.

But she also looked exactly the same as that little girl who had made Tatum feel like she actually had enough value to help someone else. She'd even taught Meg some of her songs, and how to play the guitar.

Guilt flooded her, and she shifted awkwardly as Meg stared at her. "Hey," she said. "You might not remember me—"

"Tatum!" Meg launched herself off the four-wheeler and right at Tatum.

Tatum barely had a chance to brace herself before Meg threw her arms around her. Pain shot through Tatum's arm at the contact, but she ignored it, hugging Meg back just as hard. God, it had been so long.

Meg pulled back, looked at her face, then hugged her again. "Oh my God, Tatum. It's you!"

Sudden tears filled Tatum's eyes as she clung to Meg, who was holding on so tight that Tatum felt like she'd never let her go.

Meg finally pulled back, but she didn't let go. Tears were

running down her cheeks, making fresh tears surge in Tatum's eyes. "Oh, my God. I thought I'd never see you again, and you're here!" She hugged her a third time, and Tatum laughed, hugging her back.

"Meggie," she said, through her tears. "It's so good to see you."

"Good? It's a freaking miracle. A gift." She finally released Tatum, but grabbed Tatum's hands. "Never let my brother drive you away again. Promise? I can't believe you're back." She touched Tatum's hair. "I love it long. You look so great. You're almost unrecognizable on stage, but now, you're just you. You're so normal. God, I missed you."

Tatum grinned. "You're not mad I left?"

"Mad?" Meg's eyes widened. "My brother literally asked someone else to marry him after telling you he loved you. I still haven't forgiven him."

Tatum glanced over at Brody, who was watching them. He nodded. "She's telling the truth." His voice had a hint of sadness in it. "She hasn't forgiven me."

Guilt flooded Tatum. She was responsible for a fifteen-year-rift between them? "Meg," she said firmly. "It's not Brody's fault. He..." She looked over at him, and saw all three brothers were watching and listening.

She bit her lip, not sure what she wanted to say.

Meg raised her brows. "He...what?"

Tatum pulled her gaze off Meg. "He's a protector. He saves people. It's an incredible gift that he has. When I walked away, I rejected who he was, and yet fifteen years later, I asked him to be that man for me again, and he did." She held up her cast. "Because that's who he is. And it's part of what makes him beautiful."

Meg put her hand on Tatum's cast. "I know that. He saved me. He saved all of us." She sighed. "He saves everyone. I love him to pieces, but he didn't treat you right. You were the special one for him. He had to treat you differently."

"He did what he could—"

"I spied on you that night," she said.

Tatum frowned. "What night?" God, she hoped the younger girl hadn't watched her and Brody making love. Meg had been twelve at the time. That would be horrifying. She glanced at Brody and saw the same look of horror on his face.

"The night that he told you he was going to marry Tabitha," Meg said. "*Tabitha.*"

God, Tatum would never forget that night.

"He held your hand, looked you in the eye, and told you that he loved you, but he had to marry someone else to keep her safe."

Tatum bit her lip. "I remember that quite clearly."

"I was behind Brody," Meg continued. "I couldn't see his face, but I saw yours." Her voiced softened. "I saw your face crumple, Tatum. The life literally went out of your entire body. I'd never seen someone deflate like that. I could literally see the light disappear from your soul." She touched her cheek. "And I never saw it come back. All those times, I went to your concerts, I never saw it again. Not since that day."

Tatum's throat tightened. "You've been to my concerts?"

"Forty-five of them."

She stared at Meg. "Forty-five," she echoed, stunned and overwhelmed.

"You might have left, but you were always my big sister. I was cheering you on, sending you my love every chance I got."

"Why didn't you...come see me?" Tatum could barely speak over the emotion clogging her throat.

"Because I was part of a past that had killed your sparkle.

If you wanted to open that door, you would have come back. It wasn't as if it would have been difficult for you to find me."

Tatum felt like her heart was both splitting in half, and healing at the same moment. "I'm sorry, Meg. I'm so sorry."

"Nothing to be sorry for." Meg smiled. "You finally came back. I have you back."

"Oh, God. *Meg.*" Tatum hugged her again, dragging the other woman into her arms, holding on as tightly as she could. "I'm so sorry. It was never about you. Ever. I would have loved to have seen you." She pulled back, tears running down her cheeks. "I didn't know how to come back. I ran away in the middle of the night and didn't even say goodbye. I was terrible to you—"

Meg shook her head, and there were tears on her cheeks as well. "Oh, God, Tatum. You were everything to me. I understood when you left. Brody *broke* you. You had to leave. I knew it the moment he said those terrible words to you." Her smile faded, and she clasped Tatum's shoulders. "I can see the guilt on your face, Tatum. Let it go. There's nothing to forgive. Nothing at all."

"But—"

"We were all trying to survive back then. Doing whatever it took." She smiled. "I knew you weren't going to stay with us, from the moment you arrived. You needed to be free. We were just a stop on the way. I knew it, even as a kid." She shot a pointed glare at Brody. "Of course, I didn't know you'd be leaving with a shattered heart, but other than that, I knew you'd go. You had to. Your spirit is meant to be free."

Tatum stared at Meg, surprised by her statement. "Really?"

"Of course." She touched Tatum's hair again. "You'll need to leave here again. You aren't the type to sit on a ranch all day. You'll go when you're ready, but this time, you're taking my phone number with you? Got it?"

Meg's words seemed to stab right into Tatum's chest, because she'd just been thinking that she didn't want to leave. That this might be the life she was meant for. The life that would give her peace. "Kicking me out already?" She tried to keep her tone light, but she couldn't quite keep the edge out.

"God, no. I'll keep you as long as you'll stay." Meg raised her brows. "And how long is that?"

Tatum shot another glance toward Brody. The three brothers weren't even pretending not to listen to the conversation, though they did keep glancing at her stalker to make sure he hadn't moved. "I don't know how long I'm staying," she said. "It depends on a lot of things."

"Well, before you go, promise you'll come to my house and let me cook dinner for you." Meg wrinkled her nose. "I'm not as good a cook as Bella is, but I'm decent. I'd love for you to see my home." She pointed to her left. "It's that way, still on the ranch. Promise you'll come before you leave?"

Tatum nodded. "I swear it."

"All right." Meg pulled out her phone. "What's your number?"

"I left my phone behind when I ran—"

"No problem. You'll get it back. Tell me."

Tatum rattled off her number, and then watched as Meg sent her a text. "There. When you get your phone back, you'll have a text from me." She grinned. "Something to look forward to, right?"

"Absolutely." Tatum didn't want to get her phone back. She didn't want to leave. She felt like she couldn't breathe, and at the same time, she felt like she could breathe more deeply than she had in fifteen years. "Meg—"

At that moment, she heard the wail of police sirens, jerking her back to the present, and the reason she was back with the Harts. She looked up as a police SUV bounced down the trail that they'd just ridden along. Two other police cars followed behind it, their blue lights flashing.

The horses that had been leaning along the fence bolted, and Cecil and the other horses startled, scooting sideways.

"Oh, let's get the horses." Meg hurried over and grabbed the horses that her brothers had ridden.

Tatum followed her and took Cecil's reins a split second before he scooted sideways, his head up and nostrils flaring.

"Turn off the sirens and lights," Brody yelled, walking toward the vehicles, waving his arms. "Turn them off."

The horses were all panicking, the tranquility of the ranch and the afternoon shattered by the police cars. This was her fault. She'd brought this to them. She'd left behind shadows that had weighed on this amazing family, and now she was doing it again.

She bit her lip as she watched Brody get the cops to turn off their display. Finally, after what felt like forever, blessed silence fell. The stark contrast was such a relief, reminding her of what it was like when she got back to her trailer or her hotel room after a concert, into the silence.

Silence that was her escape. Her oasis. Her respite.

She leaned on Cecil's neck and stroked him as she watched Brody talk to the cops. She saw the police look over at her, and there was no mistaking the awe in their eyes when they realized that it was Tatum Crosby standing only a few feet away. Dylan and Keegan were still guarding her stalker. Meg was soothing the other two horses.

Two different worlds colliding. Where did she fit?

Brody gestured to her. "Tatum. The cops want to ask you a few questions. You up for it?"

She took a breath. "Of course."

"I'll take his reins." Meg held out her hand, and Tatum dropped the reins into her outstretched palm.

"Thanks."

"No problem." Meg's eyes were clouded now. "I'm happy to have you back, Tatum, but I'm deeply sorry for the circumstances. I hope this ends quickly, for your sake."

"Thanks." She gave Meg a quick hug, then squared her shoulders and headed toward the police. To Brody. To her life.

CHAPTER SEVENTEEN

Brody watched as the police drove down the trail by the pasture, Hank DaVoe in the back. He could tell that Hank wasn't going to talk. He wasn't going to tell anyone who sent him.

He was either being paid too much for him to break his silence or else he knew he was going to get off somehow. Either way, they weren't going to get answers from him, which meant that this wasn't over yet.

Dylan put his hand on his shoulder. "We'll figure out what's going on. I'm going to make some calls."

Brody nodded. "Thanks."

"You got it." Dylan whistled for his horse, mounted up, and took off at an easy lope in the direction the cops had gone.

Keegan had already left to do the evening feeding at the barn.

Meg had gone home to take care of her dogs.

Which meant it was only Tatum and him.

Once Dylan was out of sight, Brody finally turned back to Tatum. She was sitting on the grass again, leaning up against the fence. Her arms were draped over her knees, and her head was back, her eyes closed.

She looked exhausted and beautiful.

Silently, he walked over and sat down next to her.

She sighed, and leaned into him, so he put his arm around her and tucked her up against his side. "How are you doing?" he asked.

"I don't know." She leaned her head against the front of his shoulder. "Is there someone else running around the ranch right now, ready to attack me?"

"I doubt it. Hank was supposed to do a better job than he did. It'll take time to come up with a Plan B." He held his hand out, palm up, on his thigh.

She looked at it for a moment, then put her hand in his.

Rightness settled through him at the feel of her skin against his. "How long usually elapses between incidents?"

"A few weeks. But obviously, last night and today was shorter than that."

Brody rubbed his thumb over her palm. "So, he's upping the pressure. I think we should be ready for the next round to come pretty quickly."

Tatum closed her eyes. "That will be fun. I'm looking forward to that."

Brody laughed softly and kissed her hair. "Can you think of anything that has happened lately that would have caused him to start pressuring?"

She shook her head. "I still think it has to be Donny. He's been getting more and more...angry...since I started really trying to find a way out of the contract. Last night, he showed up at the concert and said he was staying with the tour. I can't do that, Brody. If he stays, I can't keep singing."

Brody ground his jaw. "Singing is your soul."

"When I'm on stage, yes, I love it, but all the traveling

and touring and pressure from the label and Donny..." She was quiet for a minute. "Brody?"

"Yeah?"

"Being here, with your family, on the ranch, away from all the noise...it makes me want to not go back. Not ever."

Brody froze, his whole body coming to life at her words. How was it possible she'd just said that? "You want to stay? Here?"

"Not here, necessarily. I mean, it's your home, not mine. I want peace, and being here made me realize I never have it. Ever."

"My home is always your home."

She punched him lightly in the chest. "I know, but I didn't mean it in that way. I meant mine, in that it's *mine*. I feel like my life is always on loan to everyone around me, and it's never only mine."

Brody considered that. "I understand the need for peace and solitude. That's why we have the ranch. But I also know how music lights you up." He chose his words carefully, not wanting to put any pressure or judgment on her. "I was under the impression that music gives your soul life." He knew it did. He just didn't want to force her into anything...especially leaving.

When she'd said she didn't want to go back... His whole world had stopped for that brief moment.

She laughed softly. "According to Meg, my soul hasn't been alive since that night when you shattered it."

Guilt shot through Brody. Heavy, debilitating guilt. "I need to bring up something that's been weighing on me."

"That sounds like I'm not going to want to hear it." She snuggled more tightly against him. "So I vote to table it."

"I can't do that." He continued to rub his thumb over her palm. "When Meg said she was watching your face the night I told you about Tabitha. That she saw you crumble and the light go out of you." Those words had been like a knife to his gut.

Tatum tensed. "What about it?"

"I didn't see that. I didn't realize what I'd done to you at the time." He paused. "Even in the fifteen years since, when I've been beating myself up over it, I didn't understand, not really, what I'd done to you. I know an apology can't erase the past, but I'm so deeply sorry, on more levels than I could ever count." He felt like he could apologize every second for the rest of his life, and it would never be enough. "I won't ask for your forgiveness. I just want to free you from the pain of what I did to you."

"Oh, Brody." She was quiet for a moment. "All this time, I was never mad at you."

He frowned. "Why the hell not?"

"Because I knew you were who you were. I didn't blame you. I mean, yeah, I was utterly devastated, but it was my fault for falling for you, for believing you could be something other than you were. I spent the last fifteen years nursing a broken heart that I blamed myself for, and pouring blame into myself for leaving the way I did."

He let out a low groan. "Hell, Tatum. You were seventeen. You fell in love. There's nothing wrong with that."

"I stole the money," she said suddenly.

He frowned. "What money?"

"The money you had saved to take care of everyone under the bridge. I took it all when I left. I'm sorry. God, I'm so sorry, Brody."

Oh. *That* money. He brushed a finger over her cheeks, where a single tear had leaked free. "It was a volatile time in all our lives, and we all had a lot of baggage and trauma. We did the best we could. All of us." Except him. He could have done better. He *should* have done better.

He'd held himself out as the one they could trust and count on, and that raised the standard for him.

She looked down at their entwined hands. "Did you know that was me? Who stole the money?"

"Yes," he said quietly. "I knew that."

Her voice was thick. "What about the others?"

"I didn't tell them." The pain in her voice broke Brody's heart. He could feel the weight of fifteen years of guilt and self-recrimination, clamped down on her.

"They must have figured it out. Where else could the money have gone?"

"I didn't tell them it was gone."

She pulled away to look at him. "But how did you pay for things without it?"

He wasn't going to go there. "I managed."

She made a small sound of distress. "I can hear it in your tone. You did things you didn't want to do, because of me. Because I forced you to cross lines you hadn't wanted to cross." Anguish made her voice raspy and fragile. "I'm so sorry, Brody. I'm so sorry—"

He put his finger across her lips. "No apology needed. I was glad you took the money. I wanted you to be safe."

She searched his face. "See? The protector. Always the protector. You needed me to be safe. What else is there in you, Brody? Did you ever love me, or was it always about keeping me safe?"

He ground his jaw, and didn't answer.

She sat up and looked at him. "You didn't love me?"

He swore under his breath. "It's not that simple."

The look on her face was crushing. "You didn't...love me? You said you did. You said you loved me. I always believed that even though you broke my heart by agreeing to marry Tabitha, I never thought you loved her. I always thought it was me. Was that a lie?"

"No." He caught her wrist as she started to scramble to her feet. "I absolutely meant it. You were my light."

She pulled free and stood up. "Being your light isn't the same thing as loving me. It's not the same, Brody. There's a difference between loving me because of how I make you feel, and loving me because of who I am."

He rose to his feet. "Did you love me because I was protecting you and keeping you safe? Or did you love me because you loved the broken, terrified, vulnerable kid who had nightmares every single night that he would fail all these kids who'd fallen into his lap?"

She stared at him. "You were really that scared?"

"Absolutely fucking terrified. Every night when I went to sleep, a part of me hoped that when I woke up, everyone would be gone, and I wouldn't be responsible for anyone else. And at the same time, I was terrified I'd wake up and everyone would be gone, because then I wouldn't have anyone."

Tatum's face softened. "You never showed that side of you."

"I couldn't. I had to be strong." He walked over and took her hands. "And every night that summer, I would dream that I woke up and you were gone. Meg was right. I knew I couldn't keep you. You were born to fly, Tatum." He brushed a strand of hair back from her face. "Maybe that's why I agreed to marry Tabitha. To make you run, because I knew I'd never be able to let you go."

"And then one day, you woke up, and I was gone."

"Yeah." His gut clenched at the memory. "Worst fucking day of my life."

She smiled. "I think that's a bit of an exaggeration. I know about some of the things in your life. They're pretty bad."

"Getting the shit beat out of me by my foster parents was

bad. Getting taken from my mom because she was an addict was hell. Hearing she'd died when I was fourteen, and I was never going to get out of the foster care system? Getting beaten by my foster dad before I ran away and never went back? Yeah, those were all bad. But they were also all okay, because they made me stronger and propelled me forward to be who I am." He touched her face. "But there's nothing good about losing you," he said. "Or if there is, I still haven't figured out what it is."

She wrinkled her nose. "Well, maybe the fact that you don't have to spend your life running around the country in tour buses with me. That's good for you."

He grinned. "Yeah, that wouldn't be my thing. I'm not going to lie. I couldn't do that."

"So, see? It's right that we didn't end up together." She spread her arms and spun around. "Heaven knows, I couldn't spend my life in this gorgeous place, riding horses, and making love with a hot billionaire day after day. That would be a tragic way to live."

He laughed as she spun, her hair glorious in the evening sun. "Want to go for a ride?"

"Now? The sun will be setting soon."

"I know. It's a full moon, and it's not far. We'll be fine."

She smiled. "I'd like that, Brody. I'd like that a lot."

"Great." He knew where he was going to take her.

To the place he'd been to a thousand times, and always imagined what it would be like if Tatum were with him.

Tonight, he wasn't going to have to imagine.

CHAPTER EIGHTEEN

"Oh, Brody. It's breathtaking." Tatum sat on the massive, flat rock beside Brody, stunned by the sight before her as the sun began to dip toward the trees.

It was a glorious sunset, so bright it was as if the sky was on fire. The angle of the sun turned the rock they were sitting on to gold. Even her cast was glowing with the orange rays.

But the most magnificent part was the waterfall towering above them. The sun was casting its glorious golden rays through the dancing droplets. The cascading water was sparkling with pink, orange, yellow, and even some violet.

She lifted her face to the water, feeling the cool mist from the waterfall on her cheeks. "It feels like we're in the middle of nature's fireworks. I've never seen anything like this."

"Glorious, isn't it?" Brody was leaning forward, his arms clasped around his knees. He wasn't leaning in toward her. He was just basking in the scene before them.

Tatum turned her head, watching Brody as he absorbed the beauty. She could see he really appreciated it, all the way to his soul. The Brody she'd known when she was seventeen had always been on the move, always involved in something, never resting, even for a minute. She wasn't sure he even slept much back then.

But now...he was at peace in this moment. Not doing anything. Simply sitting.

He smiled, but didn't turn his head to look at her. "Tatum, baby. The sunset's a lot prettier than I am."

"Different pretty."

His smile widened. "I'm not at all pretty."

She tried to pull her knees to her chest to rest her chin on them, but pain shot through her hand, and she grimaced.

"Come on." He put his arm out for her, and she snuggled up on her side, using his thigh for a pillow. The rock was cool against her side, but Brody's thigh was warm and strong.

For a few minutes, they didn't speak. He played with her hair as they watched the colors change, becoming brighter and brighter, until they began to fade.

"We've never done this," she said.

"Watched a sunset?"

"Just been together peacefully."

He was quiet for a minute, his fingers never stilling in her hair. "We were both in such motion back then, desperate to change our lives."

She smiled. "I wanted to become a star."

"I wanted to become a Major League pitcher."

"Seriously?" She rested her cast on his leg. "I didn't know that."

"Yeah. I had talent, and I liked being the one that everyone was counting on. I thought it was a way out. Money is the path to safety, right?"

She nodded. "That's part of what drove me to become a star. Being rich felt safe. It would make people love me."

He nodded. "Exactly." He squeezed her hand, a reminder that he got her. He understood what drove her in a way that no one else did.

She'd made her dreams of being a star come true, but Brody hadn't fulfilled his baseball dreams. He was the kind of man who could succeed at anything he wanted, so, why no baseball? "What happened?"

"My mom died, leaving me permanently in the foster care system. I had no way out, no hope, and that started to get to me. I knew I had to get out, even if it cost me school and baseball. Then Keegan came into my foster home and got targeted by the abusive bastard running it. Keegan was the straw that broke me. For some reason, he was the one. I couldn't let him suffer. I had to protect him. So, I ran away and took him with me. He had nowhere to go, so I decided to help him and then..." He shrugged. "Baseball just kind of disappeared."

Tatum thought about that. "You didn't want to be taking care of everyone?" She'd never thought about it before. He was so committed to that role that she'd never considered any other role for him.

He laughed softly "I was sixteen when I met Keegan," he said. "I wanted to play baseball, not sit under a bridge, eat scraps for my meals, and take care of a bunch of stray kids." He grinned. "I'm a lot older than that now, and I still don't want to sit under a bridge and eat scraps for my meals."

She laughed. "And the stray kids?"

His face softened with the love that he never tried to hide. "I wouldn't give them up for anything. Family is everything."

It was the answer she would have expected from him, but the love in his voice when he said it made warmth wrap around her. "You're a lucky man."

He rested his hand on her shoulder. "In this moment, I feel like I'm the luckiest man in the world. I have everything I could ever want."

It was obvious he meant her. She didn't know what to say.

"Can I ask you something?" Brody began rubbing her shoulder.

"Of course." Tatum snuggled more closely against his thigh, watching as the last pinks faded from the waterfall, leaving it crystal clear as the light faded.

"Does the touring really drain you?"

She closed her eyes, basking in the feel of his fingers working out her tense muscles. "I used to love it. I loved seeing new places and experiencing the world. But I've been getting more and more tense lately. I thought it was only because of Donny, and that if I fixed that, I'd get my joy back—" She didn't want to say it. She didn't want to acknowledge the truth that had been eating away at her.

"And you don't think that?"

She bit her lip, but shook her head. "Being here has shown me that I need this. I need the peace that your ranch gives. Getting away from people. From obligation. I need...to be in a place where I can just be. I need to be with..." *you*. She stopped herself before she said the last word. "Myself," she said instead, which was also true. But being with Brody felt like being with herself. He was easy for her to be with, like he was a part of her soul.

But she wasn't ready to say that. Not yet. Ever? She didn't know.

He was quiet for a moment, and she could almost hear him thinking about what she'd said. Of course he would think about it. Because he cared. He listened. He helped. "But you still love the music? Performing?"

"I love it, but..." She sighed. "I don't think I can go back out there, Brody. It's not just the stalker and Donny. It's all that time alone on the road. No roots. No space that's mine." Tears filled her eyes. "I can't do it anymore," she whispered. "All I want to do is sit here on the rock with you. I can't help but think—"

"Think what?"

"If I hadn't been so obsessed with making it as a singer, maybe we would have worked. What if singing wasn't my dream? Then I wouldn't have left—"

"No. You needed to go." He paused. "I wasn't ready for you, Tatum. I wasn't ready for how I felt about you, and you weren't ready to settle down. We needed to find our own paths. I see that now."

She bit her lip. She wasn't so sure about that. Right now, she felt the most at peace she'd been since she could remember. She needed that. She could tell she did.

He continued to rub her back. "Have you ever considered a residency in Las Vegas? I'm sure you could get one. You could do your concerts, but not have to travel. That might fit your needs."

"Vegas?" She frowned. "I don't want to live in Las Vegas." She'd never really thought about it as a solution. Vegas wasn't her home any more than life on the road was.

"It's only about an hour and a half plane ride from here. We have a private plane. You wouldn't have to sleep there for even one night. It's a long commute, but for four days a week, not too bad. And our plane is really nice." He paused. "If you lived here."

"Here?" Her heart started racing. "You mean, if I lived in Oregon? You'd let me borrow your plane?"

"I would, but I didn't mean just in Oregon." His fingers stilled on her back. "I meant here. On the ranch. With me."

Silence fell after his statement. He left it in the fading rays of sunset, for her to grab onto. She could almost see the words drifting past her, waiting for her.

Brody cleared his throat. "I mean it, Tatum." He paused. "Sit up for a sec."

He helped her sit up, then he moved around until he was in front of her. He kneeled in front of her, on one knee, and then took her hand. "Tatum, sweetheart, it's been a long time since we were together. We were young back then. In love, but it was teenage love. Right?"

She nodded, watching him. He was so handsome now, so earnest. So intense. God, she loved him. She'd always loved him. She hadn't imagined those feelings. They were real then, and they were real now.

"I've held you in my heart ever since," Brody said. "But I didn't know if those feelings were still valid, still true. Did you wonder that?"

She nodded again, her heart starting to race. "I was afraid I'd built you up into something you weren't."

He smiled. "Aside from the move of deciding to marry someone else after I told you I love you and made love to you? Other than that?"

Surprisingly, she was actually able to crack a little laugh over that. "Yes, other than that." Her smile faded. "I married Donny to escape my pain, but it didn't work."

"I tried to get over you as well." Brody kissed her palm. "It didn't work, because it turns out, our souls are still intertwined. Now that we're together again, it's obvious."

She nodded once. "I feel that, too," she admitted.

Brody took a breath. "Life is short, Tatum. We've missed out on fifteen years together. I don't want to miss even a day more." He took her hand. "I'd like to ask you the question that I've been wishing for fifteen years that I'd asked you."

Her heart started to race, and suddenly, she couldn't breathe. "Brody—"

"I love you, Tatum. Your heart, your soul, your courage, your vulnerability. I love the way you laugh. I want to be the man who makes you laugh, who holds you when you're scared, and who wraps himself around you every single night for the rest of your life." He met her gaze. "Tatum Crosby, will you marry me?"

CHAPTER NINETEEN

TEARS FILLED TATUM'S EYES, and she had to cover her mouth, struggling to hold back the emotion trying to consume her. "You're proposing to me?"

"I am. I mean it, too." He grinned. "And before you ask, it's not because I have some heroic need to protect you from Donny by marrying you. My only heroic need is to love you. Don't get me wrong. I'll still protect you, but it's an even playing field now. You're rich, famous, independent, and entirely capable of saving yourself." Her face softened. "You're also vulnerable, charming, sassy. All of it, Tatum. I love all of you, and I want to be yours forever, simply because you're you."

She took a breath, not quite able to speak over the emotion threatening to overtake her. "I dreamed of this for years," she whispered. "It was all I wanted. You. Your love. Us. Together. I—" She had to swallow to try to keep from drowning in emotion. "Every time I saw your face in a magazine, I just...a part of my soul broke a little more."

"You're in magazines way more than I am," he said. "I

definitely suffered more at the checkout line at the grocery store with all those celebrity magazines lined up."

She burst out laughing, despite her tears. "You're a man. Men don't have emotions like women do."

"That's a bunch of bullshit right there." He released her hand and framed her face with his hands. "I love you, Tatum. I'll be yours forever, if you'll let me. All yours. You come first. Always."

Those words.

Those were the words she'd longed to hear from him.

You come first.

She wrapped her hand around his wrist, her heart aching with longing. "I love you, Brody."

His face softened. "I never thought I'd hear you say that again. The most beautiful three words in the English language."

His emotion was so stark that she could barely breathe. "But getting married? I—" She paused. "Marriage was terrible for me. It trapped me for life. And my heart was still broken from you until about three hours ago. I don't know how to turn that around so quickly. I don't know if...if I want to. I don't know if being married is something I want anymore."

Understanding flickered in his eyes, but there was also pain. "I wish you hadn't had to experience that," he said softly. "I wish I'd been ready to be the man you needed back then. Strong enough to love you and help you fly." He searched her face. "I still believe that, Tatum. You needed to fly. The only choice was that I could have gone with you."

"But you couldn't. You had the others."

"I had the others." He kissed her gently, his lips warm against hers. "If I had the chance to do it differently, I wouldn't be able to."

Tears filled her eyes. "Me either," she whispered.

"But..." He kissed the corner of her mouth. "Today..." He

kissed the other corner of her mouth. "We have the chance..." He kissed her nose. "To make choices again." He slid his hand into her hair and kissed her.

A kiss so full of emotion that she felt her soul lift in response to him.

She didn't want to make a choice right now. She was afraid that if she did, she'd make the choice to leave again...and she didn't want to do that. But she couldn't choose to stay. There was too much that had happened, both to herself and between them. So, she slid her hand behind his head and held him to her, kissing him back.

He went down on both knees and pulled her onto his lap, wrapping her legs around his hips. The moment she locked her ankles behind his back, he rose to his feet, standing easily despite the fact he was supporting her.

His arms were strong around her back, holding her securely, giving her the freedom to kiss him and bask in the feel of his body against hers. "I need you, Tatum," he said.

"Now?"

"Yep. Outdoor loving." He pulled back to see her face. "You good with that?"

Anticipation rushed through her. "Aren't there cameras around?"

"Not here." He navigated across the flat rock, easily keeping them both balanced, then stepped down to the grassy clearing at the edge of the waterfall's pool. Excitement rushed through her as he lowered them both to the ground. The grass was cool and soft beneath her hands, and she had a feeling that he took care of the grass and kept it thick and lush.

She was on his lap now, and he carefully pulled her shirt over her head, lifting it gently over her cast. The cool evening air was a gorgeous whisper across her skin. He grasped the bottom of his shirt and pulled it over his head, revealing his corded muscles.

She laughed as she palmed his belly. "You're even hotter than the paparazzi make you seem."

He grinned as he used one hand to spread their shirts on the grass, making a blanket. "I am very hot," he agreed. "Hot for you."

"That's such a cliché." She laughed as he pretended to toss her onto the grass, catching her before she landed.

"I'm not a cliché. I'm an original in every way." He moved on top of her, holding himself above her like he was doing a plank.

Which of course, made every muscle in his body taut.

She laughed. "You're showing off your muscles?"

"Of course. I have to use all my skills to seduce you. You're a celebrity. You aren't going to fall for just anyone. I'm rich as hell, but my fame doesn't measure up to yours. So I gotta be hot, too."

"This is true." She ran her hands over his chiseled shoulders. "I have standards. How many pushups can you do?"

"Too many for you to handle." He lowered himself just enough to kiss her, but he was still holding his body off hers, so only their lips were touching.

It was pure temptation, the way he was holding himself off her, and working magic with kisses that made her want to giggle with delight. "This is insane," she said. "How do I like kissing you so much?"

"Because I'm meant for you. Always have been." He slowly lowered himself, just enough that his bare chest was against her breasts, teasing them both.

She sucked in her breath. "Wow."

Heat flashed in his eyes. "Right?" His face became serious. "Just to be clear, I am well aware that you didn't give an answer when I asked you to marry me."

Her amusement faded. "Brody—"

"No." He kissed her before she could explain, kissing her until the heat between them was burning through her. Only then did he break the kiss. "Take what time you need. Ask me whatever questions you need. Be honest in your fears. I'm not going away, Tatum. Whatever you need from me, this time, I'm here. All the way." He kissed her again. "And if you run, I will follow. Not in a stalkerish way. Just in a future husband you adore way."

Tears filled her eyes. "That was a beautiful speech."

He smiled. "I've been practicing it for fifteen years." Before she could answer, he lowered himself the rest of the way onto her and kissed her like a man who had indeed just declared his forever love.

And she gave herself over to him. She didn't want to think. She didn't want to try to figure out answers. She just wanted to enjoy being with Brody, to allow it to be whatever it could be.

So, she wrapped her non-broken wrist around the back of his head and pulled him down, kissing him back, playing with his hair, basking in the man she'd dreamed of for so long. "Just so you know," she whispered between kisses. "I think you're a major celebrity. I feel like I need to impress you to be worthy of—"

"No." He cut her off, pulling back to look at her. "I know you're only half serious, but it's important that you never feel like that, Tatum. Ever. I might be rich and a target of the paparazzi. You might be a celebrity. But that's irrelevant to what we have together." He put his hand over her heart. "We've been connected since we were both living under a bridge, Tatum. It's not about the external trapping. It's about who we are in our hearts, and you've always been everything I could ever need or want."

She smiled, her heart turning over. "That's how I feel about you."

He grinned, a wicked gleam in his eyes. "Then let's make love, sweetheart, on this level playing field that we share." He caught her in another kiss, and this one was pure heat.

Happily, she sighed and kissed him back, giggling when his hands wandered over her body, touching her everywhere with a reverence that made her feel like the most beautiful woman in the world.

She knew that if she got old and wrinkled, he would still think she was the most beautiful woman in the world.

If she never sang another note, he would still love her.

If she became broke, he'd take care of it.

And if she became the most famous singer ever to walk the earth, he would still simply see her as who she was inside.

Because he wanted nothing from her, just as she wanted nothing from him...except for who he was.

He rolled off her and shucked the rest of his clothes, then quickly slid hers off in a move that was pure finesse and over-the-top seduction, whispering sweet nothings about how perfect every inch of her body was as he kissed his way across every curve and every dip of her body.

She propped herself up on her elbows, grinning as she watched him kiss her ankle bone. "You're a goofball."

He flashed her a wicked grin as he kissed his way up her shin. "I'm happy. It brings out the silly side of me sometimes. Too silly for you?"

She laughed as he peppered her kneecap with kisses. "Silliness makes the world a better place."

"I agree." He raised her leg and then kissed the back of her knee, whispering words of adoration to the crease on the back of her knee.

She giggled. "You're worshipping the back of my knee?"

"Yep." He kissed his way down the back of her calf. "Baby,

I've been watching you on stage for years. There isn't a part of your body that isn't longing for some admiration and devotion, don't you think?"

"Definitely." She caught her breath as he began kissing his way up the back of her thigh. Her leg was resting against the front of his shoulder, and she could feel the flex of his muscles against her skin. "You're very hot for an old man."

He laughed. "I'm not old."

"Compared to the last time I got naked with you? You're so old."

He moved her leg and pounced on her, eliciting a shriek from her as he pinned her arms above her head. "You literally got naked with me a few hours ago. I don't age that fast."

She laughed as she locked her ankles behind his lower back. "Oh, right. I forgot about that."

"You forgot?" He let out a low growl and lightly bit her breast. "I can't even express how deeply my ego is shattered by the fact you can't remember my love making from a few hours ago."

"In my defense, I do love you."

"Hah. That will never work to distract me." He paused and cocked his head. "Well, that might work. Say it again."

"I can't remember what I said."

He laughed then, a gorgeous, rich deep laugh that made joy leap through her. "Tatum Crosby," he muttered. "You're as much trouble as you ever were."

"More. I'm pretty sure I'm more."

He gave her a wicked smile. "Then we're perfect, because Trouble is my middle name." Then he kissed her and proceeded to show her all the ways in which he was trouble.

There were a lot.

And they were all good.

CHAPTER TWENTY

BRODY NUZZLED the crook of Tatum's shoulder, grinning as she leaned back against him.

In a total teenage lover move, they'd wound up both riding his horse back to the house. He'd tied her horse's reins to his saddle, and spent the ride with Tatum in his arms, leaning against his chest.

It was dark out, but the moon was full, and it easily lit the way.

They'd stayed out until almost midnight. Making love. Laughing. Talking.

It was as if they'd never been apart.

It wasn't as if no time had passed, because they were both different now. Their connection was different, but it had grown with them, even though they hadn't been together all this time.

As they neared the barn, Brody rested his chin on her shoulder, breathing in the scent of Tatum's shampoo. He had one arm around her waist, resting on her belly. She was holding onto his wrist with one hand and resting her cast on his thigh. "I'm happy," he said.

She patted his wrist. "Me, too."

"I'm telling you. Las Vegas might be the answer."

She didn't answer, and he smiled. He knew her silences. This one meant that she was thinking about it. Not ready to say anything, but she hadn't rejected the idea.

He turned his horse to the right, onto the last stretch of trail before they would be back at the barn. "Tates—"

"Tates?" She laughed. "No one has called me that for a long time. Not since you. I forgot about that."

He'd forgotten too. "It just slipped out."

"It was perfect."

"Good." He smiled as he urged his horse into an easy jog. "What I was going to say is that I want you to be happy. I want you to make whatever choice you need to make that's right for you." He paused. "If you want to stay on the road and tour, I'll go with you."

She twisted around to look at him, frowning. "You'd leave your oasis to sit on a tour bus with me?"

"In a heartbeat."

"But you need this place. The ranch. Your family. You can't leave it."

"I need you, too. I fucked it up once. I won't do that again."

She turned forward again, leaning back against his chest. "Then I won't marry you."

His gut stabbed. "What?"

"I won't let you walk away from this place. I don't want you to go off and propose to someone else after we make love again, but I also don't want you to be some spineless wuss that gives up everything to follow me around."

He laughed. "Spineless wuss? No one has ever called me that."

"Well, if you give up what you love to follow me around, then I'll call you that. And it's not an attractive trait in a guy."

His smile faded as he rode up to the barn. He could hear the tension in her voice. "What's going on?" He reined in outside the doors.

She said nothing as she dismounted, but her face was troubled.

Brody swung down beside her and took her hand. "Talk to me, Tatum. This is what I was referring to earlier. Let me in. Let's work this out together."

She searched his face. "I don't know what I want, Brody. Not from you. Not from me. Not from my life. I just know that if you give up this place to follow me around, it feels wrong. It's not who you are. It's not the man I love."

He frowned. "You don't want me to come with you?" He'd thought it was a great idea to show her that she would come first.

"No. I don't." She took a breath. "My career has always belonged to Donny. To the fans. To everyone but me. I need it to belong to me."

"And me coming with you makes that impossible?"

She held up her hands. "I don't know. I—I don't know what I'm trying to say. Or even what I feel. I just— you coming with me on tour doesn't feel right to me."

He pressed his lips together, but made himself give a casual nod. "All right." He felt something inside him begin to shut down. He'd offered her everything, and it wasn't enough. He didn't know what else to offer her. "How many weeks a year are you on the road? Normally?"

She bit her lip. "I've been on tour for two years."

"Two years *straight?*"

At her nod, he swore. "I can't imagine that. Don't you miss home?"

"I don't really have a home. I have a house that someone takes care of, but it's not a home." She gave a half smile. "This ranch is the first place that has felt like home in a very long time."

He was beginning to understand now. She needed to sing. To connect with her fans. But she'd never finished the other part of her life. "When we were living under the bridge," he said, "the most important thing I tried to do was create a home. A place to feel safe. The first thing I did when my software company sold was buy all these acres, so that everyone could have a home. We're together, but we also all have our space. Everyone needs that, Tatum. Belonging and space at the same time."

She nodded, chewing her lower lip as she listened. She was watching his face carefully, and he knew she was hearing him.

He took her hand and pressed a kiss to her knuckle. "I offer you both, Tatum. Home, and life with me. And you can handle your career how you want." He paused. "But I'll be honest with you. If you choose to be on the road and never home, and you don't let me go with you...I can't do that. That's not how I could live. My love is all encompassing. I believe in occupying your own space, in whatever way you need, but I also believe in togetherness." He put her hand over his heart. "People can't live without connection. I love you, Tates. Always, and forever. Take whatever time you need to figure it out." His fingers tightened on hers. "But if you decide it can't be, tell me, and set both of us free."

Her eyes began to glisten with tears, but she nodded. "Okay."

"Okay" wasn't what he'd been hoping for. He'd been hoping for her to tell him that they'd find a way.

But that wasn't who Tatum was. She had a free spirit that could never be tethered. The question was, how free did she need to be?

He had a feeling he'd find out soon. He managed a smile.

"How about a glass of wine? It's a nice evening. We ate early. I could bring out some appetizers and wine after we take care of the horses."

She let out her breath. "You know, I'm kind of beat. I might just go to bed after we're finished here."

"All right." There was tension between them. He'd laid it all out there for her, and now it was in her hands. "I'll take care of the horses. You go to bed."

"No, I want to help." She patted Cecil's neck. "He's been good to me today. I owe him." She paused, "I'd like to see what ranch life is like."

Hope leapt through him. Did that mean she was considering it? "All right. Follow me." As he led the way into the barn, he decided not to bring any of it up again.

He'd just let them be normal. As if the weight of their future wasn't hanging in uncertainty right now. As if—

He heard a strange sound from his left, and he paused, searching the shadows.

Tatum stopped beside him. "What is it?"

He didn't answer for a moment, waiting to hear if he heard it again.

He didn't, but a chill crept down his spine. Something wasn't right. "Stay close to me," he said. "The threat isn't over until we find out who sent Hank."

"Hank." She shivered. "I forgot about that for a moment."

"Soon you can stop worrying about it. But not quite yet." He wished he had a flashlight to see past the outreaches of their spotlights. The barn and yard suddenly felt very deserted and empty. They were the only ones outside right now.

Suddenly, the isolation that made his ranch a beloved oasis felt like a pulsating threat. Instinctively, he put his hand on his gun, but he wasn't about to start shooting at things he couldn't see. "Let's get these horses put away, and get back to the house. I want to arrange for additional security until this is solved."

Until he did, he wasn't going to sleep well.

Tatum glanced at him, and he saw the fear in her eyes. "I'm so tired of this," she said softly. "I'm so tired of being afraid."

"I know, baby. Soon." He gestured to the barn. "Let's go. I'll keep an eye out. We'll be fine."

But as he said it, foreboding trickled through him.

He always made it a point never to make promises he couldn't keep, promises like everything was going to be all right. He'd never said that to one of his bridge kids. Ever. Because he couldn't promise it.

And yet, he'd just made a similar promise to Tatum.

Was that an omen?

CHAPTER TWENTY-ONE

By the time they finished with the horses, Tatum was exhausted.

She could tell Brody was on edge. He kept pausing to listen, and he stayed close to her, moving them quickly through the steps. He'd kept his humor up, but there had been a tension to him, which had made her nervous.

And he'd completely dropped the subject of them. Not even any allusions to all his declarations, which made her nervous that he'd decided she wasn't worth the effort.

He bid her a good night at her bedroom door, giving her a light kiss that promised nothing and asked for nothing.

He was already on his phone as he walked down the hall, talking to Dylan about getting additional security.

Tatum closed her bedroom door and leaned against it, listening to his voice as he walked away. She wanted to go after him.

She wanted to run down the hall, throw herself in his arms, and let him make everything better.

And at the same time, she wanted to run away.

But to where?

Not back to her life. Not to the tours. Not to her house.

She realized she had nowhere she wanted to run to.

Somehow, despite a decade and a half of living her dream, she'd wound up with no place to call her own, no person to go to, no safe space to retreat into.

Brody's ranch was indeed the closest she'd ever come.

But did that mean she simply wanted his ranch, and not him? She felt like she had a thousand different emotions pouring through her, and she couldn't sort any of them out.

She looked around the beautiful room. The wooden bed frame was a deep, beautiful brown, rustic and elegant at the same time. The huge windows. A window seat with deep, soft pillows. A bed that he'd made—

Her gaze fell on the bedspread, and relief rushed through her when she saw her favorite overnight bag on the bed. It was the bag she'd had at the stadium with her, packed to go to a hotel that night as a treat to get off the bus.

Her heart softened at the realization that Brody must have arranged with Jackson to have it delivered, probably driven over by courier, so that Jackson wouldn't actually come to the ranch.

She was sure Jackson was safe, but until they knew for sure, they couldn't take chances.

She hurried over to it, and unzipped it. Pajamas, jeans, underwear, a couple sweatshirts. And sitting on top was her charger and her phone, with its pink case that had always made her smile.

See? She had a home. It was her belongings. The things she wore when she was alone, and not on stage.

She quickly dug through the bag and put on the pink heart PJ pants, a tank top, and her fuzzy socks. The hoodie was impossible to put on by herself over the cast, so she grabbed a fleece blanket from the bed and wrapped it around her. With her phone in one hand, she shuffled to the door and peeked out.

Brody's door was closed, and she could hear him talking.

The blanket dragging behind her, she hurried down the hall and tip-toed down the stairs to the kitchen. It was late, but she knew what she needed. What she always needed.

She unlocked the slider and opened it—

A deafening alarm started shrieking, and she yelped, holding her hands over her ears. Dammit!

Brody raced around the corner, his gun up. "What's wrong? What happened?" he shouted over the alarm.

"Accident," she yelled. "It's fine."

He gave her a look of exasperation that made her laugh, then pulled out his phone and punched a code into it. The alarm went off instantly, and he raised his brows at her. "What happened?"

She grimaced. "I just wanted to go outside and sit under the stars. You remember when we used to do that?"

He nodded. "I do. It was one of my favorite times. The stars here are amazing."

"I thought they would be. That's why I was going to do it. I just...I wanted time to think. Is it not safe?"

"I think it's fine. I called security. Everything is all set. They're sending some roving security guards over, and they should be here within the hour." He paused. "I'd like to sit out there with you, if that's all right." He held up his hand before she could argue. "To keep you safe. Not to invade your space."

She smiled. "I'd like that."

He smiled back. "All right, then. Let me grab another blanket. It's chilly out there."

"Okay." She shuffled out the door, and walked over to the huge outdoor couch. She stretched out along the length of it so she could look up at the sky, tucking the blanket all around her, and pulling it over her head.

Brody came out carrying a thick, blue fleece blanket.

She patted the couch next to her. "Come sit with me."

He walked over, stretched out next to her, and then draped the blanket over himself. Her cocoon kept them separate, but she could feel the heat and solidness of his body next to hers. He pulled out his phone and clicked a button. The outdoor lights went off, casting them into complete darkness. "Give it a moment for your eyes to adjust," he said. "It's amazing."

Tatum leaned her head against his, watching the sky. At first, she could see a few stars, then more, then more, then even more, until the dark night seemed to be alive with twinkling lights. They seemed endless, with more appearing with each passing moment. She felt tiny and insignificant, and at the same time, she felt immensely powerful, knowing that she was a part of this incredible universe she lived in. The magic of life. Of love. Of hope. Of following her soul.

Of sharing the moment with someone who understood her, who saw her for who she truly was.

"I forgot how beautiful it is," Brody said. "It's been a long time since I've done this."

"Me, too." She wanted to stay here, with him. She wanted to say yes to his proposal. She wanted to finally live what they'd begun so long ago.

But she was scared. Scared to turn herself over to anyone. Scared of giving up her freedom. Brody was a protector, which meant he wasn't a pushover. Not that she wanted a wimp, but she needed to be able to be however she wanted, whoever she wanted, whenever she wanted. Could she do that and share her life with him?

She hadn't been able to do it with Donny, but that had

been a different time, a different man, and she'd been different. And, she hadn't loved him.

"I'm going to make a quick espresso. I want to stay alert until the security gets here," Brody said. "You want anything?"

"Water would be great." Cold air drifted in as Brody flipped the blanket up and rose to his feet.

"All right." He started to walk away, then paused and turned back to look at her.

She held her breath. It was too dark to see his face, but she could feel his tightly coiled energy. "What?"

He said nothing for a moment, then shrugged. "I don't know what to say, Tatum. I'm out of words with you."

Her heart sank as he turned and walked back into the house.

He'd just disappeared inside when her phone rang, startling her. She pulled it out from under the blankets, and her stomach jumped when she saw it was Donny. Fear trickled through her, and she glanced into the house. Brody had turned the kitchen light on, and she could see him getting his espresso together.

She was safe now. On a ranch in Oregon. Brody only a few yards away, with a gun.

The phone rang again.

She took a deep breath, summoned courage, and answered. "Donny." She kept her voice low, not sure she wanted Brody to know she was talking to a man who might be hunting her.

"Tatum! You're safe? Where are you? I've been freaking out!" He sounded legitimately panicked, which Tatum found an odd response if he'd sent Hank after her.

"Did you send him after me?" Somehow, being so far out of Donny's reach, in the protective sphere of Brody, gave her the courage to speak up calmly, without feeling trapped or defensive. She felt...powerful.

There was a pause. "Him? Who?"

"The man who attacked me and broke my arm."

There was a longer silence. "Someone attacked you and broke your arm?" His voice was low and lethal. "When?"

"At the stadium. After you sent Brody away and I followed him. A man dressed as a security guard jumped me." She paused. "He said someone on my team hired him," she hedged. "Was it you? The police have him now and they're interviewing him. I know they'll find out, but I want to be prepared. I want to hear it from you."

"What the hell? Is that what you think of me?"

"Yes." She didn't hesitate. "That's exactly what I think of you. Did you do it?"

"No." He didn't hesitate. "I love you, Tatum. I'd never hurt you."

She felt the truth in his voice, a truth he believed...a truth that he was wrong about. He didn't love her. "Then what do you call stalking me, making me uncomfortable, trapping me in a contract that is killing my soul, and refusing to let me get away from you and get on with my life? That's love?"

There was an even longer silence. "Is that what I do?"

"Yes."

More silence. "I thought... It was a mistake when I cheated on you, Tatum. I wanted to prove to you that I was different. That it would never happen again. That you came first. I wanted to fix what I broke."

She watched Brody get a mug out of the cabinet. "It was broken before you cheated, Donny. I was eighteen when we got married. A child. I never had a chance to be me, to become who I wanted to be. You saw money when you looked at me, and that's how you treated me. How you always treated me."

"That's bullshit, Tatum. Our marriage started with love—"

"It didn't. I was eighteen and desperate. I wasn't capable of loving you." She watched Brody. She hadn't been able to love Donny, because her heart had been laying in shattered pieces after losing Brody. She took a deep breath. "I think...I think I used you to escape. You were my ticket to my dreams. Looking back, I never loved you, Donny, but I don't think you ever loved me, either." The words tumbled out. She hadn't meant to say them, she'd never even thought them, but as she said them, she knew they were true. All of them. Truths she'd never been willing to acknowledge or take responsibility for.

Donny was silent.

"Donny, I want you to let me go. Let me out of the contract. Let us both get on with our lives."

More silence.

"Donny?" A tinge of guilt flashed through her. She'd been married to him for a decade, which was a long time not to love someone. "I'm sorry," she said quietly.

He finally spoke. "I'm sorry, too."

"Will you let me go? Please? I'll buy you out, if it's money you want."

He sighed. "It's never been about the money, Tatum. It's just been about you."

Fear prickled through her at his words. It had always been about her? Divorced for five years, and it was still about her? Her mind drifted back to her stalker. "Donny." She watched Brody fill a glass of water from the dispenser on the front of the fridge. "Someone is trying to kill me. If it's you, you need to understand that you won't succeed. You won't have me, and you will go to prison. You have twenty-four hours to cancel the contract and sign a confession, or I will take this to the press. Understand?"

Brody was heading toward her now, with the water and the espresso.

"Tatum—"

"Good-bye. Don't call me back. I won't answer." She hung up and hid her phone under the blanket as Brody stepped outside.

He paused and looked at her. "What did you do?"

She gave him an innocent smile. "Nothing. What did *you* do?"

"I got us drinks." He set them on the table and continued to frown at her. "You have that expression on your face that you always have when you're hiding something from me."

She flipped the button on her phone to silent, in case Donny tried to call back. "Is there any word from the police? Did they find out who hired Hank?"

"No." He sat down in one of the chairs. "Dylan can't find Jackson or Ace, though. They're not at home or work. Their phones are both off."

Her stomach tightened. "It can't be them."

"It could." Empathy flickered in his eyes. "I know you want it to be Donny. He's the obvious choice, but sometimes it's the quiet ones who do the most damage. I want you to think carefully. Tell me about Victoria."

"My drummer?"

"Yeah."

"She's been with me since I was originally signed. I trust her."

"Nora?"

She shrugged. "She's been with the tour for several years, long before any of the stalking started. Donny hired her and —" She stopped suddenly.

"What?"

She looked at him. "He hired her right when we were getting a divorce. He slept around a bit at the time. Do you think he had an affair with Nora? And now she's jealous because he won't leave me alone?" She thought back to her last interactions with Nora, how she'd intervened to help draw her away from Donny. She'd thought Nora was helping her, but what if there had been other motivations?

"I'll tell Dylan to check." He pulled out his phone. "Keep thinking—" He hit send, and had just put his phone to his ear when sirens ripped through the night and the lights on the property began strobe-light flashing.

"What's that?"

Brody swore and leapt to his feet. "Fire in the barn. Fuck. We have over thirty horses in there." His phone rang and he answered it. "What? Flames? You can see *flames*? I'll be right there." He shoved his phone in his pocket. "We need to go! Come on!"

Panic shot through Tatum as she leapt to her feet. "All right!" She didn't even take time for shoes. She just sprinted after Brody as he raced down the deck steps, his phone to his ear as he barked orders.

They raced around the corner, and she gasped as she saw the roof of the barn on fire. "Oh, dear God," she whispered.

Brody didn't slow down. He just bolted down the driveway as headlights lit up the fields, streaking across the pastures toward the barn as the rest of the Hart family convened.

Fear gripped her as she ran, following Brody right into the barn. The sprinkler system was pouring water all over everything, and she had to blink as the water dumped all over her. Brody ran to the first stall, slipped a halter and a lead rope on the first horse and led him out. "Take him to the nearest pasture and turn him out there. Then come back." He paused. "Don't let go."

She took the lead rope from him. "I won't, I promise." She jogged out the door with the horse, who was dancing and skittering, his eyes wide as the sirens screamed and the smoke began to thicken.

They made it outside as a pickup truck skidded to a stop. Out leapt Bella. For a split second, Tatum froze, but Bella didn't hesitate. "Take him to the second pasture," she yelled, pointing down the driveway.

"Got it!" The horse continued to skitter, and Tatum tightened her grip as she ran down toward the gate. She got it open, hurried inside, and then locked it behind her. Only then did she unsnap the rope, jumping back just in time as the horse whirled away and galloped off.

Tatum ducked under the rails and ran back toward the barn, limping as her feet hit the pebbles. She ran up to the barn as Keegan came out of the doors, leading two horses. She was just running past him when he shouted her name.

She spun around. "What?"

"You can't go in there without shoes! It's a damned fire!"

"I don't have time—"

"Don't be a fool. Go get shoes. You'll be more help!"

She hesitated as Bella ran out, leading two horses. "He's right," Bella shouted above the sirens. "I have boots in my truck! They're on the back seat!"

Tatum nodded. "All right!" She whirled away and ran for Bella's big, black pickup. The door was unlocked, and the keys were still in the ignition. She opened the back door of the cab and climbed in. The floor was covered with several horse blankets, some lead lines, a bin of spray bottles, and other ranch gear.

She scrambled up on the seat and began to move items. She finally saw a boot sticking out from under a bag. She shoved the bag aside, and saw a pair of hiking boots. She yanked one on. It was big, so it went easily over her thick socks. The sirens were still wailing, and she rushed to tie the laces. Then she got the second one on just as the door on her side opened.

She didn't look up. "I'm almost ready—"

There was a quick movement, and then sudden pain shot through her head. She fell forward, fumbling for balance, and then pain hit again, and then there was only darkness.

CHAPTER TWENTY-TWO

An explosion echoed through the barn as Brody handed over two horses to Keegan. He spun around, swearing as sparks dripped down from the ceiling at the middle part of the aisle. His brothers Colin, Jacob, and Lucas were already pulling the horses out from the other end, but neither side had reached the middle.

Two of the middle stalls contained new arrivals, mares who had come from an abusive situation. They were high strung and bordering on dangerous, and he could hear them kicking.

He shoved the lead shank for Midnight at Bella. "Take him. I'm going for Carmen!"

He could hear the sirens outside, and he knew the fire trucks were there. Their state-of-the art sprinkler system was doing a master job, but sparks kept getting past it. He pulled out his phone as he ran and punched in the code to turn off the sirens.

Silence fell mercifully as he reached the stall. Carmen was up against the back wall of her stall, her head up, her eyes wide, her nostrils flaring. Brody grabbed a lead line off her door as she slammed her back feet into the wall again.

He unlocked the door and then locked it behind him, locking himself inside with her. She was a bolter, and he didn't want to risk injury to her by having her get free. "Hey, sweetheart." He moved slowly, steadily, keeping up a gentle crooning as shouts and footsteps echoed through the barn. "Time to get out of here, baby." A spark dropped on his arm, and he left it, not wanting to startle her by knocking it away.

It burned briefly, then faded away as Brody edged toward her. "Hey, Carmen. It's all good." She kicked again, and scooted away from him just as he reached for her halter. He swore under his breath, but kept his body relaxed. "Hey, how about a song?" He began to sing the song that he and Tatum had sung together on stage the night before.

The moment he began to sing, he saw Carmen's ear cock toward him, listening. He sang a little louder as he moved closer. He rubbed his hand over her neck, which was damp from the sprinklers. He continued to rub her neck as he moved his hand toward her head. Singing and scratching, he got to her ear, and she lowered her head slightly so he could scratch it. He kept up the song as he gently snapped the lead line to her halter.

"All set?" Bella was watching through the bars.

"Yep."

Bella unlocked the door and swung it wide. "She's the last one. The firefighters are here."

"I heard." Brody kept singing to Carmen as he led her out into the aisle. The moment she was out, there was another small explosion, and she bolted. Brody swore and dug in, but even then, she managed to drag him a few feet before he got her to stop. "Stay back, Bella."

"You worry about you. I'm fine." She followed as he led the mare down the aisle, staying out of range as the mare spun around in frantic circles. Sparks dripped down from the hayloft, and Brody swore, allowing the horse to move faster.

He didn't know how dangerous the situation was. "Bella, get out."

"No."

"I can't worry about you and the horse."

"Then don't worry about me. I can handle this."

He glanced at her as they worked their way down the aisle. Bella had soot on her cheek, and she was absolutely soaking wet, as were the rest of them. She looked determined and fierce, and he smiled.

She was right. She did have this. "All right. Thanks for your help."

She nodded. A lead line was dangling from her hand, and he knew she was ready to clip on if she got the chance. Carmen spooked again, and he started singing again. After a moment, Bella joined in, not missing even a single word of the song.

He glanced over at her, and she shrugged. "So I know her songs. So what?"

Tatum had stayed with all of them all this time. In and out so quickly, but she'd left a piece of her sparkle with them all. She mattered. To him. To his family. To the world.

Did he need to let her go? Was it selfish to keep pushing her?

With her song filling the air as he and Bella got Carmen down the aisle, it was difficult not to think of Tatum. Of what to do. Of how to handle it.

They finally got the mare outside, and Brody handed Carmen over to Colin, who took her toward the back barn, away from the fire. They had only a few stalls there, but Carmen definitely needed the safety of a stall, not a big field with other horses.

He turned to watch the building, and he was relieved

when he couldn't see any flames. The hoses were in full force, but there wasn't a raging fire visible. "It looks like it's going to be all right," he said.

"I think we got it." Bella came to stand beside him. "Tatum was running into the fire in socks," she said. "She didn't even stop for shoes."

Brody heard the emotion in her voice, and he looked over at Bella. "I still love her."

Bella nodded. "I do, too."

He sighed and put his arm around his sister. "I don't know if she's going to stay this time."

"I know."

Brody glanced over his shoulder, scanning the busy stable yard. Between his family, the firefighters, and the police, there was a lot of activity and chaos. It took him a moment to conclude that Tatum wasn't among them. He frowned. "Have you seen Tatum?"

Bella shook her head. "Not since I told her to get a pair of my boots out of my truck—" Her voice faded. "My truck's gone."

Tension ripped through Brody. "What do you mean, your truck's gone?"

"It's missing. Not where I left it." She pulled away from him. "I parked by the fence. Right where the fire truck is now." She ran across the stable yard, and Brody jogged after her, continuing to scan for Tatum.

Bella stopped, her hands on her hips. "It's gone." She spun around. "Did anyone move my truck?" she shouted.

All she received were a bunch of head shakes.

A firefighter walked up behind him. "A black truck with writing on the side?"

"Yes, it says Bella's Cantina." Relief was evident on her face. "Where is it?"

"It passed us on our way in. A woman was driving it. Almost ran right into us, which is why I noticed it."

Bella sucked in her breath. "She stole my truck?"

Shock rippled through Brody. It didn't make sense that Tatum would just leave again. If she did leave, it would be different. There would be goodbyes at least. "I'm sure that's not what happened."

Hurt was etched on Bella's face. "I have GPS on my truck. I'm going to go get my truck back. Will you drive me?"

"Yeah, of course." Tension was mounting in Brody. "Hang on." He saw Dylan walking across the yard, and he gestured him over.

Dylan broke into a jog. "What's up?"

Brody quickly explained, and Dylan swore. "She's in trouble. She wouldn't have left like that again."

"I agree."

"They said she was driving the truck," Bella said.

"They said *a woman* was driving the truck." Brody swore. "How long ago did they leave?"

The firefighter shrugged. "Maybe forty minutes. We've been here a while. Maybe less."

Dylan was already pulling out his phone. "I'll call the security team. They'll be almost here."

Bella put her hands on her hips. "Why are you so sure she didn't take it?"

"Because someone is hunting her. I brought Tatum here to keep her safe. He already sent a stalker to break her arm, and the same guy showed up at the ranch today and attacked us."

Bella's mouth dropped open, and she covered her mouth with her hand. "I didn't know. Oh, God, *Tatum*."

"Let's go!" Brody ran toward his truck, and Bella sprinted after him. He vaulted into the front seat, checked the glove box for a gun, and then turned on the ignition while Bella pulled out her phone and typed in the GPS.

"It's not that far away," she said. "It's on Old Dutch Road."

"I know where that is." He put his phone on speaker and called Dylan, giving him the location of the truck.

The silence in the truck was grim as he sped down the driveway and turned right on the main road. Brody couldn't stop thinking about the barn fire. How the fuck had he not realized it was intentional?

Son of a bitch. Frustrated, he slammed his palm onto the steering wheel as the tires sped down the asphalt.

"It's not your fault," Bella said.

"I should have realized. That barn is built too well to have it suddenly catch fire like that." His gut felt like someone had stabbed him. "I fucking let her get taken right under my nose. One job. I had one job to protect her, and I fucking blew it. That's why she came to me. Because she was in danger, and she had no one else to turn to."

All he did was protect. That literally defined him. And he'd blown it.

He gripped the steering wheel. "She told me that she couldn't be with me, because with me, she would never be my number one. She told me that I always prioritize whoever is in greatest need, and she doesn't want to be in need. She wants to be happy, and if she's happy, then I won't prioritize her. And I fucking did it tonight. I ran after the horses and stopped watching her."

The guilt and self-hate were so thick he could barely even think. "Just like before. Just. Like. Before." He looked over at Bella. "She's right. She's right. I can't be what she needs. I'll always be running off—"

"Stop." Bella held up her hand. "Just stop it, Brody."

He ground his jaw. "Don't—"

"You're wrong."

The hard inflection of her voice got his attention, and he glanced over at her again. "About what?"

"That you can't put her first. She's always been first for you."

"Not tonight—"

"A trap was set for you, Brody. A trap that no one could have ignored. It was the *horses*. And you brought her with you." Bella sighed. "You're a human being, Brody, not a machine. Maybe it's time that you gave yourself a break and let yourself be human."

"I don't even know what that means." He took a hard right, and the tires almost came off the ground. "Are we catching up?"

Bella looked at her phone. "The truck isn't moving."

Fear gripped Brody's gut. What if they'd crashed? "How far?"

"Just around the bend." They both fell silent as they shot around the bend.

"There!" Bella pointed at her truck, pulled off to the side of the road.

"Stay in the truck," he ordered as he pulled up behind.

"I know how to use a gun, too." Bella grabbed his spare gun from the glove box as he leapt out.

Brody scanned the surrounding area as he approached the truck, but he saw nothing. The truck bed was empty. He got close to the truck, and saw it was parked along the side of the road. It hadn't crashed. He reached the driver's door and pulled it open, gun aimed inside.

No one was in there.

Bella yanked open the passenger door, gun up.

They looked at each other, then they both pulled open the rear doors.

No one was there.

Brody's gut sank, and fear gripped him. "She's gone."

Bella rifled through the gear in the back. "She got my boots. She's been here." She looked at Brody. "You really don't believe she just took off? Maybe she met someone here."

He shook his head. "She didn't take off. I know it." It was different this time. He was sure of it. And even if it wasn't, he wasn't making the same mistake he made last time. "Either way, I'm going after her."

"But how? We have no idea where she went." Bella paused. "Or where she was taken. We have no way to find her."

CHAPTER TWENTY-THREE

The pain in Tatum's head was excruciating.

She let out a small gasp of agony, and tried to touch her head, but she couldn't move her arms.

Panic shot through her, and she opened her eyes.

It was dark, still night, but the moon gave her enough light to see that she was outdoors. Leaves and sticks were digging into her side. She tried to move again, but her arms wouldn't move. She realized that her hands were bound behind her back, and her ankles were tied together. Thankfully, the cast protected her wrist from the rope, but it was still aching and throbbing.

Fear gripped her, and suddenly, she couldn't breathe.

She looked around again, desperate. Was there anyone who could help? She wanted to scream, but she was afraid to, afraid that whoever had dumped her there was still close.

Movement caught her eye, and she saw a vehicle through the trees. Someone was leaning into the trunk, doing something.

She couldn't see who it was, but there was something familiar about the silhouette.

It was definitely someone she knew.

She looked around, panicked. She had to get out of there. Fast. But how? She wiggled around until she was on her belly, then pulled her knees under her. She leaned her shoulder against a tree, and somehow managed to get to her knees, so she was sitting on her feet.

She felt for her ankles, and then grimaced when she felt the hard plastic. Zip ties. There was no way to break those without a knife.

She had to move before the person came back. She had to put distance between them.

Tatum leaned into the tree, and braced herself, using the tree as leverage as she managed to get her feet under her. She was panting by the time she made it to her feet, but the second she was up, she started hopping across the leaves, praying she wouldn't trip on a stick.

It was almost like all the hopping around she did on stage during shows. Except for the zip ties and the terror that she was going to be killed, of course.

She hopped again and then her gut dropped when she heard a voice.

"Going somewhere, Tatum?"

Victoria.

Tatum spun around as her drummer emerged out of the shadows, pointing a gun at her. "Why?"

"Because I love him. I've always loved him."

"Him...who?" All Tatum could think of was Brody. He would notice she was missing. He would come after her. She just needed to stay alive until he found her. Somehow, he would find her.

"Donny."

"*Donny?*" Tatum couldn't hide her incredulity. "This is about *Donny?*"

"I thought I had him when you got divorced. He

promised me we'd get married as soon as he got free of you. But as soon as you dumped him, he decided you were the one he wanted. All that mattered was you." Victoria stopped several yards from her. "You kept him strung along—"

"I didn't! I don't want him! He's yours!" *Brody. Come find me. Hurry.*

"He won't be mine, because he's obsessed with you." Victoria sighed. "It's been tough, really, because I love what it does for my career to be your drummer. And honestly, I feel like we're friends. I wanted this to be easy, Tatum. Easy for both of us, and you never had to know. I knew it would upset you to know I'd been sleeping with him while you guys were married."

Tatum felt sick. She'd known of Donny's infidelity, but never would she have expected Victoria to be one of his women. "I trusted you." She had so few friends. So few people she would have counted on. Victoria had been one of them.

"I know, and I didn't want to betray that trust."

"Did you send Hank?" Anything to keep Victoria talking. Every minute she could stall gave Brody time to find her. She still had her phone on her. Dylan would be able to track her. All she had to do was stay alive.

"I did."

"He broke my arm." Her wrist was burning with pain from being twisted around, but she didn't dare focus on it. She kept her gaze on the gun, which hadn't wavered from her chest.

"I noticed." Victoria didn't sound remotely remorseful about it, which deepened Tatum's fear. "Donny's been freaking out since you disappeared. It made me realize it's never going to be over until you're gone. You have to go."

Oh, God. "Go where?"

"Die, Tatum. Die. Why do you make me spell it out? I'm really trying to avoid processing this right now."

Tatum's mouth was so dry she could barely talk. "I called him earlier tonight. I told him he had to let me go. That it had to be over. He heard me this time. It's over. He's yours." *Hurry, Brody. Hurry.*

"Well, we'll just make sure of that, won't we?" She jerked her chin to the left. "There's a precipice there. You're going to take a tumble. Tragic accident in Oregon."

Tatum's heart started to pound. "You'll wind up in prison, Victoria. You'll never be with him."

"Why would I go to prison for an accident that befell you?" Victoria put a bottle of wine on the ground, unscrewed the lid, and then stuck a long straw in it. "Let's drink to our success, Tatum. Four Grammy awards, eleven nominations. And so many others. We make a great team."

"Drink?" Tatum echoed.

"Drink until you're drunk. Accidents happen when you're drunk."

"I'm not going to drink." She lifted her chin. "You'll have to shoot me, and then no one will believe that I died by accident. Brody will find you."

"Brody?" Victoria laughed. "Right about now, Brody will find the note you left him on the kitchen table, telling him that you don't want to be with him, and not to follow you."

Tatum's heart sank, but she lifted her chin. "He knows my writing. He'll know it's not me."

"I've been on tour with you for fifteen years. I also know your writing, Tatum. I've been planning this for a long time. You just made it easier by coming out to Eastern Oregon, where it's so easy for accidents to happen." She raised her gun. "So, drink."

Tatum lifted her chin. "No." Brody would find her. He

would come. He wouldn't believe the note. No one would believe the note.

Except they might. She'd left him before with a note.

In fact, she'd been wanting to run since she'd first arrived. All she did was run from them. So, why wouldn't they believe it? It was actually very likely that they would believe she'd run from them again, leaving nothing more than a scrawled good-bye.

Hopelessness settled down on her, and sudden tears filled her eyes. Why had she wanted to run from Brody? From Bella? From the only people she'd ever had who actually cared about her? They'd loved her before she was rich and famous. They wanted nothing from her, except for her to love them.

Suddenly, staring into the face of Victoria made everything so much clearer about what she wanted, who she wanted, the life she wanted.

But it was too late.

Victoria smiled. "If you choose not to drink, I'll shoot you, and you'll be dead immediately. If you drink, it'll take a while for you to get drunk enough to fall off a cliff. That gives Brody time to find you. He won't be looking, and he won't find you, but do you really want to give up the chance?"

Tatum bit her lip. "You won't shoot me."

"No?" Victoria moved the gun slightly and fired. Tatum jumped as the dirt exploded next to her foot. "I'm a country girl, Tatum. I grew up with guns. I am fine with shooting you. Are you fine with being shot? Or do you want to drink?"

What choice did she have? Brody was a protector. He was *her* protector. He would find her. She had to believe. Which meant she had to give him time. "I'll drink."

"Good. Start now."

Tatum grimly hopped across the ground and dropped to her knees.

"If you knock it over, I'll shoot you immediately, so be careful."

Her heart pounding, Tatum bent over, caught the straw in her mouth, and began to drink.

Or rather, she pretended to drink.

What would happen when Victoria realized she was faking it?

Hurry, Brody, hurry.

CHAPTER TWENTY-FOUR

BRODY MET Dylan at the house two hours later.

"We've checked everywhere," Dylan said. "There's no sign of any cars. She's vanished."

Brody felt like his gut was going to shatter. "They have to be nearby."

"They don't, actually." Dylan's voice was gentle, but firm. "They could be a hundred miles away by now, and probably are."

The entire Hart clan and the newly hired security team were still out combing the hills. The police had amped up the pressure on Hank at the police station, but he still wasn't talking.

Brody sank down at the kitchen table and pressed his head into his hands, trying to think. "There must be something I'm missing," he said. "Something we didn't see." He wanted to be back out on the roads searching, but he felt like he needed to be back at the house. "What the hell, Dylan?"

Dylan was quiet for a moment.

Brody looked up and saw his brother was reading a piece of paper. "What's that?"

Dylan said nothing, but he walked over and set the paper on the table in front of Brody.

Brody,

I'm leaving. Don't follow me. I can't do this. Let me go.

Tatum

Brody met his gaze. "She didn't write that."

Dylan grinned. "I had the same thought. The writing is pretty good, though."

"Not good enough. And she'd never write that. She would have said she loved me." Brody pushed the chair back. "Someone was in the house, Dylan. Someone got in here and left that note."

Dylan was already typing in his phone. "Let's see what the cameras show."

Brody leaned over Dylan's shoulder and peered into it. They watched as a woman walked right into the slider that they'd left open.

"You left the door open?" Dylan said.

"There was a crisis. I was thinking about the horses."

"You need to get much more cynical about the world."

As they watched, a woman moved into view. Brody frowned at the black and white image. "Who is that? She looks familiar."

"That's because she's Tatum's drummer." Dylan swore under his breath. "She got a call at the time that Hank was making calls after his botched attack on Tatum. It's her, Brody. It's her."

Brody's gut was like steel as he watched her drop the letter onto the counter and then walk out. He pulled out his phone and called the one personal number he had of Tatum's in his phone.

Jackson answered on the first ring. "Tatum?"

"Victoria has her," he said. "I need to find Victoria. What's her phone number?"

"Victoria? It can't be her. She loves Tatum."

"I don't know, but she was here. What's her number?"

"Hang on. I'll share her contact with you."

There was a brief pause, and then Brody's phone dinged. "Got it. Thanks." He shared the contact with Dylan, who immediately started running it through his system.

"What can I do?" Jackson asked.

"Go through her stuff. See if you can find anything about her."

"Will do. I'll check with the team. Did Tatum get her bag okay?"

Brody frowned. "Her bag?"

"Yeah, I had it messengered to her. They left it with someone at the ranch."

"Who?"

Jackson paused. "Hang on. Okay, someone named Bella signed for it."

"All right. Thanks. Find Donny. Have him call me."

"Will do."

Brody hung up as Dylan shook his head.

"Victoria has her phone off. I can't track her."

Brody swore under his breath. "There has to be a way."

"I'm good, but I can't work my tech wizardry if there's no tech to wizard."

Brody stood up and pushed back from the table, too

agitated to sit still. "We have to find her. I need to find her." He'd lost her once. He couldn't lose her again. And this time...it would be forever. He swore and slammed his palms against the wall. "What the hell? Where is she?"

Dylan looked grim. "We'll find her."

But he didn't say the rest. Would she be alive when they did?

∽

Victoria knelt beside Tatum. "You think I'm stupid."

"I don't. I think you're my friend. My best friend." Or rather, *were*. Present tense felt a little optimistic.

"Well, then, you're stupid." Victoria nudged the bottle with her gun. "How long did you think it would take me to figure out you weren't drinking?"

"Honestly, I was hoping it would take longer."

Victoria kicked Tatum's shoulder, knocking her onto her side. "Don't be funny. I hate it when you're funny."

Tatum bit her lip against the pain as her broken arm twisted. "But I like it when I'm funny, so really, it's all about me."

"It's always all about you." Victoria pointed the gun at her. "Roll on your back, and I'll pour it down your throat."

"No, thank you." Where was Brody? He was usually better at protecting people than this. She was going to have to retract all her complaints about his protector side. Seriously. "Did you really have to endanger the horses?"

"The horses were fine. I made sure of it. You know how I feel about animals."

"I do." Tatum tried to think of how to keep Victoria talking, instead of focused on killing her. Multi-tasking wasn't always easy, right? "Remember that time when—"

"Shut up." Victoria kicked her in the cheek, and Tatum

gasped, reeling from the sudden pain. Her vision spun, and she breathed deeply, trying to stay conscious.

"Are you going to drink now?"

"No."

Victoria walked behind her and kicked her cast.

The pain was blinding. Nausea churned in Tatum's belly, and she turned her head, gasping for air. "Stop," she whispered. "I'll drink."

"Good. This is your last chance. I'm running out of patience. Get up."

Tears of pain trickling down her cheeks, Tatum managed to get herself to her knees, while Victoria watched. She hadn't been lying when she'd said she'd considered Victoria her best friend. Granted, she hadn't had many to choose from, but it would never have occurred to her that Victoria was an enemy.

Finally, she understood the gift that the Harts had been. Even after fifteen years apart, they were still there for her. Even Bella. They didn't want anything from her, other than her love.

And Brody...he was her everything, and she'd been too afraid to trust him.

Would she lose her chance?

She was running out of time.

∽

Brody was pacing the kitchen when Donny called. "Brody Hart? This is Donny. Jackson said Victoria has Tatum. Is this true?"

"Yes. What do you know about her? Did she rent a car? What kind of car does she have? We need to track her."

Donny swore. "Tatum said someone was after her, but she thought it was me. I'd never send someone to hurt her, let alone break her arm. I didn't even think of it being Victoria—"

Brody went still. "Tatum told you about her broken arm? When?"

"Earlier tonight. I didn't—"

"Tonight? How did you reach her?"

"I called her phone. She answered."

Brody stood up. "Her phone? She has *her phone*?" It must have been in the bag that Jackson had sent. "What's her number?" His adrenaline jacked up as Donny rattled it off.

He repeated it to Dylan, who went to work on his computer while Brody finished off the call with Donny, who had nothing helpful to add.

He hung up the phone, then for a long, agonizing moment, he waited.

Then Dylan looked up. "Got her."

Holy shit. He gripped the edge of the counter, fighting to stay in control. "How far?"

"Fourteen miles. We're the closest ones to her."

Fuck. Brody grabbed his car keys and sprinted out the door, with Dylan right behind him. Several Harts were still there dealing with the horses, and the fire department was making sure the fire was out, but Brody didn't stop to check on them.

He and Dylan leapt into his truck, and he hit the gas, his tires spinning out as he shot up the driveway. "Which way?"

"Right. Turn right." Dylan pulled out his phone and sent a group text to the Hart chat. "They're on their way, but we're closest."

Brody ground his jaw as he floored it, his engine roaring. "Where are we going?"

"Black Bear Butte. The top."

Brody knew Black Bear. He knew the drop off. "She's going to push Tatum over the edge, isn't she?"

Dylan pulled his gun out of his holster and checked it. "We'll get there in time."

Brody nodded, too tense to speak as the yellow lines on the road whipped past.

"She's our family, Brody. We'll make it. We're never late."

Except that wasn't true. They'd been too late with Katie Crowley. "Katie's dead because we were too late." He'd let her go. He'd failed to keep track of her. And now she was dead.

And he'd made the same fucking mistake with Tatum. *Twice.* He shouted a curse and slammed his palm onto the steering wheel. "I love her, Dylan. I fucking love her. I can't live without her."

"I know." Dylan's knees were bouncing restlessly.

"I went after the horses. She's first from now on. First. I can't split my loyalties anymore. She's it."

"She's always been it for you. You were just so caught up in protecting the rest of us that you didn't notice." Dylan leaned forward, his forearms on his thighs. "Turn right here."

Brody hauled the steering wheel to the right, and the tires screeched as the truck skidded around the corner. Ahead of them, Black Bear Butte stretched high. The cliff was on the other side. He couldn't see it from where he was.

He hit the gas and raced the truck up the back side of the butte.

"We're all equals now, Brody. We take care of each other. Fuck, we've been taking care of you since she left. Get her back and keep her this time. Trust us to help hold each other up. We got this, bro. All of us. Together."

Brody ground his jaw. "You mean that."

"I do. We've all talked about it. It's time for you to live your life. For you."

Brody nodded grimly as he whipped around a hairpin turn. "Thanks."

"No need for thanks. We're family. It's automatic."

The truck burst out of the woods, and Brody swore and hit the brakes, jerking the steering wheel to the side to avoid plowing into a gray sedan parked across the road. The truck spun out, and he fought for control, coming to a stop halfway in a ditch. "Victoria's still here. That's a good sign."

Please let me be in time.

He and Dylan both leapt out and sprinted toward the top of the cliff. His breath was quick and tight as he ran, vaulting over rocks and fallen sticks. It was straight up hill, but he didn't slow and neither did Dylan.

They sprinted over the crest of the butte, and he saw the silhouettes of two women on the edge of the cliff. They were struggling with each other, and he recognized the silhouette of the woman he loved. "Tatum!" He bellowed her name just as Victoria shoved her.

"Brody!" Tatum screamed, and then she fell over the edge, her arms flailing as she vanished from sight.

CHAPTER TWENTY-FIVE

"No!" Anguish tore through Brody as he sprinted toward the edge of the cliff. He shoved past Victoria, barely even noticing her, and raced to the edge. He leaned out, scanning the ground below, terror gripping him.

Behind him, he heard Dylan dealing with Victoria, but he didn't turn around.

He just kept looking below...searching for her broken body on the ground. She wasn't there. Hope leapt through him. If she hadn't fallen all the way...

He crouched down and began scanning the cliff below him, methodically searching each section. "Tatum! Can you hear me?"

Victoria was shouting at Dylan now, and Brody swung around. "If you killed her," he said, his voice low with threat. "You will never leave prison."

Her eyes widened with innocence he didn't believe. "I didn't mean to—"

"Quiet. Now."

Her mouth snapped shut.

Brody turned back to the cliff. "Tatum!"

This time, he thought he heard her voice, and his heart leapt. "Where are you?"

He kept scanning the cliff below, searching for Tatum, but he didn't see her. "Talk to me, baby."

"Brody!"

Hope leapt through him at the sound of her voice. "Tatum." He went down on his knees, leaning over the edge. "I can't see you, baby. Tell me where you are."

"I can't hold on much longer." Her voice was strained.

"Shit!" He leapt to his feet. "Dylan! Get my truck!"

Dylan had Victoria sitting against the front tire of her car, but he took one look at Brody's face and didn't hesitate. He held up his hand, Brody tossed him the keys, and he took off. Brody looked at Victoria. "Don't move."

Her face was streaked with tears. "I didn't mean for her to fall. I just wanted—"

"I don't want to hear it." Brody turned back to the edge, braced his hands on the rim, and leaned out as far as he could without falling, searching carefully. There were a lot of jutting rocks that she could be behind. "Tatum, you need to keep hanging on. Dylan's getting my truck. I have a cable and a winch. I'll be coming down for you, but you need to hang on."

She didn't answer.

Brody swore, looking back as his truck bounced over the rutted earth, making a road where there wasn't one. He leapt up as Dylan stopped, and was already releasing the winch on the front of the truck by the time Dylan got out. "She's down there, hanging on. I need to get her before she falls."

Dylan swore, but the two brothers set up the harness and winch with effortless speed. Within seconds, Brody was lowering himself down the side of the butte, his boots knocking pebbles loose as he rappelled down. "Tatum. Talk to me. Where are you?"

No reply.

He swore. "Dylan! Do you see her?"

"No. Tatum!" Dylan shouted. "Where the hell are you?"

Brody swore again and kept going down, but he couldn't go too fast in case he shot by her. His heart was pounding, sweat was dripping down his temples, and he'd never been so scared in his life.

Not of dying.

Of being too late.

～

Tatum leaned her face into her arm, fighting not to let go of the root that she'd slammed into and almost bounced off as she'd gone over the edge. Her fingers were aching, her arm trembling. Her broken wrist had given out almost immediately, and she was dangling by one hand.

Upper body strength wasn't her forte, which was not a win for her right now.

She tried to stabilize her breathing, fighting to summon strength she didn't feel like she had.

"Tatum!" Brody shouted again.

"Brody." She tried to shout back, but her voice was a scratchy whisper, all her energy going into trying to hang on. Her legs were literally dangling. There was no purchase for her feet.

This sucked. She didn't want to die this way. She had too much left to do.

"Tatum!"

She squeezed her eyes shut, focusing all her energy into hanging on. He would find her in time. She knew he would. All she had to do was hang on. Another second. She could make it another second. And another.

"Tatum. If you don't answer me, I swear to God, I will perform with you on stage every single song for the rest of your life. It'll destroy your career, steal your independence, and ruin everything you've ever dreamed of."

A small laugh burst out of her. "You're so weird!" The words were louder, galvanized by her burst of laughter.

"Of course I'm weird." His voice was closer now, etched with emotion that made her own throat tighten. "That's why you love me. You couldn't love a normal person. You're an artist. Everyone knows artists are crazy as hell."

"This is true." She could hear his boots scrabbling on the rock face now, and she smiled. "You're taking an awfully long time to get to me. Are you like part sloth or something?"

"A sloth. You literally just called me a sloth?" He suddenly appeared beside her, and she felt his arm go around her waist. "I'm a very agile sloth, I'll have you know."

Tears filled her eyes at the feel of his body against hers. "You have me?"

"I got you."

"No dying today, then."

"Not from this, no. Dylan's got the keys, though, so there's no telling what our drive home is going to be like."

Desperate laughter giggled out of her. "I can't let go."

"Yeah, you can." His arm tightened around her. "I'm going to swing you around so you're facing me. Put your legs around my waist."

"I can't. I'll fall." Her hand was screaming in protest, cramping. But the idea of letting go of the root felt like a bad idea on every level. "It's really high. Falling would be a bad idea."

"Tatum." Brody's voice was low.

She squeezed her eyes shut. "What?"

"Trust me."

She almost started laughing. "That's such a male thing to say. I can't just turn on trust."

"I agree, but you do actually trust me already, so you can go with it."

Recognition flickered through her. Did she really trust him? Yes, she did. Not just to catch her right now, but on every level.

"Come on, sweetheart." He paused. "Open your eyes and look at me." His voice was soft. Gentle. And commanding. "Do it now."

"You're such a pain in the ass." But she pried her eyes open and turned her head. She almost started to cry when she saw him right there, over her shoulder, strapped to a cord.

He grinned, that devilishly charming grin that still made her belly flutter. "Come home to me, Tatum."

"All right." She summoned a deep breath, then let go of the branch. She didn't drop even an inch. Brody just pulled her right over to him. She swung her legs around his waist and locked her good arm around his neck and her feet behind his back. His feet were braced on the rock, giving her almost a lap to sit on. She tucked her aching broken arm against her chest and buried her face in his neck. "You're like the best couch ever."

He laughed. "I brought you a harness. Want it?"

"Of course not. Why would I want it?" She left her face buried in his neck, gripping him with all her strength as he shifted beneath her.

"Why would you want it? Maybe because you love me and don't want to make me suffer for the rest of my life without you." He carefully began to work the harness over her hips.

"I do love you," she admitted.

"I know. And I love you." He slid his hand between their bodies, strapping her in. "Here's the thing, Tatum. When I saw you go over that cliff, I thought I'd lost you."

She squeezed him more tightly as he continued to buckle her in. "I thought I was dead. When I fell off that cliff..." She cut herself off, unable to revisit that moment when she was still dangling off the side of the rock face.

"Yeah, I know." Brody gave the harness a yank. "You're all set."

"I think I'll still cling to you for dear life."

"That's fine with me." He laughed, and she felt his arm move, probably signaling someone to pull them up, because suddenly, they began to move upward. "I love you, Tatum. Always and forever. I'm sorry I took my eye off you tonight—"

She could feel the harness tightening around her, holding her tight, so she got the courage to loosen her grip on him enough to look at him. His eyes were dark and turbulent, and her heart turned over. "I'll stay with you only if you never take your eyes off me even for a second."

He frowned. "Really?"

She laughed softly, and would have punched him in the shoulder, but that would have required her letting go, so she skipped it. "No, Brody, not really. Look, tonight, Victoria gave you an impossible choice, and I realized that I've done the same for you."

They spun out from the cliff suddenly, and she sucked in her breath as they dangled in mid-air, but Brody's arms were tight around her, and the harness was secure around her hips. She tightened her grip around his neck anyway. "I tried to make you decide between me and being the protector that defines you. I tried to force you to choose, but I realize now that the protector is part of who you are, and I love that part of you."

His brow furrowed as they dangled, inching their way up. "On the way here, I told Dylan that you were coming first. No more splitting loyalties. It's you."

She smiled and rested her shoulder against the cable, leaning in toward him as they continued to rise. "That's the thing, Brody, I realized it can be both. I realized that I can come first, even while you still protect the world."

He narrowed his eyes. "I'm not following."

"I'm not going to sit around living a safe life. I'm going to sing and maybe have that Las Vegas residency. But there are going to be plenty of times that I'm not with you, and that's okay. I need to do my thing. You need to do yours." She paused, searching his face. "But every minute of every day, I know that we're still first for each other. If I get kidnapped again, you'll drop everything to find me."

"Don't get kidnapped again. I'm too old to handle that kind of stress."

She laughed, her heart feeling lighter than it had in years. "But if I do?"

"I'll find you."

"Right. And if I don't get kidnapped? If everything is just fine, and I just crawl into bed at night on the ranch?"

He smiled, his face softening. "I'll hold you all night long."

She nodded. "Unless someone else you love gets kidnapped, and then you'll go."

"I would go," he agreed. "I'd have to. But that doesn't mean you aren't first, that you aren't my whole world."

She nodded. "I get that now. I saw it tonight."

They bumped against the rock, but this time, it didn't bother her. Dangling from the side of a cliff on a cable, in Brody's arms, she felt the safest she'd felt in a very long time. Because her heart felt safe. "I think," she said, "that I made you into a demon in my head because I was afraid of what I felt for you. Afraid to trust again. Afraid to truly love."

"I know what that's like," he agreed. "We both had lost so much. How do you trust again?"

She smiled. "You wait for the right person to show you it's safe."

He nodded. "It has to be the right person, though."

"It does." She leaned forward, smiling at him. "And you're my right person. You always have been."

"And you're mine." He leaned forward and kissed her, a beautiful, perfect kiss in a moonlight dance.

She smiled. "Thank you for waiting for me for fifteen years," she whispered.

"Thank you for coming back." He kissed her again, and her heart seemed to soar for the first time in a very, very long time...since about fifteen years ago, on a warm August day, under a bridge with a homeless boy who stole her heart and never gave it back.

And now she had him back again, and this time, she wasn't going to let him go.

CHAPTER TWENTY-SIX

Brody grabbed the edge of the precipice, protecting Tatum from the rock edge as Dylan cranked them over the rim.

Waiting for them were Bella, Keegan, Meg, and three other Harts that she hadn't seen in a very long time. She suddenly felt awkward, wrapped around Brody, trapped in a harness.

"Tatum!" Tears were glistening in Bella's eyes, as Keegan and Lucas dropped to their knees, reaching for her.

"Lucas?" It had been so long. So very, very long.

He winked at her, his scrawny teenage body now a large, muscled man who looked like he could toss her over his shoulder with just his pinkie. "Always the drama queen, Tatum. Let's go."

He held out his arms for her, and she instinctively leaned into him. He wrapped his arms around her torso and pulled her onto the top of the cliff, while Keegan grabbed the harness. She tumbled into their arms, into the bodies that she'd once snuggled with during cold, rainy nights, trying to keep warm. Tears filled her eyes, and emotion overtook her as Lucas pulled her into a hug.

She hugged him back, and then grunted when Meg tackled them. "Tatum! I thought you were dead."

Tatum laughed through her tears as Jacob helped Brody up over the edge. "I thought I was dead, too. Thanks for coming."

"We always come," Lucas said. "You know that."

She nodded, her throat tight as she looked over at Bella. "I do know that." Bella was standing back, her arms folded across her chest, her eyes bright with tears.

"Bella—" She tried to walk over to her, but the cable stopped her. She fumbled with the buckle. "I need to get this off. Help."

Keegan quickly freed her, and she stepped out of the harness. She gave him a quick hug, and another one for Dylan, still watching Bella, who was standing back, outside the circle.

Tatum limped over to her, surprised to discover that her leg was sore. She hadn't noticed hurting it when she'd fallen. "Bella."

Bella lifted her chin. "I thought you'd stolen my truck. I thought you'd left again. I wouldn't have come after you. I thought you'd run. And then you would have died."

The guilt was thick in Bella's voice, and Tatum felt tears threaten. "It's okay, Bella. I'm fine."

"I wouldn't have come after you," Bella said again. "And you would have *died*." Tears spilled out. "I was so angry at you that I didn't even see the truth. I hated you for so long, Tatum."

Tatum pressed her lips together, her heart aching at the wave of regret. "I'm sorry. I wish I hadn't left. You were all I had. I was afraid that if I let myself care, I'd never leave, and I'd never achieve my dreams."

Bella nodded. "I understand—"

"No, you don't, because I just figured it out." Tatum tried

to blink back her tears. "I was afraid to love you, all of you, because to me, family was a trap. I was afraid to trust anyone. And so I left. And then I felt stupid and ashamed, and I couldn't go back."

Bella smiled through her tears. "I was stupid not to go after you."

"I was stupid not to reach out. I'll never ditch you again, I promise. You're the sister I never had."

"More than a sister," Bella said. "You were my best friend."

"*Were?*" Emotions were flooding through Tatum. "Can we try again? Start over? Rebuild trust?"

Bella nodded. "I'd like that."

"Me, too."

For a long moment, they stood there awkwardly, then suddenly, moving as one, they reached for each other, grabbing each other in a hug so tight Tatum felt like she'd never let go. She cried into Bella's hair, for the best friend she'd walked away from so long ago, trading her in for a life where the one woman she'd called a friend had tried to murder her. "I missed you," she whispered.

"Me, too." Bella pulled back, but kept her hands on Tatum's upper arms. "Whatever happens with Brody, promise me that it won't affect us. Promise me."

She nodded. "I promise."

"Okay." Bella smiled, then they hugged again, holding tightly as years of distance and hurt finally drifted away, freeing them to live again.

She didn't know how long they would have stood like that, but Brody finally walked up to them and put his arms around both of them, drawing them against his body.

Bella looked up and smiled at him through tear-filled eyes. "Does this mean I'm going to have to stop resenting you for driving Tatum away?"

He smiled. "Yeah, but I'm sure you can find something else about me that will annoy you."

She laughed. "This is true." She punched him lightly on the shoulder. "Brothers are such a pain in the ass," she told Tatum. "Even when they grow up."

"Of course they are," Tatum agreed. "You're lucky to have them."

Keegan walked up. "You have them, too, Tatum. You're a part of us."

"Yeah, you are," Dylan shouted from the truck, where he was winding up the winch.

"Damn straight," Lucas agreed.

Colin stood up. Like Lucas, the skinny teenage boy she'd once known was gone, replaced by a tall, muscular man. He was rough, with attitude in his eyes, exactly as before. If she didn't know him, he might even scare her.

But she did know him. She knew where he'd come from. She knew his story. She knew his pain. He'd come only days after her, and she'd been there the night he'd arrived. Broken. Scared. In danger.

And now he looked like a man who no one could ever touch. A man who had made a point of becoming so fierce that he'd never be in danger again. Was that what all of them were like? So afraid of loss and being hurt that they were too closed off to ever really love?

Not her. Not anymore. She refused to be that way.

Colin looked over at her. "Welcome home, Tatum." His voice was rough and deep, laced with an edge that she suspected would never leave him. Then he smiled, showing her the same dimples he'd had as a kid.

Scary and fierce, but still with a heart of gold.

She relaxed and smiled back. "Thanks, Colin. It's good to be here."

At that moment, flashing blue lights lit up the night, and

they all turned as a police SUV bounced up the trail. The police officer jumped out as a second one pulled up behind him. "Where is she?"

Tatum thought he was asking about her, but Brody shook his head. "Victoria took off while we were rescuing Tatum." He looked around. "Did anyone pass her when they were driving up?"

"I did," Bella said. "She almost ran me off the road."

Fear shot through Tatum. "Victoria got away?"

Brody put his arm around her. "We'll find her."

Victoria's furious eyes flashed through Tatum's mind, and she shivered. "I'm sure you will, but who is she going to hurt in the meantime?"

The Harts looked at each other. "We need to get back to the ranch," Dylan said. He pulled out his phone. "I'll alert the security team. Go!"

All the Harts except Dylan and Brody raced for their vehicles. They stayed with her to talk to the police. Standing by her side.

She looked up at Brody as he spoke with the cops. He still had his arm around her, and she had a feeling he'd never let her go.

She'd almost died tonight, and they both knew it.

That changed everything.

CHAPTER TWENTY-SEVEN

All Brody wanted was a moment alone with Tatum, but he had to make sure everything was finished first.

Talk with the cops. Give the description of Victoria's car. Drive back to the ranch with Dylan and Tatum.

When he arrived, there was still the aftermath from the fire to deal with, but this time, he made sure Tatum was protected at all times. While he and Keegan went into the barn to go over the damage, he left Tatum with Dylan and his brother Tristan, who had given Tatum a big hug when he'd seen her.

Meg and Bella wouldn't leave her alone either, and it made him smile to see the three women back together again. It had been a long time. Too long.

It made him realize how much they'd all lost by playing it safe. Hiding out. From their pasts, from pain, from loss.

Keegan looked over at him as they jogged up the stairs to the hayloft. The firefighters had said that the barn was structurally sound, but Brody wasn't bringing the horses back until he made sure of it. "Good thing you went to the concert, huh?"

Brody grinned. "Yeah, you could say that."

"You guys work it out this time? For good?"

Brody opened the door to the loft. "We'll find a way." He knew it. Maybe he wasn't sure what it would look like yet, but he knew they weren't going to give up this time. "I asked her to marry me."

Keegan's face lit up. "It's about time you asked the right girl to marry you."

"Yeah, well, she hasn't officially said yes, but she's definitely starting to lean into it." He lightly punched Keegan's arm as he surveyed the loft. There were charred walls, and burned hay, but their sprinkler system and fire-proof construction had done their job well. They'd spent a lot of money on the barn with all the newest safeguards, and it had paid off. "What about you?"

Keegan kicked at a pile of soggy hay. "What about me?"

Brody looked over at him. "What about Sascha?"

Keegan's shoulders tensed. "What about her?"

"You ever think about her?"

Keegan laughed, but there was an edge to his voice. "Brody, just because you had one that got away doesn't mean the rest of us did."

"What if I found her?"

Keegan spun toward him. "Did you?"

"I have a strong lead. I'll know more in a couple days. You want me to tell you if I find her?"

Keegan stared at him for a long moment, then shrugged. "It would be good to know she's alright, but whatever." He turned away. "Barn looks solid. Let's bring a contractor in tomorrow to confirm, but I think we'll be able to bring the horses back no problem."

Brody grinned at the obvious change of subject. "I agree." He'd played Keegan's role too many times in his life not to be able to see what he was doing. Like him, Keegan had unfinished business with a woman he'd once known. Sascha was different. She'd never lived with them. But her impact had been strong...especially on Keegan.

And Brody was pretty sure he'd know where she was in a few days.

Keegan looked over at him. "Let's go get the horses settled for the night. I'll sleep downstairs in your house tonight, in case Victoria comes back."

The offer made Brody smile. Keegan was willing to sleep in his house to protect Tatum. Because they were family, to the end. No matter what. That was what they did. Who they were.

He put his hand on Keegan's shoulder, acknowledging the offer. "Thanks, but I'll have the security team sweeping all night. We'll be all set."

Keegan raised his brows. "You sure?"

"I'm sure." Brody needed to be alone with Tatum tonight. Tomorrow would be for the family, for the ranch, but tonight would be for them. He put his hand on his brother's shoulder. "Thanks for bringing her back into my life, Keegan."

His brother looked over at him as he started down the steps to the barn. "Just want you to be happy. You're always telling us we all deserve it."

"Damn straight we do." Brody had always preached it to his family, but he'd never thought about it for himself. He paused to look out the window. Tatum was sitting on the tailgate of his truck, laughing as Bella signed her cast. Meg was sitting next to her, and Colin and Dylan were sitting on the fence, also laughing.

Brody braced his hands on either side of the window frame, watching his family. Almost losing Tatum tonight had made him even more viscerally aware of the precious, fragile nature of life. He'd wasted fifteen years over a mistake he'd made. She'd wasted fifteen years being hurt over a choice that hadn't been about her.

And now...she fit. He could see it in her body language. She was welcoming the Harts back into her heart, and they were doing the same.

As he watched, Keegan emerged from the barn and walked over to them. He gave Bella a quick hug, then hopped up on the fence next to his brothers.

Colin and Tristan joined them, leaning on the truck.

Brody took a deep breath as he surveyed the gathering, remembering how many times they'd gathered under that bridge. Scared kids. Lost. Afraid. In danger. How he'd stayed up night after night to keep an eye on them, trying to figure out who he needed to keep, and who had better places to go, if Brody could figure out how to get them there.

He'd sent Tatum off with the choices he'd made, but the others out there in the stable yard? None of them had had a better place to go. And now...they had a family. A vast fortune. They had everything... Brody's gaze settled on Tatum as she laughed.

He'd thought he had everything, but he hadn't. Tatum had been missing. Now that she was back, he was complete. He scanned his family. Other than Hannah, who was a bridge kid but not a Hart, not a single one of them had found that special person meant for them. Not yet. But now that he had Tatum, he realized that he wanted that for all of them.

And he was going to help them get it.

Tatum suddenly looked up at the window as if she'd felt him watching her. She met his gaze and smiled, waving her hand at him to come down and join them.

He grinned and blew her a kiss. Hell, yeah, he was going down there. He wasn't missing out again. Not even for a second.

He smacked his palm on the window, thanking the barn

for withstanding Victoria's assault, then he turned away and headed for the stairs. For his family. For the woman who'd never left his heart.

～

It was almost five in the morning by the time the Harts finished securing the horses and cleaning up from the fire.

Tatum was exhausted as she and Brody headed up the steps to his house, but she was also exhilarated. She grinned at Brody as he punched in the code to the alarm. "I had no idea I loved horses so much."

He laughed. "They're amazing creatures in so many ways."

"I love that you rescue them and give them the home they deserve."

He raised his brows as he opened the door. "Is it even possible that we'd do anything else?"

She laughed. "No. You collect those in need and heal them. It's what you do." For the first time in a very long while, there was no resentment in her heart. Just love. Just understanding. Acceptance and admiration for the man Brody was, for the lives he had changed, for the hugeness of his heart.

He closed the door behind her, then caught her around the waist and pulled her to him. "Tatum."

She smiled up at him, resting her broken wrist on his chest. Her arm was tired and aching, but it didn't hurt nearly as much as she would have expected after the day she'd had. Maybe because she was too happy to feel pain. "Brody? I want to tell you something."

He smiled. "What's that?"

"You have the most beautiful, most compassionate, most all-encompassing heart of anyone I've ever met. You make the world brighter simply by being in it."

His smile widened. "Aw, shucks, ma'am. I'm just a good ol' boy trying to do ma best."

"And you do it so well." She stood on her tiptoes and kissed him. The moment her lips touched his, he pulled her tight against him, kissing her back. No holding back, not anymore, not between them.

She wanted to lose herself in him, but she couldn't. Not yet. "Wait." She laughed as she lightly bumped her fist on his chest. "I'm not finished."

He gave a dramatic sigh and kissed her fingertips. "What's up?"

"Thank you for saving me tonight."

The amusement left his face as he met her gaze. "I was scared shitless," he admitted, his voice suddenly rough. "Those were the longest moments of my life after I saw you go over the edge until I had you in my arms."

She nodded. "I knew you'd come. The whole time, I knew you'd come, if I could just hang on."

He picked up a lock of her hair and twirled it around his index finger. "Always. Forever."

"I know." She swallowed, her heart starting to pound. "I love you, Brody. I always have."

He smiled. "I love you, Tatum. I always have."

She knew it was fast, but she also knew it was right. They'd been through too much for too long not to know what was right. Life had made it crystal clear. "Ask me again," she whispered. "Please ask me again."

His brow furrowed in confusion for a split second, then it softened into joy. He immediately went down on one knee and took her hand. "Tatum, you've always had my heart in your hands. I don't want to lose even another minute with you. I know you want your independence, and I'll give you whatever you need, but I want to do it as your husband, and the man that the entire world knows is the one who will love you forever." He pressed a kiss to her knuckles. "Tatum Crosby, will you marry me?"

Her throat tightened as tears slipped down her cheeks. "You bet I will. A thousand times, yes."

His face lit up, and he tugged her hand, drawing her into him. She went down on her knees in front of him as he pulled her against him and kissed her. His body was warm and solid against hers, his kiss tender and beautiful, his heart beating for her.

As hers was beating for him. For always. Forever.

CHAPTER TWENTY-EIGHT

Two days later, Tatum was lying awake in Brody's arms, watching as the sun rose over the Oregon hills. The light cast golden shadows on the white barn and fences, drifting over the walls of his bedroom.

She rolled onto her side, smiling as she surveyed the incredible beauty. The ranch was endless acres of beautiful green grass, white fences, and gorgeous landscaping. Flowers. Trees. It was luxury and nature and freedom, all wrapped up into a perfect oasis.

Gratitude filled her heart. For this moment, for her life, for the chance to be with the man she loved, for the love that had been surrounding her from all the Harts.

Victoria still hadn't been found, so they'd all been alert, but she was almost glad she was still in danger. It gave her an excuse to stay where she was and not go back on tour.

She'd been touring for almost fifteen years without a break. Being home felt beautiful. The thought of going back out felt terrible to her. She wasn't sure if it was because of the whole Victoria situation, or if she simply was ready for a different life.

Brody's arms tightened around her, and she smiled as he kissed her bare shoulder. "Morning, love."

"Morning." She wiggled backwards until she was tucked tightly against him. She didn't think she'd ever get tired of feeling his body against hers. "I love this view. No wonder the whole side of your bedroom is glass doors."

"I love the second-floor deck. I'm looking forward to making love on that couch under the stars with you." He rested his chin on her shoulder, his whiskers deliciously rough against her bare skin.

Desire warmed in her belly. "That sounds like fun."

"It does, doesn't it?" He palmed her stomach. "Maybe some morning loving before we go check on the horses."

She loved that Brody and his brothers rotated care of the animals, so they all had space for themselves, while having the horses be only theirs. They had only two regular staff who worked there, because the family valued their privacy.

Just like her.

She smiled and rolled over toward him, sliding her hand through his hair. "Ravage me like you'll never let me go."

"I'm never letting you go." He pulled her against him and kissed her, a long, slow decadence that she knew she'd never get tired of. He'd just slid his hand over her bare bottom when his phone rang.

They stopped and looked at each other. "Victoria," they said at the same time.

He reached over to grab his phone from his nightstand, and tucked her against him as he answered it, putting it on speaker so she could hear it. "Dylan. What's up?"

"They got her."

Relief rushed through Tatum. "Really? Where?"

"At Donny's hotel room."

She frowned. "Donny's? He was in on it?"

"No. He called the cops on her. She broke into his room

and started ranting about them being together and how you set her up. She told him all about the things she'd done for his love, all the things she'd done to you. Apparently, he was pretty shocked by what she did and cooperated with the cops."

"When did all this happen?" Brody asked.

"They arrested her early this morning. I just got word of it, though. I expect the cops will be calling Tatum shortly. But now that she's caught, I expect Hank will start talking. It's over, Tatum. You can go back to your life."

She looked at Brody with a sinking feeling. Go back on tour?

Brody frowned and brushed the hair back from her face. "Thanks, Dylan. Appreciate the update. I love your contacts."

"Right? I can find out anything. Talk to you guys later."

Dylan hung up and Brody set the phone back on his nightstand. "What's up?"

"I don't want to go back. I want to stay here."

He smiled and ran his hand through her hair. "I love being here, so I get it. But I think you'd miss singing."

"I can sing to the horses."

He laughed and kissed her. "I was at your concert a few days ago, sweetheart. I felt the fire pouring from your soul as you performed. Or was I wrong?"

She bit her lip. "No, you were right. I do love it, but there's just so much tangled up with it. I don't want to be on this tour anymore. It's so tainted from Victoria and Donny."

"Cancel it. Take a break."

"I can't. I'm contractually obligated. Donny will never let me go."

Brody frowned. "Then I'll go with you."

"I can't ask you to do that—"

He put his finger over her lips. "If you have to go finish this tour, you don't have to do it alone. I'll be by your side.

We'll use the jet to get home as often as we can. When it's over, you can reevaluate." He winked. "I'll even sing our song with you every night. I think the fans loved it."

She laughed. "They did." Brody had made the same offer before, and it had felt suffocating. This time, it felt like a relief. To have him with her, building their relationship as she finished the tour...it felt right. Well, better, at least. "Donny might try to beat you up."

"I'm a badass. I'll win."

She laughed. "You probably would—"

Brody's attention shifted off her, and he looked over her shoulder. She rolled over and saw a car cruising up the long driveway. She frowned. "Who is that?" She already knew all the Hart vehicles, and this one wasn't one of theirs. Brody's house and the barn were the only buildings that the driveway accessed, so whoever it was wasn't here to see any of the other Harts.

"I don't know." He threw back the covers and jumped out, yanking on his jeans.

Concern rushed through Tatum, and she quickly got up, pulling on the same pair of jeans she'd been wearing the last two days. The little bag of clothes that Jackson had sent was keeping her dressed, but that was about it.

The car pulled up in front of the house. The driver's door opened, and she froze when she saw her ex-husband get out. "It's Donny."

Brody swore. "You stay here. I'll deal with him."

"No." She pulled on a sports bra and a sweatshirt. "I can do it."

He shoved his feet into his boots. "You want me to stay out of it?"

She smiled. "No. I'd like you to be by my side. Fighting battles together now."

He grinned. "All right, then." He took her hand and pressed a kiss to her knuckles. "Let's do this, sweetheart."

"All right." She finished getting dressed, took a deep breath, then headed out of the bedroom.

She'd been afraid of Donny for a long time, but no longer. She had Brody now, giving her strength. And she'd realized that if she had to give up her music, she'd be all right. She had the money, she had a partner she could trust, and she had a life beyond what Donny could control.

As she hurried down the stairs, she made the decision. She knew what she was going to say to him. She didn't need Eliana to fix her contract. She was ready to handle it herself.

As she reached the bottom of the stairs, Donny knocked at the front door.

Brody looked back at her, and she held up her hand to ask him to wait so she could open it.

He immediately stepped aside and let her pass. Her protector, but also allowing her to run free. Exactly what she needed. They had both learned and grown.

She gave Brody a quick smile as she passed him, then walked to the door. She put her hand on the doorknob, took another steadying breath, then pulled it open.

"Tatum." Donny immediately reached for her, as if to give her a hug, and she held up her hand.

"No." Her tone was hard. Unyielding. No longer asking. Telling.

And he stopped. "I'm so sorry for what happened. I had no idea Victoria was involved—"

"It's over."

She heard Brody's phone ding, and he stepped away and pulled out his phone, but she didn't look at him. She kept her gaze focused on Donny.

He frowned. "What's over?"

"I'm not going to sing again. Ever. Even one note. Not for

you. Not for anyone else. Either you let me buy my way out of the contract, or you'll never get another note from me."

His eyes narrowed ever so slightly, barely visible, but she noticed. "You have to sing. We can sue you for breach of contract."

She shrugged. "I have plenty of money. Plus, emotional distress from being almost murdered by my own band member. If I have to go to court, that's fine. Here's the thing, Donny. I don't care if I don't sing again. I literally don't. I'm done. My act is over." She grinned. "And that makes me free. You can't control me if you don't have anything I want."

He stared at her, and she saw the moment that he realized he'd lost. Like, *really,* lost. He saw that she meant it. No singing. He'd lost his cash ticket. "You little bitch." The snarl was so aggressive that she actually stepped back, startled by his venom. "I fucking plucked you out of the trash and made you a star. You don't get to take that away from me. Your money is mine, and I want it." He suddenly pulled out a gun and aimed it at Brody. "Drop the phone. You don't get to have her."

Tatum went still, shocked. "You were working with Victoria, weren't you?" Holy cow. She should have realized that Victoria wouldn't have gone down that path alone, without encouragement.

"You're going to marry me again," he said. "And you're going to change your will back. That money is *mine*."

She stared at him, and then she started to laugh. "Oh, God, did you hear that, Brody?"

Donny frowned, looking back and forth between them. "What the fuck are you laughing about?"

"That you think shooting me will get you my money. That's what this is all about? What it's all been about? My *money*? I thought you were obsessed with *me*." Her money. All he'd ever wanted was her money. Victoria had wanted him, and he'd used that to get her help.

She knew she'd been lacking in friends, but she'd had no idea how really lacking she'd been. It would be appalling, if she hadn't found her way back to the people who loved her for who she was, flaws and all.

"Tatum, you should find a guy who has more money than you do," Brody said. "Then you'll know that he wants you only for your body."

"Exactly." She didn't quite dare take her gaze off Donny and his gun, despite the banter. She was pretty sure he wouldn't actually shoot them, but all sorts of unexpected delights had been cascading into her life lately, she couldn't count it out. She could, however, try to diffuse the situation by being hilarious. "I wonder where I can find a guy who has more money than I do. I'm pretty freaking rich."

"Shut the fuck up." Donny wiggled the gun in Brody's direction. "I'll shoot him right now if you don't come with me."

"I offered to buy you out," she said. "That would have been a good deal to take."

"I want it all, Tatum. Your money is mine. Just because you were the talent doesn't mean you deserve it. I made you—"

At that moment, a handgun appeared around the side of the door and pressed into Donny's temple. "She made herself," Dylan said icily as he moved into sight. "Hands up, big guy."

Donny swore, but he raised his hands. Dylan plucked the gun from his hands and grinned at Tatum. "I love how much fun you bring into my life, Tatum."

She smiled, relief cascading through her as Brody walked up, slid his arm around her waist, and gave her a thoroughly possessive kiss designed to remind her that she was loved, and to make a point to Donny.

Since those were both excellent ideas, she kissed him back just as thoroughly, while Dylan pulled out his phone and called the cops.

By the time she pulled back from the kiss, Dylan had Donny on his knees, his hands clasped behind his head.

Brody put his arm around her shoulders. "I think you are going to be able to get out of your contract now. Eliana will be able to use this attempted murder and blackmail nicely."

At his words, the reality finally sunk in.

She was free. Free from Donny. Free from the contract that had tied her up for so long. *Free.*

Tears suddenly filled her eyes, and her legs gave out. She sank down to the floor. Fifteen years of not owning her life was now over. She'd given up love, freedom, and everything to pursue her dream...and now she had it back. Her way.

Brody knelt next to her. "You okay?"

She nodded, blinking back the tears. "I need to make a call."

He raised his brows. "Now?"

"Yeah." She felt her pockets. "I don't have my phone."

He raised his brows. "Want me to get it?"

She nodded. "I'll come with you. I want to come." She wanted to be away from Donny. Away from the past that no longer held her.

Brody looked over at Dylan. "You good for a minute?"

Dylan looked very cheerful. "You bet. Holding bad guys at gunpoint is my happy place. Cops will be here in a moment and rain on my parade, but I'll milk it for as long as I can. Maybe he'll try to get away, and I can kick his ass."

"Damn. I'll try to be back in time for that. I'd like to join you on that." Brody rose to his feet, and held out his hand to her. "Let's go, sweetheart."

"Right." She paused to look at Donny, who was looking at her with a fair amount of venom. She grinned. "It's over, Donny. Not only don't you get me, but you lost your career, and probably your freedom—"

With a roar, he lunged, but he didn't even make it to his feet before Dylan cracked him in the back of the head with his gun. Donny dropped to the ground groaning, clutching his head. Dylan grinned. "I enjoyed that so much."

"I'm not gonna lie," Brody said, as he began to lead her to the stairs. "I'm a little jealous that you got to do that to him."

Tatum grinned. "I'm a little jealous, too."

Dylan waved his gun. "If you two lovebirds hurry along, he might try something else stupid before the cops get here."

"Right. Let's go then." Laughing with ridiculous delight, Tatum spun around and raced up the stairs to Brody's bedroom, with Brody right behind her. Her phone was still on the nightstand on her side of the bed, so she hopped on the bed and flopped down as she reached for it.

Brody stretched out next to her, curiosity etched on his face. "Who are you calling?"

She held up her finger to silence him, put the phone on speaker, and hit the call button. She grinned at Brody while the phone rang. "Patience, grasshopper."

He groaned, rolled onto his back, and pulled her on top of him. She propped elbows on his chest, laughing when he kissed her cast.

It took only three rings before Ace, her bass player, answered. "Tatum! Are you okay? Jackson, it's Tatum."

She grinned at Brody as she answered. "I'm absolutely amazing. It turns out that Victoria and Donny were conspiring together to kill me for my money."

"No shit!"

Jackson came on the phone. "Hey, girl. You doing all right?"

"I am." She was so excited she could barely contain herself. "I have a question for you guys."

"What's up?" Ace asked. "Tour's over, I assume. Or on delay."

Brody frowned as he ran his fingers through her hair.

She giggled, watching Brody's face, needing to see his reaction. "I'm cancelling the rest of this tour. There's only one more month left, so it's not a big deal."

Jackson let out a small whoop. "I'm sorry that it wound up shitty for you, but I'm not going to lie. The idea of having Ace home is amazing."

"Well..." She grinned at Brody. "My pal Brody here had an idea that I'm going to follow up on." She paused for a dramatic moment, and she saw Brody start to smile.

"What's that?" Ace asked. "Don't tell me you're going to retire. My soul would die without music."

"Nope. I'm going to try to get a residency in Las Vegas. How does performing without being on the road sound?"

There was silence for a second, then they burst out in cheers. She could almost see them jumping around and hugging each other. She grinned. "I'll call you later when I have more info. Bye!" She hung up and grinned at Brody. "That private jet still available?"

He had the hugest smile on his face. "We might need to buy a second one to accommodate your daily commute, but yeah, it's available."

"Will you come with me sometimes? Not always, but sometimes?"

"It would be an honor." He caught her hair and tugged her down to him. "Always and forever, Tatum. Always and forever." Then he kissed her, and it was perfect.

CHAPTER TWENTY-NINE

Four months later, Tatum leaned on her dressing table and stared at herself in the mirror. Her heart turned over when she saw the sparkle in her eyes, the excitement on her face. Five minutes before she was supposed to be on stage, and she was glowing.

This was how it was supposed to be, how she'd never thought it would be again.

She didn't feel any fear or tension. Just pure joy and anticipation.

She was ready. She could feel it. She knew it. The magic was back.

There was a light knock at her dressing room door, and she smiled. No fear shot through her, like it had for years when she'd been on tour. Just giddiness. "You don't have to knock," she called out.

The door opened, and Brody poked his head around the door. Her heart leapt at the sight of him, and she couldn't keep the smile off her face. He was wearing a white cowboy hat, a red button-down shirt, and just enough stubble to make him look insanely hot. And he was hers. All hers.

A ROGUE COWBOY'S SECOND CHANCE

"I didn't want to interrupt your pre-show routine," he said. "I promised not to cramp your independence, remember?"

"My old routine was cringing in fear every time I heard footsteps, afraid it was Donny or my stalker. I need a new routine. Like having you kiss me like you could never live without me. That might be a good pre-show routine."

"Isn't that how I always kiss you?" A wicked gleam glittered in his eyes. "So, I can come in?"

"Yes, come in. I have a couple minutes." For her entire career, she'd insisted on being left alone for the minutes counting down to a show, but the sight of Brody made her happy. In the last four months, he'd become her foundation, the solid force of love and support that she could always count on, even when she wasn't being kidnapped.

"Great." He opened the door the rest of the way, and she saw he was holding a massive arrangement of roses. Red ones, yellow ones, salmon ones, white ones, and pink ones, in a beautiful crystal vase that was at least two feet in diameter. Behind him, two people stood with identical vases.

Her heart turned over. "Oh, Brody. They're beautiful. You didn't need to do that." She met him halfway across the room, pressing her face into the flowers. They were so beautiful, so fragrant, so perfect.

"I wanted to." He leaned over the roses and kissed her as the other two people set the roses on the coffee table and scooted out the door, leaving them alone. "Open the card. It's stashed in there somewhere."

"One more kiss." She wanted to keep kissing him, as she always did. Every time she kissed him, she felt like she had fifteen years of kisses to make up for, but she knew the endless kisses would come later, after the show, when he took her into his arms and reminded her of what it was like to be loved, and to love someone unconditionally, with all her heart.

He laughed and kissed the tip of her nose. "Open the card, sweetheart. Nora's going to be in here any second to drag you to the stage."

"All right." She wrinkled her nose in protest, but found the pink envelope as he set the incredible bouquet on the dressing table she'd just been leaning on. She recognized Brody's handwriting on the envelope, which made her smile. He never had his staff do anything for her. He did it all himself. She opened the card and read it aloud.

My Dearest Tatum,

The moment you walked past me fifteen years ago, lost and alone, I knew my world was changed forever. With the afternoon sun cascading over you, I thought you were the angel sent to save me. And you were. You still are. Every moment with you is a gift I will treasure.

It's been 182 months since we met, so I present you with 182 roses to celebrate your night tonight, the opening night of your career the way you want it.

Red roses for the passion that shines through you and lights up every room you walk into.
   Pink roses for the love we will always share, that will carry us through everything.
   White roses for the peace in my soul now that we are together.
   Yellow roses for friendship, because you are my best friend.

Salmon roses because they match the nail polish I wouldn't let you steal that time. May you forever have all the salmon-colored things you want.

I loved you before. I love you now. And I will love you forever.

Love,

Brody

"Oh, Brody. It's beautiful." Tears filled Tatum's eyes as she pressed the letter to her chest. "I love you." She tried to get the words out, but the emotions were too thick.

Brody laughed softly and wrapped his arms around her, kissing her sweetly before resting his chin on her head. "You're my world, Tatum. I want to make sure you always know that."

She held on tightly, burying her face in his chest. "I know I am. You're mine, too."

He kissed the top of her head. "When I was a kid, I didn't believe I was worth loving. I didn't have anyone who loved me. When I started saving kids, I was protecting them, but love wasn't a factor. Until you. You taught me I deserved love. Only then could I be what those kids needed. Only then could we become a family."

She pulled back to look at him, tears trickling down her cheeks. "I was the same way," she admitted. "I didn't even know what it felt like to be loved, to matter to anyone. I thought I had to be a star to be worth loving. Rich, successful, and beautiful. Only then would anyone love me."

He brushed a strand of hair back from her cheeks. "But then I loved you for being you."

She nodded. "You did, but I couldn't accept it. I couldn't believe in it. It took me until now to realize that I deserved love for simply being me." She sighed. "Why is it so hard to believe you deserve love?"

He shrugged. "Because we're human? Because we had no one to show us that we mattered? Because we refused to believe the ones who did?" He brushed her hair back and rested his hands on her shoulders. "Growing up homeless and without any support system teaches you to be strong, brave, and resourceful. But it doesn't teach you how to be loved or to love."

She tightened her arms around his waist, aware of how close she'd come to never finding him, to never allowing the love that was right in front of her the whole time. "I'm so grateful for you."

"You make me the luckiest man alive." He smiled. "We did it, sweetheart. We broke the curse of foster kids and made it together."

"We did." She smiled. "And your family, too, because of you."

"They're your family, too." He bent his head and kissed her, the same beautiful, tender kiss of unconditional love that he'd been showering her with for the last four months. "I want this for them," he said, running his finger over her engagement ring, as his voice softened. "I want them to find the one who makes them whole."

She smiled. "They will. I know it."

"I hope so." Hope flickered in his eyes. "I'm going to tell Keegan after the show that the private detective might have found Sascha."

Tatum had never met Sascha, but Brody had told her that she'd been in one of the foster homes with them and kept in touch after they'd moved under the bridge. She sounded sassy, irreverent, and determined, and Tatum was certain she would love her. "If he did find her, do you think Keegan will volunteer to be the one to go check on her?"

Brody rubbed his jaw. "I'm not sure. I can't quite read him. But if I had to guess, I'd say yes. I get the sense there is something unresolved with her, though he won't talk about it."

Tatum raised her brows. "He actually dared not to share something with you?"

Brody laughed. "These kids. I can't control them, though I do try."

She clasped her hands behind his neck, so happy that her wrist was no more than a dull ache these days. "You're just an overprotective big brother, aren't you?"

"Maybe." He laughed. "They do call me an old man sometimes."

"*My* old man." She stood on her tiptoes and kissed him. "I still think you're hot, even if you are getting old."

"Not that old." He gave her a wicked grin. "Mostly, I want to get them all partnered up with their true loves so they stop barging in all the time. I want to be able to make love to you in the living room or anywhere I feel like. It's damned inconvenient to have them all stopping in constantly."

She punched his chest lightly. "It's perfect, and you know it. That's what the Harts are all about. No personal space, just in each other's lives and business all the time."

He raised his brows. "Too much for you?"

She grinned. "Not a chance—"

At that moment, the door of the dressing room opened, and Dylan walked in, wearing a Tatum Crosby Las Vegas tee shirt and hat, along with his VIP badge. "Tatum! Go kill it out there tonight!"

Joy leapt through her. "You came?"

"It's opening night. I wouldn't miss it!" Dylan hugged her, and then she saw Keegan walk in behind him, also wearing gear from her show. "Keegan! You came, too?"

They hadn't told her they were coming. They'd given her a farewell party before she and Brody had boarded the Hart jet yesterday. And now, here they were. She loved that so much.

"We all came." As he said that, the rest of the Harts filed in behind them, carrying roses, balloons and a huge cake that said "Tatum Crosby, Love and Laughter, Las Vegas."

Meg, Colin, Lucas, Jacob, Tristan, and even another former bridge kid Wyatt Parker and his wife Noelle, who had a ranch near the Harts. Tatum hadn't met Wyatt as a kid, but she'd gotten to know him and Noelle over the last few months, and they were just as amazing as the rest of the Harts. Warmth and love exuded from every one of them, and she knew it was because of Brody, because of the standard he had set and continued to set every single day.

And now they were hers. Her family. Hers to love. Hers to be loved by.

Her throat tightened as they filled her dressing room. "You guys. This is amazing." She'd thought she liked to be alone before a show, but this? This was incredible, filling her with so much energy and warmth. She couldn't wait to go on stage and sing for them.

Ace and Jackson followed up the rear. "We've decided we're Harts, too," Ace announced. "Seeing as how we're your family, we figured it made sense."

Her throat tightened. "You guys *are* my family."

Dylan put his arm around Ace's shoulders. "Damn straight. Tatum's family is our family."

Last one into the dressing room was Bella, who was also fully decked out in gear from the show. She walked right up to Tatum and flung her arms around her. "I'm so proud of you, Tatum. You made all your dreams come true."

"All of them," Tatum agreed, hugging Bella tightly. "Including you."

At that moment, Nora walked into the room, and when she saw everyone, she swore. "Everyone out! Tatum needs to be on stage in three minutes. Honest to God, you guys are like herding cats." But she was laughing as she chased everyone out, leaving only Ace, Jackson, Tatum, Brody, and herself in the room.

"We'll be in the front row," Bella shouted. "Cheering you on!"

"Thank you!"

Nora faced down Brody. "You, too. I don't care if you've co-written half the new songs with Tatum, you still need to get out until your duet at the end." And she nodded at Jackson. "You know how Tatum likes it before a concert. You, too."

"No." Tatum spoke up quickly. "They stay. They both stay."

Everyone in the room looked surprised, except Brody. He looked pleased.

Tatum held out her hand for Brody, and he settled his hand around hers. "I want Brody here, and that means I now understand that Jackson needs to be here, too. For Ace. For me, too."

Jackson grinned and put his arm around Ace. "Our little girl is all grown up," he said. "It makes my heart so happy."

Tatum laughed. "You're only five years older than I am."

"It's a lifetime," he said, but he was smiling.

"All right then," Nora said. "Three minutes and I want Ace and Tatum on stage."

"We'll be there," Tatum said. "Thanks, Nora. For everything. You've done an amazing job with this show."

Nora grinned and blew her a kiss. "I love working with the same venue every night. It's given me the chance to create magic. And I have even more ideas. This is just the start. See you all in a few." She let herself out, leaving the four of them behind.

As the door shut behind her, Tatum grinned at the others. The rest of their band, all of them new, were in their own dressing room. This time, Tatum planned to get to know them. But right now, it was about those who had been a part of her past, who were a part of this new future. "Time for new beginnings. You guys ready?"

Jackson nodded. "I'm always ready."

Ace grinned. "This is going to be epic."

She smiled back at him, the friend that had been by her side all along, even when she hadn't realized she had him. "It sure is." She looked at Brody. "You ready?"

"Always." He squeezed her hand. "Go make history, sweetheart."

"Let's go make music," she said with a laugh.

"That, too." Together the four of them walked out, to the stage, to the fans, to the family and the love that was surrounding her, that would always be surrounding her from now on.

∽

Don't miss the next cowboy romance from Stephanie Rowe, *A Real Cowboy for the Holidays*, featuring Quintin Stockton. The rugged, loner smokejumper comes home for the holidays and discovers the true meaning of Christmas when he runs into woman he used to cause trouble with as teenagers...a woman who is now a sassy single mom in need of what only he can give. Heartwarming, steamy, and full of magic of Christmas! *One-click here to preorder your copy now!*

. . .

A ROGUE COWBOY'S SECOND CHANCE

New to Stephanie's cowboy romances? Get started on her *Wyoming Rebels* series today with *A Real Cowboy Never Says No,* Book One, in which a sworn bachelor invites a pregnant city girl to hide out on his ranch...and quickly finds himself falling hard! Skip ahead to for a sneak peek, or grab it now!

Can't wait to get started with the Quintin's story? Read a free excerpt of *A Real Cowboy for the Holidays* starting right here:

A Real Cowboy for the Holidays
SNEAK PEEK STARTS HERE

EMMA SPUN AROUND AND started to sprint across the Rollins Tree Farm parking lot to the store, and immediately ran smack into the side of a truck that had just pulled in.

She stumbled back, falling on her butt, as the pickup truck hit the brakes. God, she was such an idiot!

The driver jumped out and ran around the front of the truck. "Are you all right?"

Emma recognized his voice immediately. Quintin Stockton, the man she'd just been thinking about. She looked up, and her heart literally did a little flutter at the sight of him. He'd been a rebellious troublemaker when they were in high school, but now he was all man now. Tall, muscular, and strong-jawed. His cowboy hat was tilted at a jaunty angle, hinting at the arrogance that she had once associated with him.

Nothing scary about him anymore. Just raw, heated testosterone that made every part of her start to hum.

She kinda wanted to gawk at him, but that would be insanely rude. She was sure he'd never recognize her after so many years, so she just gave him a brilliant smile. "I'm fine. Feeling a little disappointed that I'm not strong enough to run right through a pickup truck, but I'll get over it."

His eyebrows shot up. "Nerd Girl?"

Nerd Girl. She'd forgotten the names they had for each other, back when he'd been a grumpy rebel and she'd been the overly responsible daughter-of-the-owner trying to get him to work. She grinned. "Yep. Rebel Boy, I presume?"

He still had a roguish look to him that was impossible to pin down. It was his eyes, she decided. They were the eyes of someone who would flat out refuse to play by any rules, unless he made him.

As a teenager, that had scared her.

Now? That made him deliciously attractive. She had grown to hate rules.

A smile quirked at the corner of Quintin's mouth as he held out his hand to help her up. "Rebel Boy. I forgot about that." His voice was deeper now, a richer timbre that was stunningly masculine.

She'd never thought of him as dateable material. He'd just been the irritating teenager who'd made her life a little crazy...and a lot more interesting. But only as friends. Co-workers. Co-conspirators, maybe.

But now? She couldn't stop thinking about him as a man, which was a little shocking, given that she'd been completely shut down from men for six years.

Quintin didn't appear to be looking at her as if he wanted to strip her naked, so she plastered on a friendly, neutral smile. "Well, I forgot about Nerd Girl, so we're even." She took his proffered hand, surprised by how warm it was against her freezing ones. "Didn't you run me over with the golf cart once?"

His brows shot up, and his smile widened. "I bumped you. I didn't run you over, and I felt like shit about it for years."

She laughed. "Years? Really? Because of my tiny thigh bruise?"

"It was a nice thigh. It deserved better." He helped her to her feet. His dark brown eyes searched hers with genuine concern. "You sure you're not hurt?"

His protectiveness wrapped around her like a warm, well-muscled hug. "No, I'm good." She brushed the snow off her butt and tried to pretend that she hadn't noticed the broad expanse of his chest or the whiskers on his jaw. "What can I do for you?"

A ridiculous part of her sort of fantasized that the answer would involve things that a responsible, single mom should never do with a rebellious troublemaker....

Which was both shocking and amazing...and unrealistic, of course.

But to even have that brief fantasy?

A good sign that her soul was still fighting to live.

∽

What happens when Quintin offers to help out at the tree farm for the Christmas season? Don't miss this steamy, magical holiday romance! One-click your copy of *A Real Cowboy for the Holidays* right now so you don't forget!

STEPHANIE ROWE

SNEAK PEEK: A REAL COWBOY NEVER SAYS NO

★★★★★ ***"Wow! This book was fantastic!"*** -Cindy F
(Five-star Amazon Review)

What happens when a marriage-of-convenience is the only way for a grumpy cowboy to protect the secret baby of his late best friend? Sexy, emotional, and heartwarming.

★★★★★ "I finished this book last night, and bought the

next 3 in series this morning! That's how addicted I am to the Stockton boys!" -Amanda C (Amazon Review)

★★★★★ "OH. MY. GOSH! This was the best book I've read in a really, really long time." *-jenny7 (Amazon Review)*

⁓

Chase Stockton knew he'd found the woman he'd come to meet.

There was no mistaking the depth of loathing in the gaze of AJ's dad when he'd glared at the woman in the pale blue sundress. There was only one woman Alan could despise that much, and it was Mira Cabot, AJ's best friend from childhood.

Chase grinned. After more than a decade, he was about to meet Mira Cabot in person. *Hot damn.*

Anticipation humming through him, Chase watched with appreciation as she ducked into the last row of pews, her pale shoulders erect and strong as she moved down the row. She was a little too thin, yeah, but there was a strength to her body that he liked. Her dark blond hair was curly, bouncing over her shoulders in stark contrast to the tight updos of the other women in the church. He'd noticed her flip-flops and hot pink toenails, a little bit of color in the chapel full of black and gloom.

Chase had hopped a plane to attend the funeral, but it hadn't been just to honor AJ. He could have done that from his ranch in Wyoming. Nope, he'd come here to meet Mira, because he'd had a feeling this was going to be his only chance.

He ignored the line of churchgoers waiting to be seated. Instead, he strode around the back of the last pew to the far side, where his quarry was tucked away in the shadows. As he approached, someone turned up the lights in the church, and the shadows slid away, casting her face in a warm glow, giving him his first view of the woman he'd been thinking about for so long.

Chase was shocked by the raw need that flooded him. Her eyes were the azure blue as in her photos. Her nose had that slight bump from when she and AJ had failed to successfully install a tire swing in her front yard, resulting in her crashing to the ground and breaking her nose. Her lips were pale pink, swept with the faintest hint of gloss, and her eyelashes were as long and thick as he'd imagined. Her shoulders were bare and delicate in her sundress, and her ankles were crossed demurely, as if she were playing the role that was expected of her. Yet, around that same ankle was a chain of glittering gold with several blue stones. He knew that anklet. He'd helped AJ pick it out for her twenty-first birthday.

She was everything he'd imagined, and so much more. She was no longer an inanimate, two-dimensional image who lived only in his mind. She had become a real, live woman.

Mira was eyeing the crowd with the faintest scowl puckering her lips and lining her forehead, just as he would have expected. She didn't like this crowd any more than AJ had.

Chase grinned, relaxing. She was exactly what he'd imagined. "You don't approve?" he said as he approached her.

She let out a yelp of surprise and jumped, bolting sideways like a skittish foal. "What?"

Chase froze, startled by the sound of her voice. It was softer than he'd expected, reminding him of the rolling sound of sunshine across his back on a warm day. Damn, he liked her voice. Why hadn't AJ ever mentioned it? That wasn't the kind of thing a guy could overlook.

She was sitting sideways, her hand gripping the back of the pew, looking at him like he was about to pull out his rifle and aim it at her head.

He instinctively held up his hand, trying to soothe her. "Sorry. I didn't mean to startle you." He swept the hat off his head and bowed slightly. "Chase Stockton. You must be Mira Cabot."

"Chase Stockton?" Her frown deepened slightly, and then recognition dawned on her face. "AJ's best friend from college! Of course." She stood up immediately, a smile lighting up her features. "I can't believe I finally get to meet you."

He had only a split second to register how pretty her smile was before she threw her arms around him and hugged him.

For the second time in less than a minute, Chase was startled into immobility. Her body was so warm and soft against him that he forgot to breathe. He had not been expecting her to hug him, and he hadn't had time to steel himself. He flexed his hands by his sides, not sure how to react. It had been so long since anyone had hugged him, and it was an utterly foreign experience. It was weird as hell, but at the same time, there was something about it that felt incredible, as if the whole world had stopped spinning and settled into this moment.

When Mira didn't let go, he tentatively slipped his arms around her, still unsure of proper protocol when being embraced by a woman he'd never met before. As his arms encircled her, however, a deep sense of rightness settled over him. He could feel her ribs protruding from her back, and he instinctively tightened his grip on her, pulling her into the shield of his embrace. In photographs, she'd always been athletic and solid, but now she was thin, thinner than he liked, thinner than he felt she should be.

She tucked her face in his neck and took a deep breath, and he became aware of the most tempting scent of flowers. It reminded him of a trail ride in the spring, when the wildflowers were beating back the last remnants of a stubborn winter.

The turbulence that constantly roiled through his body seemed to quiet as he focused on her. He became aware of the desperate nature of her embrace, reminding him that she was attending the funeral of her best friend, and she was no doubt being assaulted by the accompanying grief and loss.

He bent his head, his cheek brushing against her hair. "You okay?" he asked softly.

She took another deep breath, and then pulled back. Her blue eyes were full of turbulent emotion. "It's just that seeing you makes me feel like AJ's here again." She brushed an imaginary speck of dust off his shoulder. "You were his best friend, you know. You changed his life forever."

He wasn't used to anyone touching him with that kind of intimacy, especially not a woman. Women never got familiar with him. *Ever*. He simply didn't allow it. But with her, it felt okay. Good even. He shrugged, feeling completely out of his depth with her. "He changed mine," he said. "He did a hell of a lot more for me than I ever did for him." AJ had been a lifeline in an ugly existence that had been spiraling straight into hell. He knew exactly where he'd have been without AJ: dead, or in prison. It was a debt he could never repay.

She nodded, still not stepping away from his embrace. She lightly clasped his forearms, still holding onto him. "He was like that, wasn't he?"

"Yeah, he was." Unable to make himself release her, Chase studied her face, memorizing the curve of her nose, the flush of her cheeks, and the slope of her jaw. "You were his rock, you know. The only person in this world he truly trusted."

And that was it, the reason why he'd wanted to meet her. He was bitter, tired, and cynical, and he'd needed to see if the Mira Cabot his friend had always talked about actually existed. He needed to know whether there was someone in this world, anyone besides his brothers, who a man could actually believe in. Hearing that AJ had died had derailed Chase more than he'd expected, and he'd needed something to hold onto, something that connected him back to AJ and to some dammed goodness in his life.

Her cheeks flushed, and she smiled. "Thanks for telling me that. We didn't keep in touch much over the last few years, but he's always been in my heart."

He stared at her, uncertain how to respond. Who talked about things in their heart? And with strangers? But he knew the answer to that. Mira did, and that's why he'd wanted to meet her.

She finally pulled back, and he reluctantly released her, his hands sliding over her hips. She moved further into the pew and eased onto the bench. "Sit with me," she said, patting the seat beside her.

"Yeah, okay." Instead of taking the aisle seat, he moved past her and sat on the other side of her, inserting himself between Mira and AJ's dad. The old man was across the church, but he hadn't stopped shooting lethal stares in her direction. AJ wasn't there to protect her, so it was now Chase's job.

He draped his arms across the back of the pew, aware that his position put one arm behind Mira's shoulders. Not touching, but present. A statement.

He looked across the church at AJ's dad, and this time, when the man looked over, he noticed Chase sitting beside her. The two men stared at each other for a brief moment, and then Alan looked away.

Satisfied, Chase shifted his position so he could stretch his legs out, trying to work out the cramps from the long flight. He was glad he'd come. It felt right to be there, and he'd sent the message to AJ's dad that Mira was under his protection.

He glanced sideways at her as she fiddled with her small purse. Her hair was tumbling around her face, obscuring his view of her eyes. Frustrated that he couldn't see her face, he started to move his hand to adjust her hair, and then froze. What the hell was he doing, thinking he could just reach out and touch her like that?

Swearing, he jerked his gaze away from her, a bead of sweat trickling down his brow as he realized the enormity of what was happening. *He was attracted to her.* For the last decade, Mira had simply been AJ's best friend, an angel of sorts that Chase had idealized from a distance, never thinking of Mira as anything more personal than simply a bright light in a shitty world.

But now?

He wanted her.

He wanted to brush her hair back from her face. He wanted to run his fingers over her collarbone. He wanted to feel her body crushed against his again. He wanted to sink his mouth onto hers, and taste her—

Hell. That spelled trouble, in a major way.

Suddenly, he couldn't wait to get on the plane and get out of there, and back to his carefully constructed world.

He hadn't come here for a woman. He'd come here for salvation, not to be sucked into the hell that had almost destroyed him once before. Mira Cabot might be the only woman on the planet worth trusting, but that wasn't reason enough for him to risk all that he'd managed to rebuild.

Nothing was worth that risk. *Nothing.*

Like it? Get it now!

SNEAK PEEK: UNEXPECTEDLY MINE

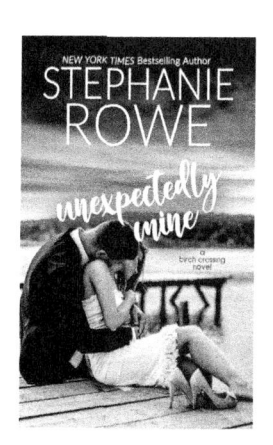

"This book wove...deep inside my heart and soul."
-Amy W (Amazon Review)

Single mom Clare is too busy for love...until a single dad rents her spare room and teaches her how to trust again.

SNEAK PEEK: UNEXPECTEDLY MINE

Clare was lifting the box of cupcakes off the front counter when she became aware of the utter silence of the general store. Even at the funerals of her parents, she hadn't heard this kind of silence in Birch Crossing.

Awareness prickled down her arms, and she looked at Norm, who was in his usual spot behind the front register. She could have sworn that there was amusement crinkling his gray eyes when he nodded toward something behind her.

Clare spun around, and there he was.

Griffin Friesé.

Her mystical knight in shining armor from last night.

Her heart began to race as she met his gaze. His stare was intense, penetrating all the way to her core. She was yanked back to that moment of his hands on her hips, of his strength as he'd lifted her. The power in his body as he'd emerged from his truck during the thundering rain and raging wind. Her body began to thrum, and his expression grew hooded, his eyes never leaving hers, as if he were trying to memorize every feature on her face.

He was wearing a heavy leather jacket that flanked strong thighs and broad shoulders. His eyes were dark, as dark as they'd been last night in the storm. Whiskers shadowed his jaw, giving him a rough and untamed look. His boots were still caked with mud, but his jeans were pressed and clean. His light blue dress shirt was open at the collar, revealing a hint of skin and the flash of a thin gold chain at his throat. His hair was short and perfectly gelled, not messy and untamed like it had been last night. A heavy gold watch sat captive on the strong wrist that had supported her so easily.

Today, he wasn't the dark and rugged hero of last night.

Well, okay, he still was. His power transcended mud, storms, nice watches, and dress shirts.

But he was also, quite clearly and quite ominously, an

outsider, a man who did not fit into the rural Maine town of Birch Crossing.

Then he smiled, a beautiful, tremendous smile with a dimple in his right cheek. "How's your daughter?"

A dimple? He had a dimple? Clare hadn't noticed the dimple last night. It made him look softer, more human, more approachable, almost endearing. Suddenly all her trepidation vanished, replaced by a feeling of giddiness and delight to see him. She smiled back. "She's still asleep, but she's okay. Thanks for your help last night rescuing her."

"My pleasure." His smile faded, and a speculative gleam came into his dark eyes. "And how are you?"

No longer feeling like a total wreck, that was for sure. Not with Griffin Friesé studying her as if she were the only thing he ever wanted to look at again. Dear God, the way he was looking at her made her want to drop the cupcakes and her clothes, and saunter with decadent sensuality across the floor toward him, his stare igniting every cell in her body. "I'm fine." She swallowed, horrified by how throaty her voice sounded. "Thank you," she said. "I owe you."

"No, you owe me nothing." He smiled again, a softness to his face that made her heart turn over. "Seeing you hug Katie was plenty."

"Oh, dear Lord," Eppie muttered behind her. "Now he's going to kill Katie, too."

Clare stiffened and jerked her gaze from Griffin. The entire store was watching them in rapt silence, listening to every word. Oh, God. How had she forgotten where they were? Wright & Sons was the epicenter of gossip in Birch Crossing, and everyone had just witnessed her gaping at this handsome stranger.

Assuming her decades-old role as Clare's self-appointed protector, Eppie had folded her arms and was trying to crush Griffin with her glare, for daring to tempt Clare.

SNEAK PEEK: UNEXPECTEDLY MINE

Astrid and Emma were leaning against the doorjamb, huge grins on their faces, clearly supportive of any opportunity to pry Clare out of her dateless life of isolation. But Norm's eyes were narrowed, and Ophelia was letting some scrambled eggs burn while she gawked at them. Everyone was waiting to see how Clare was going to respond to him.

Oh, man. What was she doing nearly throwing herself at him? In front of everyone? She quickly took a step back and cleared her throat.

Griffin's eyebrows shot up at her retreat, then his eyes narrowed. "Kill off Katie, *too*? " He looked right at Eppie. "Who else am I going to kill?"

Eppie lifted her chin and turned her head, giving him a view of the back of her hot pink hat.

"The rumors claim that you're in town to murder your ex-wife and daughter," Astrid volunteered cheerfully. "But don't worry. Not all of us believe them."

"My daughter?" Pain flashed across Griffin's face, a stark anguish so real that Clare felt her out heart tighten. Just as quickly, the vulnerability disappeared from his face, replaced by a hard, cool expression.

But she'd seen it. She'd seen his pain, pain he clearly kept hidden, just as she suppressed her own. Suddenly, she felt terrible about the rumors. How could she have listened to rumors about him when he was clearly struggling with pain, some kind of trauma with regard to his daughter?

She realized he was watching her, as if he were waiting for something. For what? To see if she believed the rumors?

She glanced around and saw the entire store was waiting for her response. Eppie gave her a solemn nod, encouraging her to stand up and condemn this handsome stranger who'd saved Clare's daughter. Sudden anger surged inside her. "Oh, come on," she blurted out. "You can't really believe he's a murderer?"

SNEAK PEEK: UNEXPECTEDLY MINE

Astrid grinned, Eppie shook her head in dismay, and the rest of the room was silent.

No one else jumped in to help her defend Griffin, and suddenly Clare felt very exposed, as if everyone in the room could see exactly how deeply she'd been affected by him last night. How she'd lain awake all night, thinking of his hands on her hips, of the way his deep voice had wrapped around her, of how he'd made her yearn for the touch of a man for the first time in a very long time.

Heat burned her cheeks, and she glanced uncomfortably at Griffin, wondering if he was aware of her reaction to him. To her surprise, his face had cooled, devoid of that warmth that they'd initially shared, clearly interpreting her silence as a capitulation to the rumors.

He narrowed his eyes, then turned away, ending their conversation.

Regret rushed through Clare as she glanced at Astrid, torn between wanting to call him back, and gratefully grasping the freedom his rejection had given her, freedom from feelings and desires that she didn't have time to deal with.

"I need a place to stay," Griffin said. "A place without rats, preferably."

Griffin's low request echoed through the room, and Clare spun around in shock. Then she saw he was directing his question to Norm, not to her. Relief rushed through her, along with a stab of disappointment.

No, it was good he wasn't asking to stay at her place. Yes, she owed him, on a level beyond words, but she couldn't afford to get involved with him, for too many reasons. Staying at her house would be putting temptation where she couldn't afford it. There was *no way* she was going to offer up her place, even though her renter had just vacated, leaving her with an unpleasant gap in her income stream.

"Griffin stayed at the Dark Pines Motel last night," Judith whispered, just loudly enough for the whole store to hear.

"Really?" Guilt washed through Clare. The Dark Pines Motel was quite possibly the most unkempt and disgusting motel in the entire state of Maine. How had he ended up there?

"Well, now, Griffin," Norm said, as he tipped his chair back and let it tap against the unfinished wall. "Most places won't open for another month when the summer folk start to arrive. And the Black Loon Inn is booked for the Smith-Pineal wedding for the next week. It's Dark Pines or nothing."

Griffin frowned. "There has to be something. A bed and breakfast?"

Norm shook his head. "Not this time of year, but I probably have some rat traps in the back I could loan you for your stay.'

"Rat traps?" Griffin echoed. "That's my best option?"

Astrid grinned at Clare, a sparkle in her eyes that made Clare's stomach leap with alarm. She grabbed Astrid's arm. " Don't you dare—"

"Clare's renter just moved out," Astrid announced, her voice ringing out in the store. "Griffin can stay in her spare room. No rats, and it comes with free Wi-Fi. Best deal in town."

Oh, dear *God*. Clare's whole body flamed hot, and she whipped around. *Please tell me he didn't hear that.*

But Griffin was staring right at her.

Of course he'd heard. And so had everyone else.

Like it? Get it now!

SNEAK PEEK: BURN

"A fast-paced, heart-racing, mind-boggling, sexy read...and I loved it!!!" -NanaX8 (Five-star Amazon review)

Don't miss this sizzling romantic suspense in which a serial arsonist targets the biological family he found through an online DNA test. In this high-stakes cat-and-mouse game set in the unforgiving Alaskan terrain, a reclusive ex-military tech expert must protect a spunky, sexy tavern hostess from the killer who has already wiped out the rest of her family.

SNEAK PEEK: BURN

"A M A Z I N G...A fast-paced adventure all wrapped up in scorching hot romance. This entire series is a must-read!" -Christa S. (Five-star Amazon Review)

∽

Mack Connor had been in Alaska for less than an hour, and he was already restless. He wanted to be back in Boston, but when Ben Forsett asked for his help, he got it.

Always.

Every single time.

No matter what.

It had been that way since they were kids, both of them trying to survive the streets, the drugs, and the gangs long enough to get the fuck out of the hell they'd grown up in. Ben had gone to college and law school. Mack had gone into the military and become one of the world's renowned experts on security tech, and all the shit that went with that.

Their connection had never faltered, even when life had blown up around them. Ben was the only friend Mack counted, and the only one he needed.

They always leaned on each other when the shit got real. Always. Until last month when Mack had uncovered a living hell...

"You okay?" Ben looked over at him, his brow furrowed.

Mack cleared his throat and looked out the window at the trees rushing past. So many damn trees. "Yeah. Fine."

"What happened last month?"

Mack shot a sharp glance at Ben. "Nothing."

"Bullshit. Something fucked you up. What was it?"

For a split second, Mack was tempted to tell Ben the truth, to rip the darkness out of him and throw it onto his friend.

SNEAK PEEK: BURN

But just as quickly, he shoved it back down inside him, deep and hard, where it couldn't see the light of day.

"Nothing." He wasn't going there. He just fucking wasn't. He hadn't told Ben about it then, and he wasn't going to tell him now.

Darkness settled in him, and he growled as he dragged his thoughts away from the nightmare that had jerked him awake every single night for the last month. "How about you?" Ben had been through hellacious year.

Ben hesitated, and Mack saw the moment that he decided not to push Mack for more answers. "Better. Mari helps. A lot."

Mack nodded. "Good." He was glad Ben had found someone who fit him. "I can't believe you proposed to her."

Ben smiled, a legit grin that lit up his face. "She changed my world, bro. She's a gift."

A sliver of envy flickered through Mack at the happiness on his friend's face. He'd never seen him like that before. It hadn't even occurred to him that either of them would ever feel that, that it could be a part of their lives. "Damn, man," he said softly. "I'm almost jealous of that stupid grin."

Ben's smile faded into seriousness. "I'm staying in Alaska. I've found peace here."

"Not coming back to Boston?" Mack felt darkness settle in him again. He and Ben had both been in Boston for the last few years, and it had settled him to have Ben around again. Having him move to Alaska? *Shit*. But he grinned at his friend anyway. "Good for you." He meant it, too.

Ben cocked an eyebrow at him. "You might like it here, too. It's an amazing place."

Mack snorted and jerked his thumb at mountains in the distance. "Where are my skyscrapers? No fucking way."

"That's what I thought, too. Things change."

"Not for me." Mack shifted, suddenly restless to get back to topics he felt comfortable with.

They'd spent the first part of the drive from the airport going over the serial killer he'd helped Ben track a few weeks ago, and now it was time to focus on the present.

"Talk to me," he said. "What do you need me for?" He knew it must be bad for Ben to ask him to fly to Alaska for it. The fact Ben had refused to give any details over the phone about why he needed him had jacked up his adrenaline even more.

Ben glanced over at him as his truck bounced over the rutted dirt road. "Mari's friend. Charlotte."

Charlotte. Mack liked the name. He wasn't sure why. It was soft and strong at the same time. He knew nothing about soft, and he didn't particularly want to, but her name seemed to settle in him whenever he heard it.

"The one who got kidnapped." He'd tracked her phone for Ben to help find her. "She doing okay?"

Ben inclined his head. "Sort of."

Mack narrowed his eyes, studying Ben. "You brought me here for her?"

At Ben's nod, Mack settled into the familiarity of business mode. "What's she into?" He unzipped his backpack and pulled out his computer. It booted up instantly, and he created a file with her name. "Her last name is Murphy, right?"

"Yep." Ben rattled off her address, and Mack entered it into the computer.

"What else?"

"That's it."

Mack looked up. "What do you mean, that's it? What's going on with her?"

"I don't know." Ben took a right, the truck lurching over a

big rut in the dirt. "It's something though. Something from her past."

Mack frowned. "A person? A man? Something someone else did? Something she did?" The last question stopped him hard. He knew all about someone who had done something bad, something that came back to haunt him. He was not getting involved with someone who had done bad shit. Not again. He cast a suspicious look at Ben. "How well do you know her?"

"Not well, but she's good. She's been Mari's friend since the day she arrived in town."

Not well. Mack closed the lid to his computer. "Look. I owe you a thousand times over, but I'm not feeling this one."

"You will." Ben slowed the truck. "I arranged for you to stay at her place with her."

"No." Mack put his computer away and zipped up his backpack. "Absolutely not. I live alone. I hate people, except for you. And even you I don't want in my space."

At that moment, Ben's phone rang. He hit the speaker button. "Hey, sweetheart."

Sweetheart? Mack frowned at his friend as a woman's voice filled the car.

"Hey, babe. We have a problem," she said. "Charlotte says Mack can't stay with her, and she's leaving town. She's inside packing right now."

Mack couldn't help but grin. He liked the fact that Charlotte was refusing to be railroaded by Ben. The woman had backbone. "See? It's been decided."

"Mack? Is that Mack?" The warmth in Mari's voice surprised him. "I'm so glad you're here. Ben's told me so much about you. Charlotte needs you."

Her words ripped the smile off his face. "Charlotte appears to disagree with you both." He tried to sound civil, but he knew he wasn't particularly good at it.

SNEAK PEEK: BURN

"She freaked out when we got here, Ben," Mari said, ignoring Mack so completely that he got a little more respect for her. "I thought she was going to leap out of her skin when I knocked on her window. She was scanning the woods like she knew someone was watching her. It freaked me out, too."

Her words piqued Mack's interest, despite his reluctance. A woman in danger was a dangerous trigger for him right now, even more than usual. "You think it was nerves from the attack?"

"No." Her convocation was absolute. "It definitely had to do with someone else. Whoever it was that she said would be coming back for her."

"Coming back?" Mack leaned forward, listening more intently. "When did she say that?"

"At the hospital, when she found out that the story had been in the papers and on the Internet. She said he'd see it, and he'd come back. She was so freaked when she got home."

Ben swore under his breath and shot a scowl at Mack, as if it were his fault.

"Joseph found me," Mari said, her voice cracking slightly. "There's nowhere to hide if someone wants to find her. We all know that."

Mack did know that. He was one of the ones who could find anyone. And he'd completely fucked it up a month ago.

"We'll talk to her when we get there." Ben's voice was gentle, gentler than Mack had ever heard him use. "You doing okay, Mari?"

"Yeah. She kind of wigged me out, but Haas is here, so I'm okay."

"Haas Carter?" Mack repeated the name, fighting the temptation to open his computer back up and add it to Charlotte's file. Ben had such praise for the old-timer Alaskan that Mack was actually interested in meeting him.

"Yes, he's here—" Mari paused. "Charlotte's coming out

the door now with a bag. Haas says he won't shoot her to make her stay. How far away are you?"

"We're here."

As Ben spoke, the truck rounded a bend, and a well-worn log cabin came into view. A second building had part of the frame up, a couple trucks were in the driveway, and an old man and a woman were next to the bigger one.

But what caught Mack's attention was the woman jogging down her front steps with a duffel bag that was twice as big as she was. On her heels was a gorgeous German shepherd, glued to her side as if it were trained to perfection.

But it wasn't the dog that riveted his attention.

It was the woman. Charlotte.

It wasn't the gorgeous dark waves of her hair. Or the rigid set of her shoulders that told him of a raw, inner strength. Or the way her jeans hugged her hips like they were made for her.

It was the way she stared at the woods, terror etched over every line of her body as she came to a sudden stop.

She spoke to the dog, who took off at a sprint, nose to the ground as he bolted into the trees.

Mack was peripherally aware that Ben and the two folks in the driveway had paused to watch the dog.

He didn't.

He watched Charlotte.

She remained still, but she wasn't watching the dog either. She was carefully scanning her property, her gaze focused and methodical, as if she knew exactly what she was looking for while she waited for the dog to finish.

After her survey, he saw her shoulders loosen infinitesimally. She then raised her gaze to the dog, who was trotting back, his body at ease, and his tail waving peacefully.

She relaxed more, and held out her hand to the dog, who

ground his head affectionately into her palm as she spoke softly to him.

The brief moment had told Mack much.

She was strong.

She was smart.

She was good to her dog.

And whoever was hunting her had been doing it for long enough that she'd developed a defense system, one that she no longer believed could keep her safe.

He swore under his breath as Ben pulled up beside an old, battered pickup truck that he assumed belonged to Haas.

Charlotte looked up and saw Ben's truck. As soon as she realized he was there, for a split second, she relaxed, a full and complete release that made her face soften.

Mack knew it was because Ben's appearance made her feel safe, and for that split second, she leaned into it, grasping for a respite from being constantly on edge. He liked that she trusted Ben. It showed she had good sense. Ben was the only person he trusted, so he appreciated that Charlotte could see that about him as well.

Then her gaze went to the passenger seat, and she realized Mack was with him.

Her jaw immediately jutted out. She pulled her shoulders back. And she set her hands on her hips. A fighting stance that made him grin.

"She's ready to kick you out before you even move in," Ben said, resting his forearms on the steering wheel.

"I see that."

Ben cocked an eyebrow at him. "What are you going to do about it?"

Mack leaned forward, watching Charlotte. She was too far away to see clearly, and he knew she couldn't see him well behind the windshield. "She believes she'll be attacked in her own home," he observed.

"I agree." Ben drummed his fingers on the dash. "What if you walk away, and that happens to her?"

Mack was unable to take his gaze off her as she stared him down. She was attitude and sass, even when she was scared shitless. He respected that. Which made Ben's question jab right into his gut and twist its blade. *What if he walked away, and she was killed?* "Really? That's the line you're throwing my way to get me to stay?"

"Yep." Ben cocked an eyebrow. "Did it work?"

Mack sighed and picked up his backpack. "Fuck you, Forsett." He grabbed the door handle and stepped out of the truck.

Ben leaned across the seat, grinning at him. "So, that's a yes? It worked?"

Mack's only answer was to slam the door in his friend's face, but he was grinning as he heard Ben's laughter.

Yeah, it had worked.

Charlotte Murphy was officially his next case.

Like it? Get it now!

BOOKS BY STEPHANIE ROWE

CONTEMPORARY ROMANCE

WYOMING REBELS SERIES
(CONTEMPORARY WESTERN ROMANCE)
A Real Cowboy Never Says No
A Real Cowboy Knows How to Kiss
A Real Cowboy Rides a Motorcycle
A Real Cowboy Never Walks Away
A Real Cowboy Loves Forever
A Real Cowboy for Christmas
A Real Cowboy Always Trusts His Heart
A Real Cowboy Always Protects
A Real Cowboy for the Holidays (Nov. 21, 2021)
A Real Cowboy Always Comes Home (2022)

THE HART RANCH BILLIONAIRES SERIES
(CONTEMPORARY WESTERN ROMANCE)
A Rogue Cowboy's Second Chance (Sept. 14, 2021)
A Rogue Cowboy Finds Love (2022)

BOOKS BY STEPHANIE ROWE

LINKED TO THE HART RANCH BILLIONAIRES SERIES
(CONTEMPORARY WESTERN ROMANCE)
Her Rebel Cowboy

BIRCH CROSSING SERIES
(SMALL-TOWN CONTEMPORARY ROMANCE)
Unexpectedly Mine
Accidentally Mine
Unintentionally Mine
Irresistibly Mine

MYSTIC ISLAND SERIES
(SMALL-TOWN CONTEMPORARY ROMANCE)
Wrapped Up in You (A Christmas novella)

CANINE CUPIDS SERIES
(ROMANTIC COMEDY)
Paws for a Kiss
Pawfectly in Love
Paws Up for Love

SINGLE TITLE
(CHICKLIT / ROMANTIC COMEDY)
One More Kiss

PARANORMAL

ORDER OF THE BLADE SERIES
(PARANORMAL ROMANCE)
Darkness Awakened
Darkness Seduced
Darkness Surrendered
Forever in Darkness
Darkness Reborn

BOOKS BY STEPHANIE ROWE

Darkness Arisen
Darkness Unleashed
Inferno of Darkness
Darkness Possessed
Shadows of Darkness
Hunt the Darkness
Darkness Awakened: Reimagined

IMMORTALLY DATING SERIES
(FUNNY PARANORMAL ROMANCE)
To Date an Immortal
To Date a Dragon
Devil's Curse
To Kiss a Demon

HEART OF THE SHIFTER SERIES
(PARANORMAL ROMANCE)
Dark Wolf Rising
Dark Wolf Unbound

SHADOW GUARDIANS SERIES
(PARANORMAL ROMANCE)
Leopard's Kiss

NIGHTHUNTER SERIES
(PARANORMAL ROMANCE)
Not Quite Dead

NOBLE AS HELL SERIES
(FUNNY URBAN FANTASY)
Guardian of Magic

THE MAGICAL ELITE SERIES
(FUNNY PARANORMAL ROMANCE)

BOOKS BY STEPHANIE ROWE

The Demon You Trust

***Devilishly Sexy* series**
(Funny Paranormal Romance)
Not Quite a Devil

ROMANTIC SUSPENSE

Alaska Heat Series
(Romantic Suspense)
Ice
Chill
Ghost
Burn
Hunt (novella)

BOXED SETS

Order of the Blade (Books 1-3)
Protectors of the Heart (A Six-Book First-in-Series Collection)
Wyoming Rebels Boxed Set (Books 1-3)

For a complete list of Stephanie's books, click here.

ACKNOWLEDGMENTS

Special thanks to my beta readers. You guys are the best! Thanks to Kelli Ann Morgan at Inspire Creative for another fantastic cover. There are so many to thank by name, more than I could count, but here are those who I want to called out specially for all they did to help this book come to life: Alyssa Bird, Anita Hanson, Ashlee Murphy, Bridget Koan, Britannia Hill, Caryn Santee, Deb Julienne, Denise Fluhr, Dottie Jones, Felicia Low Mikoll, Heidi Hoffman, Helen Loyal, Jean Bowden, Jeanne Stone, Jeanie Jackson, Jodi Moore, Judi Pflughoeft, Kasey Richardson, Linda Watson, Regina Thomas, Summer Steelman, Suzanne Mayer, Shell Bryce, and Trish Douglas. Special thanks to my family, who I love with every fiber of my heart and soul. Mom, I love you so much! And to AER, who is my world. Love you so much, baby girl! And to Joe, who teaches me every day what romance and true love really is. I love you, babe!

ABOUT THE AUTHOR

New York Times and *USA Today* bestselling author Stephanie Rowe is "contemporary romance at its best" (Bex 'N' Books). She's thrilled to be a 2021 Vivian® Award nominee, and a RITA® Award winner and five-time nominee, the highest awards in romance fiction. As the bestselling author of more than fifty books, Stephanie delights readers with her wide range of genres, which include contemporary western, small-town contemporary romance, paranormal romance, and romantic suspense novels.

www.stephanierowe.com

Printed in Great Britain
by Amazon